Cry of a Valkyrie

By

C. M. Schrecengost

ISBN (Paperback): 978-1-7377512-3-6
ISBN (Ebook): 978-1-7377512-2-9
Library of Congress Control Number: 2021918320
Any reference to historical events, real people, or real places are used fictitiously. Names, characters, and places are products of the Author's imagination.
Front Cover images by Artist.
Book Design by Designer.
First Print edition 2021
Published in Swansboro, NC

Also By C. M. Schrecengost:

Pana-Mania

Contents

Acknowledgments

To my loving family, whom supported me through the perilous journey of writing, and publication.

Cry of a Valkyrie

Prologue

"Get the hell out of there, you skank!" a confused and worried Meana hears her father yell.

Holding her daughter tight to her bosom, with tears dropping down upon the child's head, Meana's mother hears her say, "It's not your fault, Mommy. You can tell Daddy that we packed our bags because we found a new hide-and-seek spot."

Trying to mask the fear in her eyes, she looks down at her six-year-old daughter, and whispers, "No, baby. Daddy has just had a little too much grown-up juice to drink. If we play hide-and-seek in the bathroom for a while longer, he'll go lay down to take a nap, and then he'll feel much better."

Meana reaches her hands up to her sniffling mother's face, and tries to wipe away the streams of black eyeliner, and cloudy tears.

Giving her mother a kiss on the chin, Meana asks, "Is Daddy mad because he can't find us?"

Letting out a small but false laugh, her mother looks into her eyes and says, "Yes, baby, that's why. Now, just hold on to Mommy tight, and never let go."

Doing as her mother says, Meana tightens her grip and snuggles her forehead into her chest. Just then, the singular door of the bathroom acting as a shield between them and her crazed father, gives way. Splinters of wood spit out in their direction, and Meana's mother attempts to cover their faces.

Yanking her mother off the floor by her underarm, he roars, "What did you do with them, woman?"

While Meana still clings to her, she screams out in desperation, "I flushed them! I swear I flushed them!"

Seeing that Meana is still holding on to her mother, her father reaches down and rips her away, "Sit down you little shit, I'm going to go have a talk with Mommy!"

With a maniacal smile, he drags her mother out of the bathroom, and slams the fractured and splinter ridden door behind himself. Meana immediately rises from the floor and runs over to the door, placing her face against the open hole where the handle used to be, and watches her parents frantically converse.

With one hand clutched firmly around her skinny and already-bruising arm, he yanks her mother around the living room like a rag doll. Lifting his other hand, he caulks back, and rains down a concussive smack. Hearing her mother let out a deafening scream, Meana covers her ears, and cries once more. Attempting to look through her clouded vision, she continues to watch this event unfold.

"Where are the drugs, you two-timing whore?"

"I told you, I flushed them!" her mother declares, panicking, gesturing toward the bathroom.

He throws her on the couch, and then grabs her by the wrist and pulls her arm until it is straight.

"Then why do you have fresh track marks? Don't lie to me!"

Knowing that she has been caught, she lashes back in an attempt to excuse herself, "I'm sorry, baby, but I've been jonesing too, and you took my stash with you!"

Letting go of her arm, and pacing back-and-forth, he says, "That wasn't yours to use, damn it. I was supposed to sell that shit and pay Leon back. What the fuck do I do now?"

Her mother slumps off of the couch and down to her knees, grabbing him by the pant leg, and pleading, "I'll work the corner more! I'll make the money back, baby!"

Looking down at his wife with a swirling mixture of desperation and fear in his eyes, he says, "No, forget this, I'm out of here. You can deal with Leon and that damn kid," gesturing toward the bathroom.

"No, please, don't leave me behind! We can leave her, and skip town! I promise I'll do better, baby!"

Placing both hands on his head and looking to the ceiling to contemplated her offer, he responds, "No, fuck you both, I'm out of here." He then turns from the blubbering mess of a woman that still clings to his leg, and with a yanking motion, frees himself to walk to the entryway of their apartment.

"Come back! Don't leave me!" her mother cries out, while grasping at the air like a madwoman.

Meana watches her father swing the front door of the apartment open, and swiftly walk through. Not even bothering to close the door, he makes his way down the stairs, and out of their lives forever. Seeing her father leave without a second thought, and her mother hysterically crying on the living-room floor, a tear-filled Meana opens the remains of the bathroom door and quickly makes her way over.

"Mommy, it's okay. Daddy will be back for us," she says, placing one small hand on her mother's shoulder.

Removing her hands from her face and looking up at Meana, her mother wears a look of pure disgust and rears her hands back to slap her while exclaiming, "This is all your fault, you little shit! He left me because of you!"

Laying on her back in the middle of the living room, the six-year-old Meana looks up at her mother in terror, and raises her hands to defend her face before her mother bends over to strike again.

Thumping noises reverberate around the apartment as blow-after-blow lands upon Meana's arms, head, and back.

Screaming at the top of her lungs, her mother exclaims, "Why? Why did you leave me?"

Filling the living-room carpet with tears and small trickles of blood from her nose, Meana attempts to curl herself tighter into the fetal position. Her mothers labored breathing continues to increase, and her arms begin to fatigue from furiously thrashing about.

Finally, too exhausted to lash out, Meana's mother falls to her knees, and wraps her arms around her sobbing child. Trying to console her, she whispers, "Shh, my sweet. Mommy's here. I love you. I'll always love you."

Meana, having become accustomed to her mother's back-and-forth lunacy, reaches up and wraps her arms around her.

The Happening

A large, midnight-black SUV with darkly tinted windows and matte black rims lays in wait down a shadowy and mist-permeated alleyway on the outskirts of a corrupted and tainted town. A young brunette with pale skin, sunken eyes, and heavy eyeliner comfortably sits in the driver seat and takes a long, relaxed drag from her mentholated cigarette. Shaky nerves won't serve her any good here, and although she despises smoking, she knows well enough that she needs this cigarette. Continuing to take steady and lengthy puffs while observing the scenery around her, she peers into the driver side mirror and sees a badly scraped and dented, blue dumpster littered from top to bottom with a restaurant's kitchen scraps. An older woman dressed in tattered blue jeans, a soiled gray hoodie, and worn-out black combat boots begins to rummage through the scraps, struggling to prop the lid of the dumpster open. With her stomach firmly against the dumpster, she reaches toward the bottom, causing her feet to lift off of the ground. Seconds pass, and she returns to her original standing position and stops to smell the leftover food she now holds. Turning her head toward the dark vehicle lumbering in the distance, her face smooshes up, and wrinkles protrude from each eye while she squints in an attempt to look at the mysterious vehicle. Shrugging her shoulders in a lethargic manner and determining there is nothing of interest, she averts her eyes, and once again gazes upon her prize. Looking directly at the homeless woman, the young brunette perks up in her seat and grips the handle of the door.

"Is that my mother?" frantically runs through her head, and she debates leaping from the car and running down the alley to find out.

Not wanting to open old wounds, she decides that the probability of knowing the old woman to be her mother is near impossible. Attempting to avert her thoughts and calm her now-fast-beating heart, the young brunette continues to suspiciously gaze about her surroundings and sees numerous waterlogged potholes and heaps of trash bags lining the entirety of the alleyway. With legs outstretched, she leans back into the well-worn black leather of her seat, and gazes out the driver-side window at the run-down building towering above her. Shattered windows on the ground level line the tall tenement, accompanied by a surplus of graffiti reaching as high as the third floor. An equal amount of stress fractures riddles the mortar joints between each tired and worn-looking red brick. With her mouth slightly agape, she continues to look in bewilderment and wonders how this building endures the test of time. Still staring at this modern ruin, her blackened and sleep-deprived eyelids begin to feel heavy. Although months have been spent in anticipation of this night, the young brunette, while sitting in the silence, allows her mind to wander, and thinks of a past life filled with shadows and fear. For a split second, her eyes close, and the battle to stay awake begins. She knows that falling asleep now could be her undoing, and yet she can-not resist the sweet call of nothingness. Laying half in and half out of consciousness with the nearly depleted cigarette still in hand, a surge of memories washes over her, and just before her body goes limp, she slurs, "Fuck, I'm tired."

An eighteen-year-old Meana kneels with shaky hands from nervousness, and vomits in an old and piss-stained toilet. Leaning her face into the bowl, and placing her hands on either side of the seat, the toilet wobbles unsteadily. Tightening her grip on the seat, she steadies the toilet and continues to upchuck. Meana feels pain shoot through her back as it tenses with each new projectile, and lets out a faint sobbing sound. An hour of back-and-forth retching goes by, and her stomach no longer houses the hefty plate of pasta she had eaten earlier. She pushes herself from the checker-patterned, laminate floor, wiping the red-sauce-filled vomit from her mouth and blowing her nose into a small piece of tissue paper. The apartment doorbell shrieks with a high-pitched and garbled tone, and she stands motionless, questioning if she is capable of answering the door. The ticking noise of a circular, black-and-white nuclear clock mounted on a wall just outside the bathroom door, echoes throughout the house. The silence of her mother's apartment is yet again rudely interrupted with the shrieks of the doorbell.

"I need to get that damn doorbell fixed," Meana exclaims, frantically washing her hands.

Mustering up enough courage, she drags herself to the front door. She takes a single deep breath, and while reaching for the handle, exhales. She struggles to open the door, and wrenches the handle back-and-forth until the door lets its death grip on the frame loose. Meana stumbles and nearly falls flat on her back-side. Feeling her cheeks burn from embarrassment, she regains her balance and lifts her head to see a Marine Corps recruiter wearing a crisp, pressed military uniform, and holding the keys to his government-issued vehicle.

He looks her deep in the eye and energetically says, "Let's do this!"

Meana shoots him a half-hearted smile and retrieves her bag from beside the door. Slamming the tattered apartment door behind herself in frustration, she makes her way down the stairs of her mother's run-down apartment and out to the horribly maintained parking lot. His vehicle is a sheer-white sedan with nothing but a U.S. government logo on each side. Putting forth as little thought as possible, Meana opens the rear passenger door and enters the vehicle. With a loud thump, she lands in the back seat and places her singular black duffle bag upon her lap. This bag is the only part of her mother that she is willing to bring along. It was a gift many years ago when she was still but an innocent girl, and years of neglect and abuse have led her to form a bitter hole where the love for her mother is supposed to reside. Deciding now was not the time to ruminate on cloudy subjects, she brushes the thought of her mother away.

Meana did the only thing she could think of to get away from her hellish life. With only twelve days since she graduated from high school, she is eager to embark on this new and frightening adventure.

The recruiter quickly follows suit and swiftly enters the vehicle and snaps his seat belt into place. With an effortless motion, he takes the car-key and inserts it into the ignition. He turns the key, and for a moment, nothing happens. A second goes by, and he starts turning the key back-and-forth while murmuring something under his breath. With one last turn of desperation, the vehicle roars to life, and Meana can see the recruiter nervously looking at her through the rearview mirror.

"Nothing to worry about," he says, chuckling away the incident.

He throws the shifter into drive, and the car creeps forward. Meana steals one last glance at the apartment she is leaving behind, and they turn onto the open road. The vehicle twists and turns, navigating down the tight-and-bumpy roads of New York City, and Meana feels a sense of dread come over her as the distance from the apartment increases. Her mind begins to race, and she starts to panic; she formulates excuses to exit the vehicle, and allows scenario in which she is able to back out of her contractual agreement to fill her heart with fear. Luckily, her thoughts are abruptly interrupted when the vehicle hits a wide-and-deep pothole so violently the recruiter says, "There goes my damn paycheck," and then lets out a loud, obnoxious sigh.

Time drags by, and the exhaustion of excessive worry washes over her, and she nearly succumbs to the blissful pleasure of a nap, when, all of a sudden, the hotel in which she will be staying, comes into view. With a couple of excessively loud thumps, the vehicle pulls into the hotel parking lot. They arrive at their final destination, and Meana steps from the car and retrieves the lone black bag that she had been strangling throughout the ride. The recruiter and her briskly walk through the hotel lobby and ascend to the third floor via elevator before Meana has any time to glance around. The elevator doors open, and the recruiter leads Meana down a *long-and-dusty hallway with Victorian-style carpets and cheap sconces on the walls. The hallway is ill lit, and as Meana peers down the passageway, her vision plays a trick on her. The hallway seems to elongate itself, and slightly twists from left-to-right. She briefly stumbles while walking down this ominous hallway of despair. The recruiter ushers Meana to her room door with one hand placed on her left shoulder, and pulls a room key from his pocket with his other.*

He then looks her in the eyes and says, "The bus will be here at 0400 sharp. I don't recommend missing it."

Having said all he needed to, he hands her the key, drops both hands down toward the floor, and performs a military drill movement called "right face." Looking down at the key, while the recruiter casually walks away, Meana silently inserts it into the hotel-room door. She turns the knob and is immediately struck in the face by a musty-and-damp odor that can only come from excessive age.

"Great," she whimpers, and slinkies her way toward the bed, sits down with a hard thump, and leisurely tosses her bag onto the armchair nearby. "Damn, I need a nap," Meana says, throwing herself back onto the rock-hard bed, and beginning to close her eyes. She feels the weightlessness of sleep wash over her, and makes no attempt to fight it.

With a hypnic jerk waking her and bringing her mind back to the present, a more-seasoned Meana, gazes at her extinguished cigarette, lets out a sigh of disappointment, and pulls another from her pack and strikes a match. She takes a long drag from her newly lit cigarette, and then pulls a well-tuned and oiled pistol from the center console of the SUV, and checks the round count in the magazine. After performing a quick quality check on the matte-black pistol, she inserts the magazine and loads a round into the chamber with a smooth and effortless motion.

She turns her attention to the windshield and can see a fortified wall with a solitary guard in a small, unsecured brick guardhouse in the distance. The guard-house sits outside a dark and forested estate that Meana has been watching for some time now. The shadows of her dark world lay beyond the large steel gates that stare her in the face.

"This will work," Meana reassures herself, turning her attention to the guard once more.

The guard is a female, approximately the same size and weight as Meana herself. In the guard's possession is an older model AR-15, a worn-looking radio, and the standard black pants, black shirt, and black cap uniform. The guard has the rifle lazily slung around one shoulder, and never appears to look up from the phone in her hand. Meana averts her eyes from the gate guard and opens the glove box. Pulling out a blueprint from inside, she unfolds it, and starts to read the legend in an effort to locate the gate control assembly. She squints her eyes to clear the cloudiness of exhaustion, and then continues to skim through the detailed layout of the main gate's power grid. There is a silent darkness all around her, and the only sound to be heard, is the scrapping of Meana's finger-tips tracing the lines on the blueprint.

The silence is broken in an abrupt fashion, when Meana exclaims, "Aha!" She taps the paper and proceeds to take a picture of the spot of interest. A couple quick taps of her fingers, and Meana sends the picture of interest to an unknown number. With the same speed she had grabbed the blueprint, she folds it and stuffs it back into the glove box. Meana steals a glance at her watch to see how long until midnight. Only five minutes left until midnight, and only five minutes until her plan goes into effect. With a silent shift of her body and an even-quieter sleight of hand, Meana stands outside the vehicle, and wears an all-black uniform, and flak jacket resembling that of the gate-guard. She makes her way to the end of the alley in which she has been waiting, and pulls a sleek, black radio from her pocket. She glances at her watch once more and counts down the seconds until midnight, "Five, four, three, two, one."

She triggers the key on the radio and says, "Alpha Team, we are a go. Proceed with Operation Cry of a Valkyrie."

Hearing a double-clicking tone of acknowledgement over the radio, she turns her sights to the guard at the gate. The street lights above the main gate and the lights of the guard-house flicker, then die. Meana works her way across the poorly graded street, and presses herself against the brick exterior of the guardhouse.

She can hear the female guard questioning, "What the hell is going on?"

Just when Meana is about to step from the shadows, the guards radio goes off loud-and-clear, "Gate Guard, report. We lost visual of the front-gate. The cameras are down!"

The guard scrambles out of her chair in surprise, and nearly trips as she grabs the radio to respond and says, "Gate Guard to Command, I'm checking on the main power-box now. I'll report back in five minutes."

A loud and gruff voice responds, "Make it quick. How do you copy?"

"Solid copy on my end," the guard replies scoffing and mocking the voice on the radio.

Meana fiddles with her watch, mentally noting the current time, and realizes that she has less than five minutes to complete her plan of action. With the lights out and the guard-house heavily darkened, Meana slides her way in through the front door and sees the guard scrambling to find her phone. The guard shuffles around, bumping into the table where her phone was and knocking over a chair as she reaches down to pick it up. Turning the light of the phone on, she illuminates the entirety of the small building. With the guard clearly in sight, Meana moves closer with predatory swiftness. She effortlessly grabs the young woman from behind and places her in a choke hold.

A well-placed forearm against the guard's jugular allows Meana to apply pressure with ease. She tucks her face in between her own arm and the back of the guard's head, and steadily keeps her hold firm. With her face well protected and grip strong than ever, all that's left to do is wait for the guard's life to cease.

The guard flails around in a desperate attempt to save herself, and while gasping for air, she hoarsely cries out, "Please. Please, don't kill me."

Feeling her heart sink at the sound of this innocent woman struggling for her life, Meana makes a split-second decision and changes the style of choke hold. No longer crushing the guard's jugular, she restricts the carotid arteries of the neck and reapplies her hold. The blood that was once pounding through this young guard's neck stops, and the supply to her brain diminishes. The guard's body quickly goes limp, and she is rendered unconscious. Ensuring not to drop the guard, Meana gently drags the body to a small utility closet and sets her down with the utmost care.

Looking upon the unconscious woman, pity washes over Meana, and she says, "I won't make you a casualty of my war."

She looks around the small space and sees an orange six-foot electrical cord sitting on a low-leveled shelf. She reaches down, picks it up, and binds the guard using a taut-line hitch knot. If the guard wakes earlier than expected, then she will be unable to break free, as this knot tightens the more, she struggles. Meana pulls a black bandana from her right cargo pocket and ties a gag around the guard's mouth and head. She gives the bandana a tight squeeze and steps back to look at her handy-work. Satisfied that the she will be unable to get loose or scream for help, Meana relieves the guard of her cap and radio. Unclipping the radio from the guard's flak jacket, she stops to gaze upon the face of her captive. Seeing that the young woman's hair is slightly in her face, Meana gently reaches down and presses the loose hair behind the guard's ear. She stands upright, turns her back to the guard, and proceeds to shut and lock the door. Unclipping her flashlight and turning it on to look around, she quickly picks up the fallen chair and places it back into its original position.

She takes her own radio out of her back pocket, hits the key, and says, "Alpha Team, initiate phase two."

A double-clicking tone of acknowledgment is heard, and the lights of the guard-house begin to illuminate.

Instantly the gruff voice on the radio chimes in and says, "Command to Gate Guard, we have a visual on the gate again. Maintain your post and stay off your damn phone. How do you copy?"

Meana steadies her breath and mimics the tone of the gate guard, "Solid copy. Gate Guard out." She then places the guard's radio on the table, gently takes a seat where the guard was once sitting, and very subtly adjusts her cap to sit a little lower on her face. Meana pulls the other radio from her back pocket and with a soft yet stern voice says, "Bravo Team, in T-minus twenty-seven minutes, initiate phase three."

Two clicks of acknowledgment fill the empty static of the radio, and Meana returns it to her pocket. With twenty-seven minutes to spare and waves of exhaustion weighing her down, Meana begins to reminisce on times long past.

Controlling the Chaos

An eighteen-year-old Meana is woken by a screaming Marine Corps drill instructor, dressed in starched green trousers, a wrinkle-less, tan, short-sleeve button-up uniform layered with decoratively colorful ribbons, and a "Smokey Bear" style cap, that has come aboard the hot and crowded bus she has been a captive on for the past four hours.

"Everybody, wake the fuck up and pay attention!" the drill instructor shouts at the top of his lungs. "When I call out your name, you will respond with, 'Here, sir,' and nothing else. Do you understand me?" Pausing to observe the motionless bus, the drill instructor turns his nose to the sky and takes a large sniff of the air.

"Smells like shit and fear in here!"

Not a single person dares to respond, and only a fraction of a second goes by before he starts screaming again, "When I speak, you will respond with, 'Sir, yes sir, 'Sir no sir,' or 'Aye-aye, sir!' Do you understand me?"

This time the women on the bus respond with a meek and half-hearted, "Sir, yes, sir."

The drill instructor and his furrowed brow continue to vocalize, "Scream at that top of your lungs, or so help me, you will never step foot on my yellow footprints!"

The women increase their volume to an acceptable level, shouting, "Sir, yes, sir!" Without so much as a second thought, the drill instructor enthusiastically continues with roll call. Time melts by and he calls the last of the names and begins to vocalize the next set of instructions.

"When I say move, you are going to line up single file on the yellow footprints outside of my bus, and from then on out, you will be known as recruits. Do you understand me?" he says while pointing to the multiple rows of yellow footprints painted outside on the ground.

"Sir, yes, sir!" the newly labeled recruits shout in an unorganized and random fashion.

"Get off the bus, now! Move, move, move!" the drill instructor screams as his voice cracks, causing him to pause for a split second just before pushing and shoving recruits off the bus in an effort to mask his own embarrassment.

Meana and her fellow recruits begin to scurry off the bus as if their lives depended on it. She approaches the narrow and grossly steep opening and attempts to take a slow and well-placed step through the bus's door, when all of a sudden, she is sent flying forward. Before she hits the ground, she manages to glance back and see the maniacal smile of the drill instructor and his outstretched arm.

With a loud and sickening crack, she hits the freshly paved asphalt. She lies there, feeling lifeless, and her only thought is, *"Dickhead."* She can hear a slight ringing in her ears, and the sounds around her seem to muffle altogether. She lifts her already-tired and aching body from the ground, and gray clouds roll in, causing the sky to darken. Noticing the quickened pace of the dimming light, Meana fixes her gaze to the sky with astonishment and is simultaneously smacked in the back by a fellow recruit.

"Better stand on a set of footprints before he gets off the bus," whispers another female recruit.

Meana is still in a daze, and stumbles to the first available pair of yellow footprints. She places one foot on a print and is knocked out of her spot by two female recruits fighting for the same set. Once again, she ends up plastered on the asphalt. However, this time the drill instructor is standing over her, and his furrowed brow looks upon her with great disdain. Meana gazes up in fear and looks at his face, while the gray sky cries out with a great and terrifying bolt of lightning that illuminates the sky with an assortment of purples, reds, and yellows. The sound of thunder is so loud, the screams of the drill instructor are drowned out, and Meana lays helpless without a clue as to what she is supposed to do.

The drill instructor reaches down and pulls her up by the collar of her shirt, and all at once, his voice is loud and clear, "I said get up and get back on the yellow footprints, maggot!"

Meana hesitates, but manages to choke out a pitiful "Sir, yes, sir."

The drill instructor releases his Titan-like grip from her shirt and turns to yell about the history behind the yellow footprints to the newly commissioned recruits.

"Thousands of Marines before you have stood where you now stand, and you will carry on their tradition of excellence and courage." He stops to catch a breath before continuing again, "You are now aboard Marine Corps Recruit Depot Parris Island of South Carolina, and you have taken the first step to joining the finest institution of warriors known to mankind, the United States Marine Corps!" He looks away from the recruits and points to the front of the recruit-receiving barracks. "Walking through the doors ahead of you will be an acceptance of the challenges to come, and those doors are the portal leading you to the chaotic world known as Parris Island!"

Meana seizes the opportunity to look around, and marvels at the giant set of doors. They are completely wrapped in silver, and in the center of each door rests a Marine Corps emblem, seemingly bigger than her entire body. Mid gawk, she is interrupted by a set of hands, pushing her forward. She stumbles and regains her balance while realizing that the disorganized herd of recruits are making their way toward the silver doors of the damned.

The drill instructor yells out as they press forward, "No civilians will ever walk through these doors! They are only for those willing to accept the challenge!"

Once again, a tremendous flash of lightning litters the sky, only this time its vibrant colors refract off the silver doors and are distorted enough to reflect what could be the fires of hell. Meana instinctively tries to step back but the giant silver threshold open, and the platoon of female recruits are rushed inside. She crosses the threshold of the underworld and sees a team of female and male drill instructors standing nearby. The drill instructors quickly and aggressively guide the recruits to the desks spread out among the tight room. As the recruits settle into their seats, a lone female drill instructor approaches the front of this classroom-like formation. She has a face made of iron and a gaze that cuts to the bone. The group of recruits sit silent and deathly still while the lead drill instructor raises her hand toward them with all her fingers extended outward and her elbow firmly locked. Opening her mouth to speak, the air of the room changes, and the temperature skyrockets. Meana is sweating profusely and attempting not to touch her face as the lead drill instructor feeds the recruits instructions faster than they can process them. Her voice sounds like she has been smoking cigarettes since birth, and Meana has a difficult time understanding anything that comes out of her mouth, but still, she dares not look away.

Before anyone has a chance to raise their hand and ask any questions, the lead drill instructor starts yelling, "Get up out of my seats, and move!"

Her command ends, and the other drill instructors that have been stalking around the recruits like they are prey, attack in full force. A surge of green trousers, tan tops, and Smokey Bear-style caps come crashing down upon the recruits, and the still-scorching stiffness of the air is drastically changed. There is stomping of feet, slapping of desks, grown men and women screaming at the top of their lungs; it is complete and utter chaos. The sound level of the entire building jumps so high, any commands that are being given all blurred together. In all the confusion, the female recruits are being ushered to an area with old-school, corded, black telephones mounted along a long brick wall. Recruits gather in squiggly lines behind each telephone and are being screamed at to pick the handset of the telephones up and call their emergency contacts. Taped to these black telephones is a small paper that has a set of sentences the recruits are to read verbatim. Meana stands in line to wait for her turn, and sees the walking sacks of veins in uniforms screaming at recruits and throwing spit in every direction imaginable. Recruits are picking up the handsets and dialing the numbers to their emergency contacts and yelling the scripted message at the top of their lungs as they were instructed. Less than a minute passes, and it is time for Meana to step up to the telephone. Before she could even take a step forward, a female drill instructor that's approximately five feet and two inches, with olive skin, and jet-black hair turns and gazes at Meana with black, pit-like eyes and immediately screams at the top of her lungs.

"Hurry up, buttercup! You think I give a shit about your time! You're in my house now! Move!"

Meana does as she is instructed and briskly steps to the telephone. She pauses and stares at the telephone, and turns to face the female drill instructor that has been breathing fire down her back.

"Ma'am?" Meana says.

"What the hell do you want, recruit?" the angry woman lashes back.

Meana takes a deep breath and whimpers, "I don't know who to call." The face of the female drill instructor turns purple, and Meana instantly realizes she has made a grave mistake.

"I?" screams the drill instructor. "You are no longer an I! From here on out, you will say, this recruit! Do you understand me?"

Feeling the color drain from her face, Meana screams, "Aye-aye, ma'am!" at the top of her lungs and turns to face the phone once more.

The drill instructor then yells, "I don't give a rat's ass if you have anyone to call!" She picks up the handset and thrusts it at Meana and proceeds to say, "Punch in whatever numbers you want and just start screaming!"

Meana reaches out and takes the handset from the female drill instructor and does exactly as told. She punches in a random set of numbers and screams at the telephone handset at the top of her lungs even though there is no one on the other end of the line.

"I have arrived at Marine Corps Recruit Depot Parris Island, and I am safe!"

Meana sets the handset down and quickly runs to get in line behind the other recruits waiting along the brick wall opposite the phones. She takes a moment to catch her breath and stands as straight as she can muster. The fear of any drill instructor catching her slouching or looking around is like ice running through her veins. Her heart is pounding, and adrenaline slithers through her body while she looks upon the remainder of the recruits on the telephones getting slaughtered by saliva missiles and ear-rupturing screams.

The last of the recruits finally finish screaming their lungs out, and the large group is corralled out of the telephone area and into a classroom. The drill instructors continue to scream and slam about as the recruit's squeeze through the doorway of the classroom a dozen at a time. Without being told to, they all take a seat at their own desks; and as fast as the drill instructors appear, they vanish. The door slams behind the last of the recruits, and with all eyes facing toward the front, they see an older, heavyset gentleman with long, graying hair and thick stubble on his chin. Knowing that he must be a civilian, the recruits allow themselves to slouch a little into their chairs.

Noticing how relaxed the women in the room have become, the gentleman says, "I wouldn't do that if I were you. They're still watching you through the doors. They'll pounce on anyone they see slouching, as soon as you all step back out of this room."

Bodies quickly snap back to upright positions, and Meana can see fear swelling throughout the plain white walled room. With the gentleman satisfied that it was a good time to move forward with his instructive class, he pulls a laminated piece of paper out of a light-brown, one-strap leather bag and holds it high into the air.

"If you look down on your desk, you'll see this paper with two banking choices." He pauses to catch his breath, already wheezing not but a few sentences into his monologue. "Choose one, and whatever the choice, the money you earn in boot camp will be transferred to that account." A recruit in the back of the room raises her hand, and the overweight gentleman, annoyed at an interruption, looks her straight in the eyes. With no pause between breaths this time, he completely ignores her risen hand and says, "No one is allowed to use a pre-existing bank account. You must use these choices."

The recruit gently lowers her hand and averts her gaze toward the laminated sheet on her desk in embarrassment. Meana takes the time to look at her own sheet and notices that the paperwork has a line down the middle, and on either side is a picture of a bank and a description of their services. She also notices that the pictures and descriptions are exactly the same and that the only difference is, one is black and white, where the other is in color.

Without meaning to, she lets out a loud scoff of disapproval and immediately bites her bottom lip afterward. The gentleman looks directly at Meana, and with a squished and annoyed-looking face, raises his hand and points an oversized sausage finger at her. Meana stares at this grotesque finger in bewilderment and wonders what he could possibly have to say. Seconds go by, and not a word has been said, and just when Meana is about to exclaim, "What?" the door to the classroom is ripped open, and three tall, angry-looking female drill instructors burst through in unison. Meana, now knowing what the finger meant, takes a large gulp of her spit and feels the color in her face dissipate. With them screaming commands at subsonic tones, Meana stands and sits over and over again as the drill instructors slam their hands on the desk and spit loogies of terror into her eyes.

Meana is attempting to respond to each command given, but is unable to keep up as she erects her body over and over again, screaming, "Aye-aye, ma'am," as fast as possible. With sweat pouring down her face and her shirt drenched, the drill instructors quickly turn around and run out of the door, slamming it as they do. Meana, having learned her lesson, sits in her seat quietly for the remainder of the man's class. He wears a smug smirk while going over the banking information and proceeds to go over the legal documents they needed to sign before officially starting their training. With his endless talking complete, the man picks up his belongings and makes his way to the door.

A drill instructor opens the door for him, and when he passes, the male drill instructor says, "Sir," and gives the robust man a nod.

The drill instructor briefly comes into the room and shouts, "Sit in your seats, and don't move a muscle! I better not hear a peep out of you until I get back. Do you understand me?"

Knowing how to respond, the female recruiters scream in a more-organized fashion, "Sir, yes, sir!"

He briskly walks out of the classroom and gently closes the door behind himself.

The recruits sit for what seems like hours, in a deafening silence. A subtle clearing of a throat or shifting in a seat can be heard, and Meana is appreciative of every one of them. Each sound lets her know she indeed still has her hearing and she has not fallen asleep. She casually glances out of the corner of her eye and can see other recruits sitting as straight as possible, but their heads are bobbing up and down as they battle exhaustion.

Meana feels her eyes crossing and sleep taking over. A female drill instructor quickly opens the door and screams, "Stop bobbing for dick!" and then slams the door before getting a response.

All the recruits somehow manage to sit even straighter than before as they realize they are still being watched.

Yet again, what seems like hours passes by, and Meana can feel her bladder swelling inside. She can see legs shaking back and forth all around the classroom and can hear the groans of her fellow recruits as they too, struggle to hold it in. At that exact moment, the same female drill instructor from before enters the classroom and instructs the recruits to stand and make their way out into the hallway in a single-file line. With a newfound speed, every female recruit in the room shoots up and is lined against the wall just outside the classroom. The female drill instructor enters the hall and walks down toward the first recruit in line.

"Follow me," she growls in a low but still-hostile voice. The recruits follow her down the hallway, and within a few quick turns, they stand in front of the female restroom. The drill instructor looks back at them with an angry look and says, "This is called a head. You will go in five at a time, and as one comes out, another goes in. Do you understand me?"

The female recruits yell at the top of their lungs, "Yes, ma'am!"

"Shut the hell up!" the female drill instructor says, attempting to regulate her own tone of voice. "You are not authorized to yell in the hallways from here on out. Now get moving."

Not a word is said as the first five recruits sprint toward the head. Meana has somehow found herself in the back of the line, and even though each female is running in and out at a quicken pace, she feels a horrible pain in her stomach and bladder as the swelling sensation continues.

"Please don't piss yourself, please don't piss yourself," she repeats in desperation, inched closer and closer to the head.

Finally making it to the front of the line, she runs inside, throws herself on a toilet, and begins to relieve her bladder in the doorless stall. Halfway through relieving her bladder, the female drill instructor marches into the head and loudly screams, "Hurry the fuck up!" and starts counting down from one hundred, "One hundred, ninety-nine, ninety-eight, seventy-four, seventy-two, seventy, forty-three, forty!"

Meana knows that she has never excelled in math, but she was damn sure there was no reason to count down from one hundred and skip half the numbers. She clenches her abdominal muscles tightly in an effort to squeeze out more urine, and a harder flow of liquid can be heard hitting the water in the bowl.

The female drill instructor pauses from her counting and says, "That's what I'm talking about. Now get the fuck out!"

Meana replies with a soft, "Aye-aye, ma'am," knowing she'd have to take what she got.

With pants pulled up, she stands and steps out of the stall and is rushed out of the head. She gets back in line and stares down at her hands in disgust.

"I didn't even get to wash my hands."

Many more hours pass while Meana and her fellow recruits are moved around the building multiple times, filling out paperwork and eating their first boxed chow for lunch. The box chow consists of a dry ham-and-cheese sandwich, two hard-boiled eggs, and one oatmeal-flavored cookie in a small, white cardboard box. They did not, however, get to eat the cookie.

A female drill instructor orders them all to throw it in the trash and clearly states, "You haven't earned a damn cookie yet!"

Not feeling the temptation of starvation taking hold, the other recruits stare down at their dry sandwich and funny-smelling hard-boiled eggs in disgust. However, Meana, empty's the contents of a salt packet onto an egg and stuffs it into her mouth. Hearing the groaning and low complaining of the other recruits in the room, she shrugs her shoulders looks at a fellow recruit staring her down in disbelief. Wearing a blank expression, she shoves the other egg into her mouth.

With their five-minute chow time completed, the recruits are uplifted from their location and marched to a separate building about one-half mile away. Meana and her fellow recruits walk in a gangly formation, attempting to stay on step with each other as the hot summer sun burns them to a crisp and the drill instructor melodically screaming, "Left, left, left, right left!" Thinking to herself, *"This is the worst walk of my life,"* she trudges along, barely keeping in formation. They arrive at a building similar to the recruit-receiving barracks, and Meana can see the exterior is made of the same old red brick, but this time there are no special doors to greet them, just a set of plain glass double doors. The drill instructor plucks a recruit from the formation and has her hold the door as the rest of the recruit's march inside in a single-file line. They find themselves located in a storage-type facility with mounds of shoe boxes and uniforms nearby.

The drill instructor screams, "You're going to stay in line, and you're going to follow the instructions of the people before you. Do you understand me?"

"Ma'am, yes, Ma'am!" the recruits scream in a much more organized manner than before.

They look about and see a group of civilians standing by and ready to size them for their uniforms. The recruits are guided to the start of the line by a nice civilian woman that tenderly calls each of them "Baby." One by one, the recruits are fitted for their uniforms, and once completed, they receive two sets of green camouflage uniforms, three tan camouflage uniforms, two seabags, two pairs of boots, and many other items to start their journey.

Forced to stuff their newly acquired items into the seabags with haste, each recruit is instructed to carry them toward the entryway of the building. Lifting her seabags with a loud groan, Meana whispers to a nearby recruit, "Each of these weighs a metric shit ton." The fellow recruit looks to her with fear in her eyes and doesn't say a word.

All the recruits are ushered outside and back into a gangly formation. They have one large seabag on their backs and another hanging loosely from their front. Each recruit struggles to see past the oversized seabags as they trek toward the main building. Even though the sun is starting to set, heat waves emerge from the ground in every direction. Feeling her temperature skyrocket and sweat engulf the entirety of her body, Meana's legs start to cramp. Her pace dramatically slows, and she falls behind.

She attempts to catch her breath, and the female drill instructor screams, "Each and every one of you that falls out will have to do this march again if you don't catch up!"

Meana looks back, thinking she is the only one to fall out, but in doing, so she can see that half of the formation is behind her and walking at a snail's pace. Each recruit is sweating non-stop, with ghostly faces and slumped shoulders, looking like they are ready to keel over at any second. Meana, not feeling so bad about herself, summons the energy to push on and manages to catch up to her original spot in the formation.

They reach the building, and Meana thinks all is done when, out of nowhere, the drill instructor screams, "Turn around, we need to get the weak bodies back in formation!"

Feeling her heart sink and hearing a slew of depressed sighs, the formation swings a wide U-turn and marches back toward the uniform facility until all the fallen recruits are brought back into formation. Farther from the main building, the formation in totality turns and marches forward once again. An eternity seems to pass, and Meana can feel a painful kiss from the sun forming on her forehead. The sounds of heavy breathing fill the air while the last of the recruits finally make it to the building. The formation is dismantled and ordered to walk up a flight of stairs in a single-file line to an empty room on the second floor of the recruit-receiving building.

"Get those ass' moving. I don't have all day to wait on you!" says the female drill instructor that has been stuck with the recruits all day. She then has them drop their gear inside the empty, white, laminate tiled room and orders them to take a seat on top of their seabags. She then says, "I'll be back soon. Don't you dare fall asleep," and she turns about and walks out of the door.

Literal hours pass in this empty windowless room, and recruits stare about in a desperate attempt to stay awake.

"Does anyone know what time it is?" a random recruit closest to the door says.

Another immediately fires back, "Shut up! If she comes back and sees us talking, we're dead!"

Giving each other nasty looks, the recruit closest to the door stands and walks circles in a desperate attempt to stay awake.

Meana decides that she, too, is going to stand and walk about, and just when she fully erects herself, a female recruit looks at her and says, "I'm dying of exhaustion too, but I wouldn't risk getting up."

Meana throws her a cold look and walks around anyway. Even more time passes by, and the drill instructor finally returns. She pulls two recruits from the room and has them run down stairs and back up with the next set of box chows. The recruits greedily dig into their boxes; this time no one makes a face of disgust. The room is silent as the drill instructor waits outside and allows the recruits to finish their chow. Returning once more to have them toss their cookies away, the female drill instructor starts screaming at the recruits to stand up and pick up their gear.

Once they have done so, she looks around the room and says, "It's 0500! Welcome to day two of hell week!"

Checking In

Steady breath and rock-solid hands grasp Meana with confidence. She looks into a plain, stainless-steel mirror mounted on the wall of her newly assigned barracks room and admires herself more than ever before. Smiling while peering into the mirror, Meana mentally readies herself for this monumental day. In a matter of a few months, she has successfully completed the thirteen-week boot camp, four-week Marine combat training, and the six-week admin course required of her. Having committed to this new life of excellence, she is anxious to check-in to her first duty station.

Many early hours have been spent on measuring the solitary ribbon on her standard-issue Alphas uniform and ensuring her Corfam shoes and brimmed cap have the perfect shine. She earned the National Defense Service ribbon by enlisting into the military during a time of war, and even though she is a long way away from having a large stack of her own ribbons, her confidence is at an all-time high. With an unwavering gaze into the mirror, she checks the razor-sharp crease that runs down each leg of her trousers and ensures that her form-fitted jacket is lint-free. Mounted on each sleeve of her uniform jacket is her rank, and it is represented as a singular scarlet-colored chevron with a green secondary color on the inside. Although she is only a private first class, she feels immense pride in the uniform she is wearing and once again measures the lone ribbon on the left breast of her uniform. Feeling certain the uniform is exactly as it should be, she begins to recite the Marine Corps general orders in the mirror.

Twenty minutes swiftly goes by, and she still stares into the mirror of her twelve-foot-by-sixteen-foot barracks room composed of flaky white walls, scuffed, ivory-colored tiles, and a smell to kill. On each side of the room is a sole twin-sized bed, one old metal wardrobe cabinet, and a faded-green chair that has even more stains than her mattress. Body musk and an old urine smell still waft in the air from the prior tenants, and yet Meana couldn't be any prouder of her new domicile. She looks herself in the eyes one last time and turns toward her small, twin-sized bed. She walks in a very stiff and cautious manner, ensuring not to move any piece of the uniform out of place. She calmly picks up her military identification card from the bed and places it into the left breast pocket of her uniform. She awkwardly reaches down like an ill-lubed robot to secure her phone and car keys and with extreme caution, stands, and makes her way to the door. From head to toe, her body screams in agony and pleads to be set free, for each step taken is another chance to unravel her tightly fitted uniform. Gently stepping one foot after another, she can feel the shirt-stays beginning to rub the thin skin upon the back of her knee raw. *This is going to be one long and painful morning,*" she thinks to herself, continuing her path to the door. Taking a full minute to reach the threshold to freedom, she has the doorknob in one hand and cautiously turns her wrist in an effort to resist turning her arm. Successfully opening the door, she takes two well-placed steps and plants both feet outside of her room.

Just before closing the door, Meana hears her more-seasoned roommate yell out from under the blankets, "Have fun, boot!"

Meana pauses and manages to suppress the majority of her irritation with a deep breath, but her anger still shows when she slams the door behind herself and briskly marches down the exterior walkway of her first-floor barracks room. Allowing the irritation to seep in further, she forgets that her uniform desperately needs to stay clean, and cuts through the twenty-foot patch of grass between her door and the start of the parking lot. She lifts her feet higher to avoid the unmaintained Dallis-grass and finds herself at the end of the patch in just a few seconds. Stopping at the edge of the grass to take another deep breath, she shakes her hands at her side and violently dispels her anger. She uncomfortably makes her way to the other end of the parking lot without, messing up her uniform and somehow managing not to sweat the hairspray out of her perfectly formed hair bun in the ever-increasing southern humidity. With her faded silver sedan ahead, she continues to push forward until she is but five feet from her driver door, and just when she raises her hand and pushes the button to unlock it, she hears a revolting squish sound come from under her shoe. Meana stops dead in her tracks and dreads to look at the mysterious formation that clings to the sole of her right Corfam dress-shoe. With eyes like razor-sharp daggers, she lifts her shoe and cuts through the darkness of the early morning to look upon the fresh dog feces that encrusts the entirety of her sole and forces its way around the edge.

Staring at her shoe in horror, her heart pounds and she shouts, "Fuck!"

Frantically looking around for anything to wipe her shoe on, she sees a small clump of weeds sticking out of a crack in the asphalt. In a panic, she attempts to wipe the dog feces from her sole on the small patch of weeds, but to no avail. She finally decides to wing it and removes her Corfams. With no choice but to throw her shoes in the trunk of her car to hide the scent, she hits the trunk-release button on the car remote, but nothing happens. She hits it over and over again and comes to the conclusion that the remote battery must be dead. She lets out a frustrated sigh and decides to open the trunk manually with the key. Briskly making her way to the rear of the car while wearing nothing but her black uniform dress socks on her feet, she suddenly feels another squish underfoot and immediately knows that she has stepped in yet another pile of dog feces. Only this time the substance seeps through the socks and makes its way in between her toes. Meana, more frustrated than ever, lets out a loud scream of frustration and throws her Corfams at her car. The shoes bounce off the vehicle with a loud thud, leaving a small dent and a smear of dog feces in their wake.

Minutes pass as Meana stands frozen in place with her face buried in her hands. Finally deciding that it is the time to fix the predicament she has gotten herself into, she makes her way to the back of the car with a walk of defeat. Standing in front of the trunk, she inserts the key. She turns it with ease and lets out a victory sigh as the trunk opens.

"Fucking finally," she exclaims, staring at the black interior lining of her trunk.

She turns her attention to her shoes and bends over to pick them up. As she does, one of her shirt-stays pops and hits her in the back of the knee. She doesn't sigh. She doesn't wince. She simply picks up her shoes and throws them in the trunk of her car. She then removes her socks and throws them to the wayside as she slams the trunk closed. Meana opens the driver-side door of her car and checks her watch to see if she has enough time to drive back to her barracks room. Unfortunately, it took her fifteen minutes to walk across the parking lot, and she knows that she no longer has enough time to swap out her socks and wash her feet and shoes. Making a split decision, she closes the door of her vehicle and inserts the key into the ignition. The car roars to life, and Meana, knowing that she will likely be late to check in to her unit, throws the car into drive and stomps on the gas. The car tires screech, and she rips the wheel to the right and then to the left as she makes her way out of the parking lot and to the Combat Logistics Regiment 29 building.

Pulling into the regimental parking lot, her car stops with a loud, screeching halt. Throwing the vehicle into park, Meana frantically unsnaps her seat belt and jumps out of the car. She manually pops the trunk and pulls out the feces-encrusted shoe.

Realizing that she has no socks and her feet smell like dog shit, she quietly stares out into the distance and says, "I am so fucked."

With no other choice, she throws them onto her feet and closes the trunk of her car. Lifting her chest in an attempt to show false confidence, she walks to the entrance of the all-brick regimental building and opens the doors. Entering the building, she soon realizes that it is no more than a warehouse filled with shelf after shelf of communications gear. Wooden crates of broken communication gear litter the building, and one hundred feet to the left is an office space that looks to have been commissioned after the building's original erection. There is not a person in sight, and she finally decides that she's going to walk into the office with confidence and start asking about the administration's platoon that she is to check-in to. However, her nerves take hold as she walks over to the main door of this small, makeshift office space. She attempts to shake off her nerves by violently shaking her hands at her side. With her nerves slightly calmed, she turns the handle of the door and enters the office. The office space is half full, and exhausted-looking admin Marines sit inside their cubicles, clicking away on the keyboards of their desktops. She looks about in an attempt to find anyone with a higher rank than her own when the entry door suddenly slams behind her. Standing awkwardly by the entrance, every Marine in the office stops and turns to stare at the noise maker who has entered their space. Moments of silence pass, and a young corporal in a tan digital-camouflage uniform stands from his desk and makes his way to her. Meana, starstruck and gawking at the young Marine, envisions a younger Colin Farrell with oceanic-blue eyes effortlessly walking with swagger in her direction. Standing only five feet and nine inches tall, with medium-faded, jet-black hair, and oliv-tan skin, he throws a debonair smile at Meana, and she begins to sweat.

He stands before her and asks, "You need help, boot?"

27

Meana, hearing only muffled noises in the distance, continued to stare into his vibrant-blue eyes. The young man looks around at his fellow Marines, and they all snicker at the new girl standing before them in awkward silence.

"Earth to boot!" he says a little louder than before.

Meana snaps back to the present and stammers, "O-o-oh, my ap-p-p-pologies, Corporal. I'm here to check in."

Letting out a loud laugh, he says, "Yeah, your green pickle suit gave that away. That's why I asked if you needed help."

"Yes, Corporal, that would be fantastic. Who do I need to report to?"

Looking at her uniform and hair thoroughly, he says, "Gunny is going to have a field day with you." He circles behind her and stops mid-way, covering his nose and saying, "You smell like shit."

The other Marines in the office laugh hysterically as this new Marine is being chastised not five feet from the entrance of the office. With all the noise and commotion going on outside, the gunnery sergeant opens the door to his office and stands ominously in the doorway, trying to figure out the source. Seeing a lumbering figure in a formfitting tan camouflage uniform, Meana's casual sweat becomes a downpour.

Seeing the frightened look on her face, the young male Marine turns to look at Gunny and smiles maniacally as he whispers to her, "You're fucked now."

The gunnery sergeant with his eagle eyes spots the new Marine and says with a loud and booming voice, "Get over here."

Meana walks like her life depends on it and assumes the position of attention with a few feet between her and the gunny. He steps from the doorway, and she can see every detail on this muscle-bound, rich-Umber-colored man. His face looks smoother than any shave she has ever seen, and his eyebrows are nicely plucked.

Meana allows her mind to wonder and thinks to herself, *"Does he go to a beauty parlor for those razor-sharp eyebrows?"* He continues to fill the gap between them, and Meana takes a loud and obvious gulp of her spit, allowing her nerves to climb higher and higher. Standing before her, he immediately starts to inspect her uniform.

He berates her with corrections in a stern voice, "I see you're not wearing any socks, and I can also see that you've managed to sweat the majority of your hair-spray out and have frizzy hairs in every direction." He pauses and takes a large whiff of air. "How about next time you wipe your ass before putting your uniform on, Marine," he says in disapproval.

With that comment, the Marines in the office can hold in their laughter no longer, and they let loose. She loses her bearing and glares at gunny with her piercing green eyes, and for a moment, he hesitates. The Marines in the office hoot and holler, while Meana and the gunny stand in a locked-down stare, neither drawing so much as a breath.

In the distance, the young corporal sees the tension mounting between the two and quickly intervenes, "Excuse me, Gunny. I'll be more than happy to take this Marine back to her barracks room to change into her camouflage utilities."

Without breaking his intense gaze, Gunny slightly turns his head and says, "You do that, Corporal Pierce."

The young corporal reaches out and clasps one hand around Meana's arm and firmly pulls her away from the Gunny, while simultaneously saying, "Let's go, Marine. We need to have you changed and ready to start your check-in process. It'll be a long one."

Illusionary Intimacy

Months of sitting in the same cubicle has left Meana bitter. She comes in everyday with the same exhausted look that haunts the faces of her fellow Marines. The endless cycle of an admin Marines life: sit, type, upload documents, answer the phone, cry in silence, and repeat. This mundane existence is not what she signed up for. Meana averts her eyes from the political article upon her desktop computer screen and gazes to her left at the wall not but twelve-inches from her face. Upon this dirty white wall are chunks of peeling paint and a slanted poster of a young Marine wearing his dress blues uniform and brandishing a finely oiled and shined M1-Garand. His expression is of discipline and sheer will-power.

"What a load of shit," she quietly says to herself, turning back to her computer screen, maneuvering the mouse around, and opening her work email, only to see there are thirty unopened emails to read.

Letting out a frustrated sigh of defeat, she angrily pushes the mouse away from herself and rubs her temples. Every day that she sits in front of this computer, she feels a pressure grow above her brow until it feels like her head is about to pop. She continues to rub her temples vigorously and moves her hands to the base of her skull where it meets the neck. An inflamed feeling fills her neck, and she rotates her head in circles, attempting to alleviate the tightness.

During the first rotation, her neck cracks like thunder, and the sound is so loud she stops mid-turn and questions, "What the actual fuck?"

Returning her hands to her desk and allowing them to rest motionless on the flat surface, she peers down at the items she has gathered around. On this all-black, particle board desk lay a stapler, a few paper clips, her computer screen, mounds of files to sort through, and her weapon of choice, a black ball-point pen. Looking at her desk in disappointment, she reaches into the right breast pocket of her tan camouflage uniform and pulls out a small desk key. Inserting the key quietly, she unlocks and opens the top right-hand drawer to her desk. She pulls out an all-black notebook with nothing but the Marine Corps logo on the front. Carefully placing the little black book on the desk, she casually reaches for her pen and suspiciously looks about the office. Finally determining that there is no one close enough to read the contents of her black book, she flips open the lid and continues to flip until she has reached the first blank page. She shakes the black-inked pen in her hand, ensuring that there is plenty of ink at the tip for writing, and she begins.

Journal entry 42:

> *He has eyes like the ocean that pierce through to the very depths of my soul. With one look, I am mystified and standing in a trance. His breath is like the mist of a fine sea breeze washing over me on a hot and humid day. When his sweat beads and runs through those chiseled pecs and down his rippling torso, I reciprocating between my thighs. What I wouldn't give for one touch, for one taste, for him to hold me in the loneliest of nights. At*

night, as I lay in my bed, his hands are my hands, and I maneuver them all around the curvature of my body. They gently graze my skin as they dance up my shirt and caress my breasts. With my shirt lifted, I imagine him bending forward and engulfing one of my nipples with his soft and luscious lips. My body tightens, and I can feel the fluids inside me begin to flow. He continues to suck on my nipple, and gently slides one hand down my torso and undoes the belt around my hips. With my pants undone, and zipper wide open, he slides one hand down under my panties and massages my clitoris in a smooth rotational pattern. I curl my toes and tilt my head back as the pleasure I feel causes my body to shudder in approval. Reading my mind, he relieves his lips from my nipple and begins to lightly kiss my torso as he pulls my skin-tight jeans and hot-pink panties down. With his head firmly between my legs, his tongue dances around, and the up-and-down motion on my clitoris makes my body tense with pleasure. The shuddering of my body continues while I rhythmically grind back and forth on his face. I inch closer and closer to my climax and instinctively tighten my thighs around his head. He gives no effort in relieving the grip I hold on his head, and he continues to kiss my lips profusely while increasing his speed at a slow and steady pace. The sweat that has formed between my breasts trickles down each side and I arch my back in anticipation of my climax. The pressure between my thighs tightens, and my body reaches an all-time high as it releases, and I begin to cum profusely. I wiggle my body back and forth harder, grinding on his face. All of my worries, and all of my stresses are washed away as his tongue continues to push my climax to its limits. Coming down from my sexual high, my body becomes completely loose, and I lay on the bed with legs shaking uncontrollably. He gives my vagina one last kiss and lifts himself from between my thighs and shoots me one of his infamous debonaire smiles.

Continuing to journal with passion in her eyes, she bites her bottom lip, and sweat forms above her brow and on her upper lip. She lays down her pen and scoots her chair back in an attempt to calm herself down. Nothing seems to be working, so she stands from her chair, and with arms raised high, she fans her face with open hands.

In the distance, and bored, Corporal Pierce swivels in his chair and see's the newly promoted Lance Corporal Crane strangely standing and waving her hands about. He rises from his chair and lethargically makes his way over to her cubicle. Unaware of his presence, Meana continues to fan herself in an attempt to cool down in the already-humid office. A sweat bead rolls down her back, and she can feel her green undershirt begin to stick to her skin.

Corporal Pierce stands three feet behind her and says, "You, okay?" Meana, with cat-like reflexes, just narrowly misses slapping Corporal Pierce in the face as she speedily whips around to face him. "Holy shit, Crane, you almost slapped me!" he exclaims in a playful voice.

With a look of horror upon her face, Meana frantically says, "I'm so sorry, Corporal. I didn't mean to!"

He lets out a small laugh and waves his hands about in a nonchalant manner. The air thickens between them, and Meana feels small stings of lightning in the air while she gazes into his oceanic-blue eyes. Her lungs feel tight, and her palms begin to sweat, and she stands silent. She opens her mouth in an attempt to reciprocate his playful banter when suddenly she remembers that her journal is lying open on top of her desk for all to see. She giggles uncontrollably as her nerves take hold, and all thoughts start to cloud in her mind.

Corporal Pierce gives a look of confusion and takes a step back, casually saying, "Okay, I'll just leave you to all that craziness over there." He briskly turns and walks away, whispering to himself, "Females."

Defying gravity itself, she whips around and slams the book shut so hard a large boom reverberates throughout her cubicle, and the Marines around her look up from their cell phones in curiosity.

"Can I help you?" she says with flare to her voice, and the Marines nearby simply look away and go back to their mobile phone games. "That was way too close," she says while packing the small black book into the digitally camouflaged backpack she brought to work. "I guess I can't bring this in to the office anymore. That was just stupid of me," she says, wiping the sweat from her forehead and looking at the shine upon her hand.

She sits back down at her desk, tosses the key into the drawer, and slowly closes it in an effort to not attract any more attention to herself. She clasps her fingers together and bends them in an outward motion, forcing them to crack.

"I guess it's time to get back to my article," she says, and places her hand back onto her mouse and begins clicking away.

Meanwhile, she is unaware that Corporal Pierce is gazing over the edge of his cubicle, watching her every move in curiosity. *"What a strange girl, but she is kind of cute,"* he thinks to himself, stealing one last glance at her before turning back to his social-media page that sits open on his computer screen. He types her name into the search bar of the social-media page, and amazingly enough, she is the first option to pop up in the long list of accounts to populate. He gingerly moves the pointer of the mouse over to her name and clicks the *Send friend request* button. Just before logging off of the social-media page, he smirks at the monitor and then continues to click over to his work program.

After aimlessly clicking about her work computer, Meana decides to pull out her phone and scroll through her social-media applications. She feels her cheeks blush when she sees the friend request from Ian Pierce. She turns around to steal a glance at him, and when she does, he is looking right at her. She snaps back toward her computer and hits the Accept button on her phone screen. Feeling butterflies in her stomach, she decides that maybe she is going to take the initiative. She maneuvers her way around the app and to Ian's profile. She clicks on the message icon and types, *"Let me know if I'm overstepping my boundaries, but were you just checking me out?"* She stares at the phone with wide eyes and waffles the idea of sending the message. Chickening out, she reaches for the Lock-Screen button of her phone with the index finger of the same hand that holds the phone, and the meaty part of her palm hits the send button. After clicking the Lock-Screen button, she hears the message-sent notification ping and stares at her phone in horror. She fiddles around with the phone and somehow forgets how to unlock the screen. Getting frustrated with the phone, she shakes it violently and finally manages to get the screen unlocked. With the app still open, she sees that she indeed sent the message even though her intent was to back out. Frozen in place, she continues to stare at the screen with a look of terror. Her mind races with excuses, and for a second, she contemplates telling Ian that the message was intended for someone else. She places her phone down on top of her desk, and with both hands, she clasps them over her mouth in disbelief. Not daring to turn around, Meana grabs the mouse to her computer and pretends to be working. Only a moment goes by, and she feels a slight breeze at her back.

Before she can turn around to look, Ian leans over her shoulder and whispers, "Checking you out is an understatement. I was full-blown gawking at your beauty."

Meana's body tenses as the sweet whispering breath of her office crush surrounds her like a fine aroma in a room of filth. She feels her temperature rise, and her thighs begin to quake with excitement.

Without turning around, she decides to play cool and says, "So you got my message? Took you long enough to walk over here."

Ian continues to lean over her shoulder and places one hand on her desk, pressing his chest against her back.

He looks around the office to ensure no one is watching and says, "If you're not busy tonight, how about we go out for dinner or something?"

Meana, unable to control her excitement, nearly yells out, "Yes," and leaps in her chair.

Keeping his composer cool and concentrated, Ian asks, "I'll stop by your room around six?"

She looks him deep in his eyes and bites her bottom lip while nods her head in agreement.

Ian removes his hand from her desk and leans back to a standing position.

He throws her a wink and a crisp smile just before exclaiming, "Damn it, Crane, how many times do I have to show you how to do your damn job?"

Meana hesitates for a second before catching on to the game and replies, "I apologize, Corporal. I'll get my shit together," and throws him an equally devious smile.

Ian walks back to his desk with a lean to his strut. Meana turns her body around just enough to watch his butt bob up and down while he makes his way to his desk, and she lets out a dreamy sigh and wipes the sweat from her upper lip.

The First Date

Meana stands outside her barracks room clothed in an all-black, formfitting dress with sequin patterns scattered around the chest and torso. Fiddling with her room key as she waits for her date to arrive, Meana continues to stand outside, looking like she is standing guard. Told that their date was to be a surprise and to ensure she was outside and ready by six, she glances down at her thin-strapped, silver-plated watch and checks the time. It is six-ten and he is nowhere to be seen. She sways side to side and gradually becomes more nervous.

"I hope he's not standing me up," she says, looking around, hoping to spot him.

Unfortunately, he is nowhere to be found, and Meana is forced to wait longer. Five more minutes dredge by, and a loud, all-black Ford Mustang slowly pulls up to the edge of the parking lot, and a young male Marine rolls the passenger-side window down and cat-calls at Meana. She looks up from the ground in disgust and squints her eyes in an attempt to see the driver. Forced to move closer, she takes a few steps, and the driver becomes clearer, it is Corporal Pierce. The look of disgust quickly washes from her face, and she smiles in return.

"Come on, we're going to be late!" he yells to Meana through the window.

She quickly makes her way to the car, cutting through the patch of grass in front of her room and ensuring not to get dirt on her vibrant-red, single-strapped, two-inch heels.

"Be gentle with the door, she's my baby," Corporal Pierce says to Meana with a deadly serious look on his face.

She gently opens the car door and sits in the passenger seat, and then cautiously closes it. Sitting in the passenger seat, she can smell and see the midnight-black leather interior of this modern Mustang and is blinded by the large LED screen that sits in the dash of the car.

"You like?" he asks, seeing her look about.

"Oh yeah, it's awesome," she says, trying to convince him and herself that her statement is genuine. Meana fastens her seat belt, and Corporal Pierce pulls out of the parking lot. "So where are we going-" she says just before pausing and realizing that she has no clue what to call him.

"First off, it is a surprise, and second, you can call me Ian when we are together," he says with a smirk on his face.

Meana, stuck on the word "together," feels her cheeks becoming red and says, "Sounds good to me."

Blowing through a few stop signs, Ian presses on, rarely letting off of the accelerator. Continuing to drive off base and out into town without turning the radio on, they sit in silence.

Realizing that the air seems stiff and awkward, Ian glances at Meana and says, "We are only about ten minutes out. I'm excited for you to see where we are going."

Feeling a little more confident in herself, she looks at him and says, "Such a big surprise for a first date," and she throws a smooth smile in Ian's direction.

Reciprocating with an even-bigger debonair smile, Ian takes his right hand from the wheel and places it on Meana's left knee. Instantly Meana's body temperature rises, and goosebumps appear on her arm as she is slightly aroused by his touch.

Feeling her body slightly jerk, he says in a forceful and somewhat-questioning way, "I hope this is all right?"

Actually, enjoying the feeling of his rough, calloused hands on her knee, she lets out a whisper, "Yes."

Ian's hand remains on Meana's knee without any attempt to creep closer up her thigh, and within a few quick minutes, they finally arrive at their destination. Meana looks out into a large parking lot filled with an assortment of cars and sees a huge circular tent in the center. She clearly recognizes the all-white, canvassed circus tent and brandishes a smile from ear to ear while continuing to stare with a glimmer in her eyes.

He gracefully pulls into the parking lot, and looks over at Meana to observe her facial expression, and seeing her brimming with excitement, he says, "Almost looks like you've never been to a circus."

Meana's facial expression quickly changes, and she stares at the floorboard of his car in embarrassment.

"I, uhm, never have."

Wearing a face of pure bewilderment, Ian exclaims, "What? You have got to be kidding me!"

Feeling even worse than before, Meana looks out the car window at the white circus tent and says, "It was always just my mother and I, and we couldn't afford to go out and enjoy events like this."

Silence strikes the air and Ian pulls the car into a spot on the edge of the parking lot, throws the shifter into park, and sits motionless.

"I'm sorry, I didn't mean to make this awkward. I just feel like I can be open with you. Is that crazy?" she says, turning in her seat and looking Ian dead in his radiant blue eyes.

"No, you're not crazy. I felt a connection from the first moment I saw you, and hey, don't sweat the awkwardness. It's why I like you." She feels butterflies fluttering in her stomach, and her heart warms with every word that leaves his mouth. Ian stares back into her crème-de-menthe-colored eyes intently and asks, "Shall we go inside?"

Meana turns in excitement and looks at the circus tent and says, "Yes, let's!"

The pair carefully exit the vehicle, and Meana notices that Ian has parked crooked and is taking up two spots.

Observing her staring at the lines, he says, "I had to get the passenger door repainted after someone struck it with their car door. I'm not doing that again."

She simply shrugs her shoulders and smiles while she waits for Ian to walk over to her side of the car. Standing side by side, they casually walk toward the tent, and Ian reaches his hand out and looks Meana deep in her eyes. Looking down at his hand in confusion, Meana can see he has one finger outstretched more than the others and wonders what he is pointing at. She looks about the floor, and while doing so, Ian turns away from her and drops his hand. He wears a disappointed look, and Meana, still confused, walks beside him with an eyebrow raised high. *"What was he pointing at?"* Meana thinks to herself as they approach the entrance of the tent. Ian allows Meana to walk in front of him as they breach past the threshold and enter the large white tent.

Bubbles fill the air, and disco lights flash about in the small lobby area, and joyful music blasts from speakers hanging on metal beams above their heads. Ian gestures for Meana to stay to the side of the tent and walks up to a small foldout table where the ticketing personnel are staged. He pulls his wallet from the back pocket of his black jeans and flashes a red-and-blue credit card at a young woman handing out tickets.

"I'll take two tickets, please and thank you," he says to the young woman, wearing a flirtatious smile.

Meana sees how he unhesitatingly smiles at every young woman that passes by while waiting for the ticketing woman to hand him their tickets. Not sure if he is flirting or just being friendly, Meana decides to shrug it off. Grateful to be at the circus for the first time in her life, Meana quietly stands to the side and awaits Ian's return. As she waits, she looks around, admiring the colorful flashes of lights, the low-lying mist, and the clown in the corner making animal balloons.

Finally returning from the ticketing line, Ian pokes Meana on the shoulder and asks, "Are you ready to go sit down?"

Without saying a word and still wearing a smile on her face, Meana nods at him, and they begin to walk to the entrance of the large benched area. Just inside the entrance, Ian hands their two tickets over to a man standing guard, and Meana is unable to make out his words as he explains to Ian where their seats are located. The music inside the larger area is so loud Meana has great difficulty understanding anything Ian is saying. She simply nods and follows him to their seats. To her surprise, he has purchased front-row seats, and they descend into the lower-leveled area right in front of the stage.

Approaching their seats in a quick fashion, Meana looks at Ian and mouths, "Holy shit, thank you."

Just before sitting, he performs a small bow, and they both let out a giggle in unison. Sitting comfortably in their front-row seats, the lights begin to fade, and the music is lowered until it eventually fades out.

A spotlight illuminates a small portion of the stage, and a very energetic man stands at the ready and begins to talk to the crowd, "Ladies and gentlemen, thank you for coming out today to watch the Cirque De Italia water circus!" He takes a few steps forward and closes in on the edge of the stage. "Tonight, you will see magnificent feats of aquatic acrobatics, aerial acrobatics, and much more. Without further ado, let's welcome our first performers to the stage!"

Just when the man finishes his speech and takes a bow, the music blares once again, and two women dressed in all-white leotards that are decorated with red, green, and blue rhinestones appear from the darkness around the edges of the stage. The overhead lights turn and focus on them, and the sparkle radiating from their costumes draws the attention of every person in the crowd, and they erupt with immense cheers and applause. The two women raise their hands in approval and enter the center stage.

An hour and half later, Meana is left speechless from looking upon the multitude of lights and crazy acrobatic routines.

"Holy shit, that was amazing!" she exclaims with such glee.

"I'm glad you liked it," Ian says, casually placing his arm around her and resting his hand just above her hip bone while they make their way back out to his car.

Knowing that he is inching closer to her, she allows it and places one of her hands on top of his. They laugh and joke as they trudge their way through the crowd outside the tent and eventually to the car. Meanwhile, Ian is getting more friendly with Meana by the second. They approach his precious black car, and Ian pulls the keys from his pocket but hesitates to unlock the door. Standing in front of the passenger door, Ian lets his grasp on her hip go and smoothly turns Meana to face him.

"I hope you appreciate this little gift I gave you," he says with a smile.

Meana knits her brow at the comment he has made and says, "Why, yes, I did enjoy myself, and I do appreciate the length of difficulty you went through to bring me here."

Ian stares into Meana's eyes and inches himself closer until they are standing toe to toe.

"Does that mean I get a kiss?" he asks with an unwavering smile still upon his face.

Feeling a little uneasy at how close he is and the fact that he is essentially guilt-tripping her into a kiss with his comment, Meana looks for a way out. She questions her own resolve while teetering with the idea of backing away or kissing him, and at the last second before his lips make contact with her own, she takes a step back and thuds against the car. A high-pitched screech rings out as the alarm sounds, and all the vehicle's lights begin to illuminate in sequence.

Instantly turning away from her, he cries out, "Watch the damn car!" then pushes her to the side and thoroughly inspects the passenger side door while turning the alarm off. She lets out a sigh of relief and looks at him inspecting his car with a slight look of pity on her face. He looks up from the blackened paint job and to Meana. "Get in the car please," he says, with a hint of irritation in his voice.

She nods at him, agreeing to enter the car, and opens the passenger door while he poutingly makes his way to the driver side. He gently opens his door, as does she, and they both silently take their places in their perspective seats. He starts the car without saying a word, and angrily throws the shifter into reverse and begins to pull out of the parking spot. Meana sits quietly in the car and steals glances at his emotionless face during the stagnant and silent drive back to the barracks. Twenty minutes pass by in the dark and cold vehicle, and without looking up from her seat, Meana can feel the tugging force of his speedy turns into the barracks parking lot. He stops the car in a handicapped parking spot that is in line with Meana's room door.

"Aren't you going to get in trouble?" she says, deciding to break the silence.

"Nah, I park here all the time," he says, smiling at her with his ever-shifting mood change.

Meana glances around the car, looking for the individual he is focusing on, and determining that it is her, returns her gaze to meet his.

"I'm sorry about my attitude earlier. It's just I have spent a lot of time and money on this car, and it pains me that you don't see the value that I do." Meana once again knits an eyebrow in his direction, only this time he takes notice. "Well, what I mean is, while I value my car greatly, I'm beginning to see how I should be valuing you more."

Hearing Ian's comment, Meana feels her cheeks blush, and simultaneously her body temperature rises.

She takes a quiet breath in and out to steady herself and says, "That's good to hear."

She decides to give him another chance and slightly leans herself toward him. Taking notice of her hint, he, too, leans forward, and learning his lesson from before, leans only half-way for the kiss. Meana, feeling herself get ever warmer, finishes her lean and engages in a passionate and steamy kiss. Locking lips and twisting tongues as they go at each other's faces, a couple of minutes melt by, and Ian maneuvers himself over to her side of the vehicle. Meana, wanting to move slower than him, lifts her right hand and places it upon his chest to prevent him from moving.

He disengages the kiss and asks, "What's wrong?"

Looking him deep in his majestic eyes, she says, "Not a damn thing. I just want to savor the moment first, and well, I'm, ah-"

Looking at her with a puzzled face, he asks, "Ahh what?"

Mean looks down to the floorboard of the car and folders her arms across her chest in embarrassment and says, "I'm a virgin."

Ian sits back into his seat, and Meana looks over to him and can clearly see a large bulge in his pants. She lets out a smirk, and her embarrassment begins to wither. He sits in his seat silent for roughly thirty seconds, and Meana, feeling the weight of the air rushing down on her, reaches for the handle of the car.

"Wait!" he shouts. "I'll take you on more dates, and if you feel up to it, I'll show you how I make passionate love."

Meana blushes and replies, "I'm okay with that," and she opens the door. Just before closing the door behind herself, she looks back at Ian, and they smile in unison. "Thank you for the lovely date. I'm looking forward to having more," she says with a genuine look of affection.

"Yeah, me too," he says, throwing her a wink.

Floating on butterflies, Meana gently closes the car door and makes her way to her barracks room. She opens the door while still in a love-struck trance, and closes it behind herself as she hears the roar of Ian's car pulling away.

Cautionary Tales

Meana arrives at the office the next day, dressed and ready to go to work, while still floating on cloud nine from the night before. She swings the office door open and looks around for Ian and turns her attention to his desk. Seeing him sitting in his nice, black roller chair with his feet on the desk, hands clasped behind his head, and headphones in his ears, her heart skips a beat. She replays the date from the previous night over and over again, and even though he had a lapse of judgment with his comments, he turned the night around and made it one to remember. She pushes forward and is gleefully bound for his desk when, all of a sudden, she hears two female Marines chatting to her right. With the whispers distracting her from her daydreams, she turns to look at them. Two lance corporals, Elizabeth Cortez, and Victoria Mendoza, sit in close proximity to each other while staring at Meana. Having notably similar traits with their olive skin, midnight-black hair, and dark-brown eyes, Meana wonders if they may somehow be related. *"That's racist, Meana,"* she thinks to herself while letting a smile out in their direction.

Mendoza, being the more brash of the two, nods her head in an upward motion toward Meana and says with a staggeringly macho voice laced with a heavy accent, "You got a minute to talk?"

Recognizing a New York inner-city accent from a mile away, Meana decides that she will at least attempt to get to know a fellow New Yorker.

With a few steps, Meana stands over the two Marines, and the mousy-voiced Cortez says, "Please sit. This will just take a minute of your time."

Getting a weird vibe from them, Meana sits in a chair nearby just after moving it an extra foot away.

Mendoza smiles and says, "Don't worry. We don't bite. Well, she doesn't," winking at Meana and pointing toward Cortez.

Cortez smacks Mendoza on the arm and says, "I know we haven't been with this unit long, but we both noticed you're goo-goo-eyeing Corporal Pierce, and well, we have some cautionary tales for you if you're willing to listen."

Meana feels a bit of irritation rise inside and readies herself for the jealousy of these two women.

"How can you have any tales if you are new to this unit and the Corps like me?"

Mendoza lets out an obnoxiously loud laugh and exclaims, "Don't let our ranks confuse you, boot! Cortez has been in for over two years already, and I used to be a corporal before I was NJP'd just after re-enlisting!" Pausing to catch her breath after laughing up a storm, she continues, "I'm in my fifth year, and let's just say, I have some experience with that asshat over there," gesturing in Ian's direction.

Meana, feeling defensive, lifts an eyebrow and says, "Oh, well, why do you care what or whom I do with my time?"

Cortez's face turns red and her anger rises, while she says as calm as possible through her gritted teeth, "We are just trying to look out for a fellow female warrior, and the outcome of your life will be your problem, not ours."

Mendoza lets a wicked smile take over while looking at the eve-reddening face of Cortez and says, "Doc said to breathe in and out when you feel like you're going to pop, so do it!"

Looking upon yet another circus before her eyes, Meana scoffs toward the pair and crosses her arms in disbelief.

"So, you two, with all your issues, want to lecture me about dating that dreamy hunk of a man over there?" She asks, looking toward Ian with stars in her eyes.

"The fuck you say?" Cortez spouts out, failing to control herself.

Mendoza raises a hand to Cortez and proceeds to give Meana a stern history lesson.

"That hunk you refer to, got my rank stripped away after I reported him for sexual harassment." She takes a deep breath to calm herself before starting again, "I filed report after report with my command, and nothing happened as I watched that peacock strut around the office. In my fit of anger, I slapped the wrong person and was demoted for it. I've only recently picked up lance corporal again, and all the meanwhile, he gets transferred to a cushy unit where he gets to play king dick. Not only that, but somehow we're forced to face him once again."

With eyes a little wider, Meana turns to look at Ian, and allows herself to wonder if he is capable of such a thing.

"Nah, he exhibited an extreme amount of restraint with me and was a gentleman all night, I don't believe either of you."

Finally blowing a head gasket, Cortez shoots straight out of her chair and storms off to the farthest corner of the office. Mendoza watches the event unfold and then turns to Meana after seeing Cortez take a seat.

"Look, she's usually the calm one, and I'm the one stomping about, but we both came from the same unit he did, and she was one of his victims, just like me." Turning her gaze from a stern look to a more-sincere one, she says, "I understand that he is actually very good-looking, but just watch yourself with him. He has a tendency toward anger when he doesn't get his way, and if you don't believe me, just ask around."

Before Meana has a chance to respond, Mendoza calmly lifts herself from her chair and walks over to Cortez in the quietest manner she can.

Meana is left sitting in her chair, staring at the crumbling white walls of the office in disbelief.

"He did get fairly angry when I bumped the car, but I can see how that's justified."

After a minute of contemplation, Meana rises from her seat and gazes in Ian's direction. Turning away from his computer screen to rub his eyes, he pulls his headphones out of his ears and sees Meana staring at him from a distance. Waving his hand like an excited child seeing a parent after a long time, Ian stands from his chair and gestures for her to come over. Meana, with Mendoza's and Cortez's voices echoing in the back of her head, decides to drown them out with the butterfly feeling that re-emerges from the pit of her stomach. She casually makes her way to him and can hear a loud scoff from Cortez off in the distance.

Not even willing to give her a second thought, Meana smiles at Ian and says, "Good morning, Corporal. Good to see you again."

Unable to control his face, Ian's smile grows by the second and he playfully says, "Good to see you too, Lance Corporal," and shoots her an obvious wink.

Letting out a small giggle and staring into his eyes, Meana says, "I've been thinking, and I'm always ready for another date when you are," and just before he can respond, she raises her hand to stop him and says, "Let's make it a simple dinner date instead, and this time I'll pay."

Only hearing "I'll pay," come out of Meana's mouth, Ian protests, "It's a man's duty to pay for a woman, and I'm not about to let you pay for your meal when we go out!"

Standing motionless, Meana feels a small sense of irritation rise yet again, and she says, "I'm more than capable of paying for myself, thank you very much."

Scrunching his eyebrows together, Ian leans forward and stares Meana dead in the eyes and says, "This is not up for debate. I will pay for the meal."

Flashing back to all the times her mother snapped at her in the same manner, Meana lowers her head to look at the floor and says in a weak manner, "Okay, I'm sorry."

Feeling good about the outcome, Ian says, "We'll talk about it later," and gestures to Mendoza and Cortez staring from the corner.

Meana turns to look at the woman and then looks back to Ian and nods just before walking away and sitting down at her desk. Without looking back at Ian or the women, Meana pulls her ID card from the front left breast pocket of her tan digital uniform and inserts it into the computer. Immediately after punching in her password and pulling up a web browser, Meana types in a few words, hits enter, and begins to read a political article relating to New York. Meanwhile, Ian stares at the back of her head like he is trying to drill a hole, and after a few seconds of breathing in and out, he calms himself and returns to his seat.

Off in the distance, Mendoza and Cortez sit angrily in the corner with their arms crossed and steam coming from their ears after watching the event unfold.

Turning to look at Cortez, Mendoza says, "This dumb bitch is going to get hurt if she stays with him, and the fucking good ole boys club is going to help him out as usual."

Closing her eyes in an effort to ebb her anger, Cortez says, "We can-not control her actions. We can only try to be the voice of reason when she needs us."

Widening her eyes and leaning forward in her seat, Mendoza whispers, "You mean you want to befriend her in an effort to drive them apart?"

Opening her eyes and shrugging her shoulders in Mendoza's direction, Cortez says, "Maybe not befriend her, but let's try acting nice and see where that takes us. After all, we don't have the best track records," letting a small and false smile emerge.

Mendoza rolls her eyes and leans back into the chair, saying, "Fine, fine. I don't know how I let you talk me into these things."

Cortez places one hand on Mendoza's knee and says, "Oh, yes, you do," winking at Mendoza and shooting her a mischievous kiss.

Mendoza lets out a dreamy sigh and clasps her hands behind her head as she stares out in the distance at Meana and lowly says to herself, "I won't let you be another victim."

Going to War

It has been a year since Meana was assigned to the Administrations Platoon of Combat Logistics Regiments 92. A lot has happened between her and Ian as they keep their office romance a secret. Meana, having love in her heart for him, rises early every morning to get him food from the chow hall. She performs her morning routine of standing in line, ordering the food, waiting for it to be cooked, and then quickly grabbing it in an effort to hastily make her way back to her vehicle. She drives to the regimental building and exits the car. She enters the regimental warehouse like she does every morning, holding two large cups of coffee from the chow hall while balancing a Styrofoam *to-go* box filled to the brim with a large, golden ham-and-cheese omelet, freshly crisped bacon, and perfectly cooked hash browns on her forearm.

She steadily walks to the door of the makeshift office where the admin cubicles are located, and realizes her hands are too full to open the door. Looking around for a place to set the food down, she soon realizes that the small table that's usual outside of the office space is nowhere in sight. The only choice she has is to turn her back to the door, and push it open with her hind quarters. She bumps the door a few times with her butt and hopes that the door isn't fully closed. However, she is not that fortunate, and she is forced to twerk her butt against the door handle in an attempt to get it to move. A full minute of grinding on the door goes by, and finally, her back left pocket flap

53

manages to catch the door handle and turn it successfully. The door swings open and slams against the interior wall of the office with a frightening thud. Wincing like she is the one feeling the slam of the door, she proceeds to enter the empty office space and is pleasantly greeted by the only face in sight.

"Hello, girly," Ian says from the other side of the office. "Did you get my breakfast?" he asks with an eager smile on his face.

Blushing and wearing a huge smile Meana jokes, "You know I did, fool."

She happily makes her way to Ian and struggles to put the two cups of coffee and the weighted Styrofoam box down on the small empty spot of his desk.

Ian watches her struggle and continues to smile while he says, "You're an angel," and changes the subject by saying, "Oh, by the way, Gunny wanted me to ask you if you had a chance to complete the work orders from yesterday?"

Meana looks at Ian with a serious look and comments with a hint of confusion to her voice, "You said you were staying late to finish those last night." Wearing an irritated face and a lifted eyebrow, Ian lets out a great, long sigh. Afraid of upsetting and disappointing Ian, she immediately changes her tone and says, "Don't worry about it. I'll just sit down and get them knocked out real quick before Gunny has a chance to ask about them again."

Ian gives Meana a look of approval and then starts to open the Styrofoam *to-go* box upon his desk. As if the gates to Valhalla opened before his face, Ian's eyes widen with glee at the sight of the feast before him. He takes a deep, long sniff of the golden omelet, and Meana swears she can see drool form at the corner of his mouth. The moment is short-lived, and he lets out an even-larger sigh and dramatically starts slamming filing cabinet doors and rummaging through his desk.

Meana, who is sitting at her own desk, turns around in her chair and asks, "What's the matter?"

He snaps back in an irrationally irritated voice, "You forgot the damn utensils!"

Saying, "Sorry, sorry, sorry," over and over again, Meana frantically searches through her own desk for any utensils that would be of use, and like a light bulb going off in her head, remembers Gunny keeps a box of plastic utensils in his office. She stops looking through her own desk and turns to inform Ian, "I know Gunny keeps some in his office I believe there in his desk drawer."

"Well, I guess you better get in there and start looking, since you're the one that forgot to grab some!" Ian exclaims with an extreme look of annoyance.

Meana turns from Ian and starts walking across the cubicle-filled space toward Gunny's small, enclosed office. She peers through the door window to see if anyone is inside. The coast looks clear, and she reaches for the door-knob. With the handle firmly in her grip and turned half-way, there is a loud slamming noise behind her. She jumps into the air and let's go of the handle while looking back with a frightened face.

"Phew," she says, seeing it's just Ian slamming stuff around in frustration.

She turns her attention to the office space once more and proceeds through the door. Reaching through the doorway and flipping the light switch on, she can see the gunnery sergeant's office is littered with motivational plaques given to him from his prior units, and on his desk sits a large name-plate and an even-larger bald eagle statue. The desk is made of pure oak and looks to have been polished. The shine from the desk is blinding, and it's obvious that Gunny must clean and shine it every day. Remembering her task at hand, Meana steps forward, inching closer and closer to the desk while her heart starts to race and her palms sweat. She makes the mistake of looking the eagle statue dead in its eyes. She freezes in place and starts to stare this inanimate object down. She notices that the statue has great detail and is, in fact, hand carved.

The eagle clutches a small detailed and tattered American flag in his beak, and with his head tilted back, seems to be presenting it. The detail of the eagle and flag are beyond anything Meana has ever seen before. Every feather looks perfectly crafted, and the mixture of browns and golds that make up the eagle's coat are stunning. Even the white of the eagle's head is perfectly tinted to show the realism of an aged and experienced eagle. She lifts her right hand and approaches this magnificently carved statue. Her hands are shaking, and her breath is irregular as she inches forward. With fingers outstretched, she gently caress' the eagle's head. Just then the office door slams, and Gunny is standing directly behind her with only two feet of distance to separate them. He towers over her, standing about six feet and three inches tall with his umber-colored and smooth-looking skin. His green digital-camouflage uniform is formfitting and there is not a wrinkle in sight. Meana looks back at the gunnery sergeant with shock and awe, and as if the Gunny's stare casts a spell of petrification, Meana is unable to move a single muscle. Moments slip by, and she can hear the *tick, tick, tick* of the clock sitting upon Gunny's desk. She regains her senses and quickly snaps to the parade rest position. She stands with feet shoulder-width apart, hands behind her, with the left over the right and sitting in the small of her back. She lifts her chest in an effort to seem confident, but she feels that Gunny can see straight through the facade.

"Good morning, Gunny," she says with a shaky, yet confident voice.

"Is there any good reason for molesting my eagle, Crane?" Gunny asks through the large and full mustache that sits upon his upper lip.

"My apologies, Gunny. I was merely admiring the quality of the statue," she says, gesturing in the statue's direction. Before Gunny can say anything else, Meana inserts, "I was wanting to report on those work orders from last night."

"Yes, I saw that they weren't marked *completed* or *closed* yet. Any reason for that?" he says, walking toward his desk with long and confident strides. Meana perks up her stance a little, and her mind starts to race with excuses.

"My apologies yet again, Gunny. I somehow completely overlooked them, and when I got back to my barracks room, I cracked open a cold one, and let's just say the drinks kept on coming," she says, mimicking the motion of drinking a cold beer and cracking open another.

The excuse works beautifully, and Gunny stops walking to his desk and changes the direction of their conversation by asking, "Are you saying that you have a drinking problem, Crane?"

"I wouldn't say it's a problem, Gunny. I just enjoy a beer like any other Marine," Meana says in an attempt to keep this conversation from getting too serious.

Gunny lets out a small frustrated sigh and says, "Get those work orders done before chow." He then pauses and looks at her with a serious look and says, "Dismissed."

She quickly snaps to the position of attention and says, "Dismissed. Aye-aye, Gunnery Sergeant." She takes a step back, performs a right face, and briskly marches to the closed door and opens it. Breaching past the doorway, she turns around and with a big smile says, "I'm sorry, Gunny. Do you happen to have any plastic utensils I can commandeer?"

Without looking in her direction, he opens the drawer to his polished oak desk and starts to rummage through it. Meana stares at Gunny, and for the first time, she notices that his smooth bald head has the same kind of shine that his desk does. Her smile changes from being forced, to being genuine, and she struggles to hold in laughter. After five or so seconds of looking for utensils, the gunnery sergeant holds a black plastic knife in his hand. He sits down in his plush black leather chair and spins to face Meana. He lifts his left arm up and points it at her with all of his fingers outstretched and his elbow locked out.

Lifting his right arm and still clutching the plastic knife, he caulks his arm behind his head and proceeds to throw the knife with strength and accuracy and shouts, "Frag out!"

The knife goes hurling through the air, spinning end over end, and Meana raises her hands in an attempt to protect her face. She can hear the knife cutting through the air with a loud whistle. She spreads the fingers over her eyes in an attempt to see the incoming projectile and instead see's the Gunny sitting in his chair with a huge grin as he mimics the sounds of the knife cutting through the air with a whistle. Meana lowers her hands and notices the knife is no longer airborne, and in fact, only made it halfway across the office. She stands in the doorway, snickering at the fact that she has fallen victim to a silly joke.

Gunny's smile fades and he says, "Pick that shit up and get back to work."

Meana's smile dissipates as well and she replies, "Aye, aye, Gunny," and proceeds to pick up the plastic knife and exits the office silently. Standing just outside of the office doorway, she looks at the plastic knife in her hand. Meana lets out a sigh of disappointment and knows that Ian will throw a fit. Regardless of the outcome, she walks over to Ian's desk where he is sitting, with a pouty expression.

She approaches him with a false smile and jokes, "Can you believe this is all Gunny had in his office?" and attempts to ebb his anger with a small chuckle.

Ian, however, is not amused and smacks his lips in disapproval as he angrily stands from his chair and says, "Forget it. I'll just get the shit myself!"

He trots over to the gunnery sergeant's office door, and just before knocking, adjusts his uniform to ensure everything is in place.

He then proceeds to knock on the door and recites the proper acknowledgement, "Good Morning, Gunny. Sergeant Pierce requesting permission to speak to you."

Gunny turns from his computer monitor to face the door and replies with a smile on his face, "Come on in, Sergeant!"

Ian confidently walks into Gunny's office and brashly says, "I know Crane was just in here, and she was supposed to ask for a fork for my chow." He then pauses to asses Gunny's expression before continuing, "You don't happen to have a fork I can get, would you, Gunny?"

The gunnery sergeant looks at Ian with a stern face but then jokingly says, "Shit, why didn't she just say that," as his face transitions to a smile once more.

Gunny opens the same drawer he had rummaged through before and within seconds presents Ian with a black plastic knife, spoon, and fork. He reaches out with all the utensils in his hand and motions for Ian to come grab them.

Ian walks toward the desk, and Gunny asks, "You need a napkin too?"

"No, I'm good on the napkin, Gunny, but I appreciate it," Ian says, throwing Gunny a debonair smile.

He proceeds to take the utensils from the gunnery sergeant and does a half-hearted salute with the utensils and a smile and turns to walk away.

Making his way for the door, he hears Gunny yell from behind, "Don't forget to start your draft picks for our fantasy league. I can't have you slacking again!"

Ian turns his head and upper torso toward Gunny while maintaining his course for the door and says, "Thanks for the reminder, Gunny. I'll do it as soon as I finish my chow," and walks out of the office.

Peacocking with his chest puffed high, he is greeted by Meana standing a few feet from the entry door to Gunny's office and waiting to see what the outcome is. He raises the utensils and waves them in her face while walking to his desk and scoffing in her direction. Meana stands confused and irritated, replaying the scenes of her own office visit with Gunny and can't believe the difference in outcomes. After a moment of brooding, she decides to let it go and proceeds to walk to her desk and take a seat in her old and musty cloth stationary chair.

Pulling her military ID out of the left breast pocket of her uniform, she turns to Ian and says, "Enjoy your meal," with a genuine smile.

He, however, does not make any effort to acknowledge her existence and continues to click away on his social-media page and eat his breakfast. She then turns around with a disappointed look and inserts her military card into the card reader and punches in her password to begin the work-day.

Twenty minutes tick by, and the rest of the Marines in the office come walking in from their morning chow, and just as the last one enters the door and sets her bag down, Gunny emerges from his office and says, "Sergeant Pierce, come here!"

Ian replies, "Yes, Gunny," and quickly stands up, walks over, and assumes the parade rest position.

Gunny leans forward and is face-to-face with Ian as he whispers, "Let the Marines know that at 0730 we are having a mandatory meeting in the warehouse," and then walks away before Ian can answer.

Ian watches Gunny walk to his office and shut the door and then turns around to say, "Listen up, shit birds!" He then takes a deep breath and loudly vocalizes, "In twenty minutes, it's going to be 0730. I want each and every one of you to form up in your appropriate squads out in the warehouse, right now!"

The platoon of admin clerks responds with a low and exhausted, "Aye, aye, Sergeant," and slump their way out into the warehouse.

One by one they begin to line up in their squads, with the assigned squad leaders in the front of each row. Four rows of Marines stand at parade rest and await further orders. Ian walks over to the newly formed platoon and stands out of the formation and places himself front and center as the face of the platoon. He, too, assumes the parade rest as they all wait for the Gunny to come out of his office to attend the meeting. Fifteen minutes pass by while the platoon stands in the silent warehouse, and Ian can see that they are beginning to become uneasy. He looks upon the platoon and sees the exhausted looks on their faces and can hear the consistent clicks and pops of old and worn-down knee-caps moving around.

With sternness in his voice, he says, "Hang in there, everyone. I'm sure Gunny will be out soon."

Low grumbles of disapproval and some sighs can be heard all around, and Ian's face quickly drops, and he realizes how full of shit he sounds. Time continues to melt by, and it is 0800 as Gunny opens his office door and slinkies his way through the warehouse door. He opens the exterior office door and enters the warehouse with an excited look on his face.

As he approaches the platoon, Ian snaps to the position of attention and yells out the command, "Platoon, attention!" and performs an about face and looks away from the platoon.

With lightning precision, all the Marines snap to the position of attention in unison, and there are no longer any exhausted faces in sight. Instead, they have been replaced with the facade of prowess and attentiveness they know their leaders expect. Every Marine stand stiff like a plank of wood, with their feet facing forward and heels together at a forty-five-degree angle, each of them with hands clenched into fists and thumbs touching the side seams of their trousers and chests puffed up high. Meana stands midway down the first squad and stands tall and proud with her brothers and sisters as the Gunny makes his way to the front of the platoon.

Gunny stands in front of Ian and yells out the command, "At ease!"

Ian quickly performs an about-face movement and says, "At ease!" to the platoon and then performs another about-face movement and faces Gunny as he, too, moves to the *at-ease* position.

With all the Marines standing in front of him, Gunny forces himself to stand a little taller and says, "Good morning, Marines!"

The platoon replies in unison, "Good morning, Gunny!"

He takes a deep breath and continues with, "I have some exciting news to share with all of you." He pauses to observe the faces of the Marines before him.

He can see them wiggling around like children in anticipation of the news he has, and from the back of the platoon, he hears a Marine whisper, "I bet his good news is us working late and mopping the top of the cargo containers in the rain again."

Gunny's face changes to a sterner look, and he yells, "Lock it up!" and then picks up where he left off. "The good news I have for you is," he takes another second to pause and soak in the anticipation, "We're going to be deploying in the next coming months!"

Looking upon Gunny and watching his mouth move, the faces of the Marines before him light up with excitement, and they all let out a loud roar of approval and scream their battle cry at the top of their lungs, "Oorah!"

The gunnery sergeant reciprocates with his own battle cry, "Oorah!" and stands a foot taller, wearing the biggest smile ever seen. He proceeds to say, "I thought you'd all like that shit!" He takes a few steps forward and says, "The regimental commanding officer will be sending the word out soon to have a regimental formation to inform all of the Marines at once. I wanted you all to hear it from me first."

As her fellow Marines are reveling in the joyous news that has been revealed, not a word can be heard from Meana. She stands silent as ever and stares off into the distance with her palms sweating and her breath becoming heavy from anxiety. For her, this is not a joyous moment, but instead it means that once again her life will be turned upside down and shredded into pieces. Standing directly behind her midway down the second squad, Mendoza fixes her eyes upon the gloomy Meana. Shouting her battle cry in unison with her fellow Marines, Mendoza looks over to Cortez, who is standing directly to her left and nods for her to look toward Meana. Casually stealing a glance, Cortez lets out a low-leveled sigh and nods in approval toward Mendoza as she rolls her eyes. Mendoza smirks at Cortez and punches her on the shoulder and then shouts, "Oorah!" once more as the entirety of the platoon lets out one last battle cry before being dismissed and ordered back towards their morbid office space.

Cortez and Mendoza walk side-by-side and make their way to Meana as she slowly drags her feet behind herself and stares at the floor.

Placing one hand on her right shoulder with a firm yet supporting grip, Mendoza says, "Hey, girl, some of us are getting together to celebrate the news, and you are invited!"

Raising her eyes from the floor, Meana lethargically turns to look at Mendoza, and Cortez says, "It'll be a small get-together at a friend's house off base, and from the looks of it, you could use a beer and some good company," turning and looking at Ian as he throws a scolding glance at her from a distance.

Widening her eyes and tightening her lips to ensure another spite-filled comment doesn't slip out, Cortez pauses and peers into Mendoza's fiery eyes with an apologetic look.

Mendoza looks Meana in puffy eyes and says, "Anyways, it starts around 1800. I'll stop by your room around that time. How does that sound?"

"Yeah, yeah, that sounds-good," Meana blurts, still in a fog after hearing about the deployment and letting thoughts of losing Ian in some random battle, ravage her mind.

Rolling her eyes behind Meana's back, Cortez looks to Mendoza and gives her a playful wink, and the two walk away from Meana and back into the office. Still slumping her way to the cubicle and watching the plethora of Marines whiz by her, Meana thinks to herself, *"We are finally in a really good headspace together, and now this. What did I do to deserve this?"*

She is abruptly interrupted as Ian gives her a smack on her back and says, "Hey there, Corporal. Aren't you excited for the deployment? Seems like everyone has a fire lit under their ass' again!"

With saddened eyes, Meana looks at Ian and allows his blue crystalline gaze to ignite a small sense of hope in her heart.

Showing minimal amounts of glee, she says, "Yes, Sergeant, I am excited. I just need to get some things in order before we leave."

Not noticing her pain, he says, "Bah. We have plenty of time before shipping out to wherever we're getting sent."

Obviously not getting where she is coming from, Meana doesn't pursue the issue any further and half-heartedly smiles at him while he breaks their gaze and runs off into the office. She stands in front of the office door with one hand pressed against the cheap particle board that makes up its structure. The spark of Ian's eyes is short-lived, and her heart darkens once again, and she thinks, *"I just want to spend time with him. I wish the world would just stop getting in the way."*

Carne Asada

Laying in her small twin-sized bed with her green Marine Corps sweats on, Meana stares at the barracks room ceiling. With one arm across her forehead, she sulks in the irritation of hearing about the deployment and thinks, *"Thank goodness it's Friday, and I don't have duty. I can finally relax a little and get some sleep."* She allows her eyes to close, and the already ill-lit room darkens. Just then a loud knock on her door reverberates throughout the room, and her body shudders with surprise.

"Fuck me!" she exclaims out loud, rising from her bed like a zombie.

Dragging her feet and projecting scuffing noises, she reaches for the door and opens it. Standing there in a crop-top black leather jacket, tight blue jeans, black Nike Air Force 1's, and a plain white shirt, is Mendoza.

"Girl, didn't I say be ready by 1800?" she says loudly while looking Meana up and down in disapproval.

Looking at the bulky black G-SHOCK watch upon her wrist, Meana says, "But it's 1910. We're already super late."

"Psh-nah, girl, when you're rolling with Hispanics, late is on time. Now get dressed, and let's go. Cortez is waiting in the car, and she's going to be pissed if I return without you."

Turning from the door and leaving it wide open, Meana makes her way to her small metal wardrobe cabinet and pulls out a few articles of clothing. Mendoza looks upon the sad creature before her and pulls her phone from her back pocket to text, "This chick is so depressing. I have to get her dressed. Give me like five minutes." She presses the send button, and her phone lowly chimes, indicating that the message has been delivered.

"All right, girlfriend, you're killin' me, and I already struggle with being patient," she says, walking into Meana's room and rummaging through her wardrobe cabinet.

"Hey, not cool!" Meana says with a little sass.

Not bothering to look up from her scavenger hunt through the drawers, Mendoza jokingly says, "How many times have I whooped your ass in the MCMAP pit? Don't make me open a can of whoop ass right here!"

"Yeah, right. You've only gotten lucky once, and even then, I was just having a bad day!" Meana retaliates in an equally playful manner.

Mendoza smiles and knows that as long as she can keep the jokes rolling, Meana won't be able to slip back into her depressive state.

"Aha! Here we have some basic clothes that I can approve of," she exclaims, pulling out some faded black jeans, and a mustard-colored shirt with blue and red rhinestones and floral patterns across the chest.

"Those are hideous! I only bought them because I basically had nothing to wear after boot camp was over!" Meana says, staring at the mustard-colored shirt with a face of disgust.

Allowing her mouth to frown, Mendoza says, "It'll help brighten up your pasty ass. Lord knows you could use some color."

Meana looks down toward her arm, and realizing that Mendoza speaks the truth, shrugs and raises both hands to accept the shirt and pants.

"I guess, I'll be right back," she says, walking to the small barracks room bathroom and closing the door.

Mendoza reaches for her phones once more and texts, "Found some decent clothes for her. She's getting changed. I can't wait to see her face when we get there!" Just as she hits *send*, the bathroom door opens and a less-depressed-looking Meana steps forward, dressed in her new attire.

"I have to say, I remember these looking a lot worse on me."

"Well, sometimes it takes a small change in perspective for you to appreciate what you have," Mendoza says while gesturing for her to put her shoes on and make her way to the door.

Within seconds, Meana slips her custom Harry Potter-themed Vans onto her feet and makes for the door.

Mendoza steps back and raises her hand as she takes a small bow and says, "Your Highness."

Letting out a small giggle of approval, Meana shoots back, "Peon," with her head lifted and taking graceful steps out of her room. She takes her key from her pocket and locks the room door, just before they turn and proceed to the red sedan waiting at the closest edge of the parking lot. Meana breaks from her royal facade and asks, "Everyone just loves parking in those handicapped spots, don't they?"

Mendoza looks over to the car and says, "Well, do you know any handicapped Marines that are still active? I sure as hell don't."

Raising a finger to her chin and assuming a modified "thinking man" pose, Meana says, "I never thought of that. What a waste of space."

Mendoza shrugs as if to say, "I don't know what to tell you," and they quickly proceed to the car. They reach the passenger side of the vehicle and open their perspective doors and slide their way into the car. Cortez sits in the driver seat, and for the first time, Meana sees how small she really is. Still looking upon Cortez while buckling her own seatbelt, Meana thinks, *"She can barely see over the steering wheel! We are going to die!"*

Seeing Meana stare her down with a worried look on her face, Cortez jokes, "Don't worry. I brought my favorite books to sit on. I should have no problem seeing over the wheel now!" and gives her a devious smile.

"Phew. For a minute I thought someone had let their kid chaperone us around!" Meana says, chuckling from her own joke in the process of telling it.

"Oh shit, Lizzy!" Mendoza loudly says while laughing so hard she struggles to breath.

Cortez mocks Mendoza by mouthing her words and pretending to laugh as she does and throws the shifter in drive.

"All right, you comedians. Let's get this show on the road."

With Mendoza still dying of laughter in the front passenger seat and Meana giggling to herself in the back, they make their way out of the barracks parking lot and onto the main road leading out into town.

They whiz by the guard standing post at the front gate of base, and Mendoza swivels around in her seat to say, "I meant to tell you earlier, but you can call us by our first names if you're comfortable with that. I'm Victoria, and she's Elizabeth," gesturing toward Elizabeth and herself.

"Sounds good to me. Might take me a few times to get it right though. We call each other by our last names so much that it becomes so natural."

Victoria raises her hands and begins to flap about and says, "Crane!"

Meana lets out a laugh and says, "Hey, we don't get to pick our names!"

"Don't mind this jokester. She's always making a scene!" Elizabeth shouts, in an effort to be heard over Victoria and jabbing her in the ribs with her small first to silence her.

Victoria stops screaming about and turns from Meana while sticking her tongue out at Elizabeth. She proceeds to plug her smart phone into the auxiliary cord lying about the center console of the vehicle and plays a vibrant and energetic playlist full of reggaeton music. Meana sits in the back seat while Elizabeth and Victoria sing along to the music and sway about in their seats.

Roughly twenty minutes pass, and Elizabeth turns down a gravel road tucked away from the main highway. With not a single street lamp in sight, Meana looks about the dark and wooded area. Perking up in her seat, she looks out the windshield of Elizabeth's car and sees a large, highly illuminated house coming into view. The house looks like it belongs in an old Western movie. The exterior is a sandy-tan color, and the roof has deep-orange clay shingles in an orderly and tidy fashion. Its construction is based on a hacienda-type architecture. Meana looks upon the house and wonders how an attractive home such as this can be unseen in the ever-growing realm of Jacksonville. So used to seeing modern, cookie-cutter homes mixed in with the older, worn, brick homes, she feels out of place.

"Where the hell did this house come from?" she asks with an amazed look.

Victoria spins in her seat once more to look at Meana, and with a huge grin, says, "An old friend of mine from my first enlistment decided to stay in J-Ville and signed on with some contractors. Let's just say she makes more than the three of us combined."

Slowly pulling into the long, paved driveway leading up to the house, Elizabeth says without averting her eyes from the windshield, "That's the understatement of the year. This chick probably has bags of cash laying around like some old-school drug lord!"

Victoria turns to smack Elizabeth in the arm before muttering something in Spanish that Meana can-not understand. Finally reaching the end of the drive, they see groves of people holding red cups, and dancing to the reggaeton music blaring from the huge speakers sprawled out along the front lawn.

"I thought you said it would be a few people," Meana mumbles, noticing that every person in sight has olive skin and dark hair.

"It's mostly just Hispanics, but I'm sure there are some other white people out and about," Victoria jokes, looking at Meana with a devious smile.

"Somehow, I doubt it," she thinks to herself while still staring out the front windshield. The car comes to a slow stop, and Meana can feel the weight of the car shift.

She unbuckles her seatbelt and reaches for the door, when Victoria turns to her and says, "Just hang with Elizabeth and I, and you'll be just fine. Maybe we'll hit the dance floor later and try to shake loose that stick up your butt."

Looking at Victoria with an ever-growing nervous look, Meana whimpers, "Okay."

The three simultaneously exit the vehicle and line up side by side as they approach the side entrance to the home. Just a couple steps from the large glass sliding door, and waving to every person they pass, Elizabeth reaches for the handle of the door.

Before she can open it, a tall, slender woman bursts out and screams, "Vicky!" She quickly steps forward in her five-inch heels, raising her hands high up in the air in excitement.

"This is the Marine? She looks like a supermodel," Meana quietly says to Elizabeth while watching Victoria and the tall woman hug.

Elizabeth nods to her and rolls her eyes as Victoria stands with her arms down and her friend squeezing her tight.

Finally releasing her grip, the tall lady says, "It's so good to see you. You're going to be so excited! I got the best mobile taqueria around town to cook for us."

Elizabeth, showing more interest, says, "Hell yes. Where is he now?"

"Around the side, past the pool, and towards the corner behind the DJ" the tall woman says, pointing her narrow finger.

"Come on, Meana. Let me show you one of the most important parts of our culture," Elizabeth says, intertwining arms with Meana and ushering her around the corner of the house.

"What about Victoria?" asks Meana.

Rolling her eyes, Elizabeth says, "Don't worry about her. She'll probably be in the same spot when the party's over. Her friend is very, very, very long-winded."

The two women walk around the corner with their arms still locked together, and as they approach the pool, a strong and delicious smell permeates their nostrils.

"What's that smell?" asks Meana.

Smiling, Elizabeth responds, "That's the mobile taqueria, finest smell in the lands."

"It smells amazing," Meana says in agreement.

They continue along their path and dodge a few partiers jumping into the pool and others dancing near the DJ. They stand near the taqueria, and before them lays an assortment of meats. The sizzling of the grill fills Meana's ears, and a spark in her eyes ignites as she looks down at the splattering of grease and browning of meat.

"I didn't realize I was so hungry, but now that I'm standing here, I feel like my stomach is trying to eat me," she says without averting her eyes from the delicious assortment before her.

Looking at Meana with a large grin, Elizabeth loudly says in an effort to be heard over the music, "Other than family, the Hispanic culture values food like no other. It can mend the heart and reunite lifelong enemies. Hispanics from every venture of the globe take immense pride in preparing food, and you, my friend, are about to taste some of that passion."

With drool about to stream from her mouth, Meana leans toward Elizabeth and says, "Sign me up!" and then pauses.

"What?" Elizabeth shouts, noticing Meana standing puzzled.

Raising both hands up, she says with a childish tone, "I don't know which one to try first!"

Just then the taqueria looks up from slicing and flipping the meats, vegetables, and rice, and yells, "Listen here, mama. You can't go wrong with a little bit of everything. I recommend a Blanca like yourself try the carne asada!"

Staring at him with extreme confusion, Meana opens her mouth and says, "The wha-"

He lets out a loud laugh and shakes his head, muttering something in Spanish under his breath.

"It's like steak. You can add some rice, vegetables, sauce, or whatever else you want. So how about it?"

Without saying a word, Meana awkwardly smiles and lifts up three fingers to the man. He nods his head in silence and prepares three small carne-asada-style tacos for Meana with a little bit of everything.

Handing her the Styrofoam plate, he says, "Enjoy! I'll see you again in a few minutes!"

She caulks her head to the side in confusion to his statement and takes the plate.

"Thanks," she says, turning from the taqueria and walking a few paces out of the way while Elizabeth orders and receives her plate.

Standing in the only empty spot on the deep-green lawn, Meana lifts the plate to her face and takes a big whiff of the tacos.

Approach Meana with her own plate in hand and a small cup of hot sauce, Elizabeth excitedly says, "Eat up!"

No longer hesitating, Meana lifts the small and perfectly folded taco to her mouth and takes a greedily large bite. Instantly her mouth is filled with the flavorful juices from the meat, and her eyes widen in amazement. She looks up from her plate, and Elizabeth nods in approval and smiles as she, too, digs into her tacos. Meana turns her attention to her plate, and within minutes, devours the entirety of her tacos.

"I'll be right back," she says to Elizabeth, and scurries back to the taqueria.

"I told you, you'd be back!" he playfully says to her.

"If it's not too much to ask, I'll take three chickens, three pork, and three more of the carne asada please!" she says with a huge smile on her face.

"You got it!" he says, flipping the meats and sides while placing the tacos on her plate. "Here you go," he says.

Meana, already running back to her small patch of grass, yells out, "Thanks!"

Approaching Elizabeth with haste, Meana eyeballs her plate and nearly rams into Victoria, who stands next to Elizabeth.

"Damn, girl, you almost ran me over! That plate for me?" she says, pointing at Meana's plate.

"Hell nah! That's her second plate of food! I think she's in love!" Elizabeth playfully says.

Victoria shrugs and says, "More power to you" and then walks over to the taqueria for her own food.

An hour ticks by, and the party never once slows down. People continue to dance to the music, and even more people than before have jumped into the pool. Beer bottles and empty liquor bottles riddle the lawn, and all Meana can focus on is the delicious food that she consumes. Taking the last bite of her numerous plates, Victoria reaches out and snatches the plate from her hand.

"Holy shit, girl. At this rate, you're going to start growing a food baby! No more food for you!"

With sadness pouring from her eyes, Meana looks up at Victoria and melancholically says, "Okay," and then lets out a loud sigh.

"Time to work off some of those calories you just ingested," Elizabeth says with one hand outstretched toward Meana.

Nervousness stiffens her body, and Meana's upper lip starts to sweat at the thought of trying to keep rhythm with the reggaeton music

73

blaring from every corner of the house. She looks upon the glistening bodies of the hot and sweaty people dancing to the fast-paced beat, and her knees begin to weaken. Victoria can see that Meana's expression has worsened and shakes her head at Elizabeth.

"Forget dancing. Let's just shoot the shit in the car and head back to the barracks. You look like you're going to pass out anyway!"

Meana and Elizabeth wearily shake their heads in agreement, and the trio makes their way back to Elizabeth's car, only stopping every twenty or so feet to say farewell to another of Victoria's friends. They eventually make it back to the small sedan and depart the party in a swift fashion.

Elizabeth, sitting straight in her seat, in an effort to see over the steering wheel, says, "So how did you like the party, Meana?"

Looking out the back passenger window and staring out into the night sky, she replies, "Honestly, not really my scene, but the food was absolutely amazing!"

Victoria, sitting in the passenger seat, smiles and says, "Hell yeah, it was."

"Well, I'm glad you at least liked some aspect of the party, even if all we did was stand in the corner, stuffing our faces and watching someone walk around and converse," Elizabeth says, turning her attention from the road and fixing it upon Victoria.

Looking confused, Victoria shoots Elizabeth an awkward look and shrugs her shoulders. Noticing the playful interaction of her two new friends, Meana smiles and thinks to herself, *"I wonder if Ian would have had fun at the party?"*

The Departure

Months of training, months of pushing herself to the limit and hardening her body, have left Meana in the best shape of her life. She not only squeezes in a morning run before her everyday standard physical training with the platoon at 0600, but also during her chow time and after work. There is only one week left until they ship out on deployment, and she doesn't know if she will have the opportunity to work-out as much when she gets to their destination. She is attempting to take advantage of her current situation and mold herself into a lean and mean, athletic killing machine. Her heart pumps loud, and the veins in her neck pulsate as she continues speeding down her current running path. Sweat drips from every pore in her body, and the slight breeze of the fall weather kisses her skin.

She rounds a corner out of the wooded trail, and steps onto the main asphalt road leading to the barracks. She stares out ahead at the sky while the sun continues to rise, and readies herself for one last sprint. She steadies her pace, takes in a few deep breaths, and when she feels her body relax, she rapidly increases her pace. In a dead sprint, her footsteps are more cat-like than ever. Having mastered her running form after months of pushing herself, this sprint no longer challenges her. Not satisfied with the results thus far, she pushes even harder. Each step feels like she is about to take off like a plane. Her body glides with each well-placed step, and the scenery around her blurs while she blazes down the road. She makes her way to the barracks parking lot in no time and decides to run all the way to her room. While continuing her pace, she sees a platoon of Marines running by on the sidewalk, and quickly throws them a wave. Assuming no one saw her, she averts her gaze from the platoon of Marines and turns her full attention to running across the parking lot. Within no time, she arrives at her room door, and sees Ian leaning against it and fiddling with his phone. He smiles while staring at the screen and scrolls through some pictures without ever looking up.

Slightly out of breath, Meana heaves out, "Well, good morning, good-looking," and he looks up from his phone in bewilderment.

"Oh shit, you crossed the parking a lot faster than I thought you would," he says, managing to slip his unlocked phone into his pocket before she has a chance to see what he's looking at. He throws a smile in her direction and Meana gracefully accepts it as she walks over and heavily kisses him on the lips. Liking the energy he is getting from her, he continues to smile and asks, "Your roommate in?"

Without saying a word, Meana shakes her head no and devilishly smiles at Ian. She swiftly pulls her key from the small pocket of her running shorts and unlocks the door. Looking at Ian with passion in her eyes, she placing one hand on his chest, and pushes him through the threshold. Slamming the door behind them, she immediately unbuttons his uniform blouse. He aggressively kisses her, and in his haste, he accidentally bumps their noses together. They both wince for a split second just before giggling, and without any further hesitation, begin to lock lips again. Meana, having finished unbuttoning his blouse, watches the uniform top slide off his upper body.

Taking in the sight and seeing his bulging abdominal muscles, Meana stops and says, "No undershirt was a good choice."

She slides a hand up his abs and across his rippling pectorals and guides him backward to the bed. With the back of his legs against the bed, she gives him one firm push, and he lands flat on his back. With her prey laying right where she wants him, she places her hands on the bottom of her shirt, and with one swift movement, removes it completely. Ian attempts to sit up and speed the process of unclothing along, but Meana pushes him back down on the bed and proceeds to undress herself until she is completely naked. Standing bare before him, Ian gawks in disbelief.

"You like what you see," Meana asks in her sexiest voice.

"Fuck yeah, I do, baby," Ian exclaims in response.

Meana walks in a line, foot over foot, making her way between his legs. She unbuckles his pants and begins to pull them off, when, midway, they get caught on his large erection. Meana shimmies his pants off despite the intrusive erection, and without taking off his boots, she leaves his pants around his ankles. Forcefully pulling his boxers down, she is presented with a large and veiny penis. Reaching with one hand, she firmly wraps her fingers around his shaft and strokes it back and forth. Neither of them says a word and Ian lays back, staring at the popcorn ceiling above. Meana, firmly between Ian's legs, bends forward and wraps her plush and moist lips around the head of his penis. Ian lets out a hushed moan of approval, and Meana works her mouth back and forth along the great girth of his penis. She steadily increases her pace and simultaneously strokes him with one hand. Ian's body shudders while Meana thoroughly plays with his penis. Just as she sees he is getting close to his climax, she stops and stands.

"Not yet, baby," she teasingly says.

Ian lets out a playful, "You're killing me," and Meana turns around and pushes her ass out toward his erection.

Placing her feet between his, she squats. Using the sweat from her morning run and the fluids of her horny vagina, she slips his raging cock inside herself. Rhythmically grinding, she works the entirety of his penis inside herself, and initiates the reverse-cowgirl position. She grinds back and forth, with ease, and Ian crunches his torso up and places his hands on her hips. Meana places her right hand between her moist thighs and begins to rub her clitoris as she continues to steadily ride Ian.

"Holy fuck," Ian says, feeling a burning climax begin to rise. "I'm about to cum," he says, but it seems as if Meana does not hear him.

She increases her pace and rides harder and harder, simultaneously increasing the pace of the clitoral rubbing. Her body slithers back and forth, and she places her left hand on Ian's knee while vaginal fluids seep from inside. Cumming with great intensity, Meana lets out a series of loud moans. In unison, Ian lets out a small moan and Meana continues to hump her way through her orgasm. Finished, Meana sits up straight and playfully wiggles her ass and looks back at Ian with a smile.

"You bad girl," Ian says just before laying completely back on the bed in satisfaction.

Meana carefully shimmies her way up and off until Ian's rapidly deflating penis falls out of her vagina and slaps him in the leg.

"Thanks, babe," she says, kicking her clothes towards the small closet of her barracks room. "I'm going to shower. I'll leave the door open so you can clean up," she says while walking toward the six-foot-by-four-foot bathroom that houses her shower. Ian lays on the bed with a wide grin, and hears her turn on the shower.

Letting seconds pass him by, he lets out a loud groan while sitting up from the bed and hearing his knees crackle and pop. Stiff legged, with pants around his ankles, Ian makes his way to the bathroom and proceeds to urinate. Having relieved his bladder and pissed on Meana's seat, he shakes it out and grabs a few baby wipes from a little white container on top of the toilet.

Wiping away her vaginal fluids, he says, "I'm going to head back to my room. I'll see you at the office."

"Sounds good," she says, scrubbing her body with the *Lovely Lady Lavender* body wash she bought at Walmart.

78

Taking in a large whiff of her body wash, Ian smiles, then flushes the toilet and makes his way out of the room without another word. Still scrubbing her body and applying shampoo to her hair, Meana allows her mind to drift off and random thoughts of fighting take hold.

The next week goes by in a normal fashion with no abnormal events, and it is time for the unit to deploy. The entirety of the regiment stands outside in the dark at 0400 with a plethora of bags at their feet. Marines are staged and ready to board the buses that are set to shuttle them to the Air Force airport where they will be departing. Each platoon leader takes the roll and verifies that every Marine is present and coherent. Once satisfied, they report their completion and stand fast in wait for the buses just like everyone else. Two boring hours pass by, and while the watch on Meana wrist strikes 0600, the buses pull into the large parking lot and stop with a loud hissing sound as the brakes depressurize.

Hearing the brakes even from where she is sitting, Meana excitedly stands and nearly trips on her seabag and shouts, "About damn time!"

Every platoon that makes up Regiment 92 stands, and in a single-file formation, they make their way to the buses and lethargically board one at a time. Fifteen minutes have passed, and every single Marine that once sat in the parking lot of the barracks, is loaded and settling into their overly cramped seats. Meana sits in the back of the bus with some of the other female Marines, and clumsily places her bags in the small space available at her feet. With the Marines packed in like sardines, the bus driver turns the key in the ignition, and the bus roars to life. Hearing the brakes hiss once again, she knows that they are mobile, and she curiously looks about and sees the grim faces of the

Marines sitting around her while they turn to look out of the dark bus windows. A deafening silence fills the air, and the tension is at an all-time high, and Meana knows that for many of the Marines, this is a goodbye from their loved ones. Torn away for close to a year with nothing but occasional calls and social-media messages when command allows it, she places her arms across her chest and rubs them as a cold chill shoots through her. Knowing that some young child will be growing up with an absentee parent, Meana can't help but relate her life to theirs and wonder if they will feel the same as she. All these thoughts rattle around in her head, she leans back and tries to relax while turning her mind to thoughts of Ian. Feeling a little more comfortable, she closes her eyes and allows herself to drift off to sleep.

An hour and a half later, Meana is woken by the shutter of the bus abruptly stopping and the air brakes hissing for the last time. They have arrived at the Air Force airport, and it's time to get off of the bus and stage their gear. In unison, the Marines stand and dismount the bus in an orderly fashion as their leadership yells about and points them in the right direction. They follow a young man in an Air Force uniform to a large building with rows of putrid-green chairs inside. It is a huge hanger that has been fashioned into a wanna-be airport terminal. The Marines are walked to their designated rows and offload their gear by the seats in which they have chosen.

The man in the Air Force uniform shouts, "Everybody, please pay attention. In a minute, we are going to hand out clip-boards and pens!" Meana and other Marines stare at this man with curiosity, and she wonders why he sounds so soft-spoken. The man continues on, "Please fill out these forms and return them carefully! Make sure to read the *do not bring* items list and ensure to discard any items that match the description!" Each Marine wears a look of irritation as this man continues to drone on. "Make sure to keep these papers with you at all times! We will begin boarding in an hour or so, and I will collect them from you when you pass through security."

The sleep-deprived and grumpy Marines let out an exhausted "Rah" in acknowledgment to what the man has said. The gentleman in the Air Force uniform purses his lips and makes a surprised face as if he wasn't expecting the Marines not to give a shit.

He turns and briskly walks away, and when he does, a Marine in the back of the room exclaims, "Finally!"

Multiple Marines break out in laughter, and Meana can see the Air Force gentleman's face turn beet red as he continues to walk away without daring to look back. She sits in her uncomfortable plastic and non-cushioned chair, leaning back and tilting her head to the ceiling.

As she does, Ian appears and leans forward to say, "Kill me now. We haven't even gotten in the air yet, and I already feel like I'm about to pass out from exhaustion." Meana lets out a small giggle, and Ian proceeds to take a seat directly behind her. "Holy shit, these chairs are uncomfortable," he belligerently says out loud so that the Air Force officials standing by can hear.

Yet again, multiple Marines burst out in laughter and they watch a slew of Air Force members muttering to themselves and staring back with disgruntled looks. Meana pushes her head farther up until she is looking at Ian, and without saying a word, she lifts a finger to her mouth and singles for him to be quiet. He turns from laughing at the Air Force members and looks upon Meana with a serious face as he raises one hand and mimics zipping his lips shut. Satisfied, she readjusts herself in her chair until her level of comfort increases and then, once again, falls asleep.

Far from Home

Three months have passed, and violent rays of the midday sun beat down on the empty mounds of sand that litter the entirety of Meana's view as she looks outside the perimeter wall of the small, undisclosed forward operating base she has been assigned to. Standing in a pill-box located at the front gate of the small compound, Meana begins to feel weighed down by her flak jacket, Kevlar helmet, mounds of ammo, and standard M4 rifle. Wanting to place the rifle down and take a nap, she lifts her head and takes a deep breath to fight the urge to sleep. Looking up at the ceiling of the small pill-box, Meana can see the tan-colored block that shapes her surroundings. Not a crack in sight, and yet this pill-box has sat in this exact location for years. The military found it in the vastness of nothingness and decided to set up a forward operating base right next to it.

"Leave it to the Corps to pick a place with no water and no vegetation," she thinks to herself. Feeling more awake, she looks out the small window of the pill-box for any activity, and to no surprise, she sees nothing but heat waves rising from the sand. Deciding that the coast is clear, she turns her back to the exterior perimeter of camp and looks out the back opening of the pill-box. She watches the plethora of tan-colored tarp tents flapping in the wind, and the sand in the air wiping about.

She observes the makeshift sand-filled walls of the camp and says, "I can't believe we rely on really big sandbags to form our walls. Seems like a safety hazard to me."

Feeling stressed about standing guard duty at noon in a mini oven of a building, she reaches down into the right cargo pocket of her tan military digital-camouflage trousers and pulls out a soft pack of Turkish Blend cigarettes and a small red lighter. Tapping the pack against her hand until a single cigarette is hanging out, Meana feels sweat beads roll down the back of her neck. Ignoring the sweat, she grabs the lone cigarette from the pack and puts it between her lips. She lifts the lighter up to the end of the cigarette, and with a few strikes, lights the cigarette and puffs away. Plumes of toxic smoke fill the pill-box, and Meana watches the smoke it makes its way out of the small slitted windows. Taking a slow long drag of her dirt-flavored cigarette, she closes her eyes and allows her body to relax. Still facing the interior of the forward operating base, she opens her eyes and looks upon the Marines walking around the camp. Left and right, small groups of Marines are standing about, smoking cigarettes and cracking jokes as if they have no care in the world. Meanwhile, Meana is counting down the minutes until she is relieved from her post. Looking forward to returning to the air-condition filled admin tent and resuming her job, she lifts the cigarette and takes a series of long drags. She allows her mind to drift off and continues to look at the interior of the camp with her back to the outside world and a memory running through her mind.

The sun shines down and kisses Meana skin as she lays on her towel, taking in the joyous rays. The sound of waves crashing in the distance and seagulls chirping fills the sweat and salty air. She takes in a big breath and exhales with complete satisfaction. Wearing nothing but her tiny red-and-white, polka-dotted, two-piece bathing suit and a pair of big, bug-eyed sunglasses, Meana opens her eyes and looks about the beach. She sees a young girl, maybe four years of age, running around,

chasing the seagulls that occasionally land to steal food from the visitors that are foolish enough to walk away from it. Her mother is in the background, taking pictures of her while she runs about and lets out multiple loud screams of joy, which are followed by hysterical laughter. Meana can't help but smile and says, "One day," to herself, continuing to watch the mother and daughter enjoy their day at the beach. Minutes pass by, and Meana averts her gaze to all the vacationers lining the beach. As she does, she sits up and reaches for the blue cooler nearby. Lifting the lid, she reaches deep into the ice and pulls out a beer. She closes the lid to the cooler and grabs the bottle opener she has hanging from the handle. Popping the lid of beer with a smile on her face, she hooks the bottle opener back onto the handle of the cooler and proceeds to take a sip of her ice-cold beer. Feeling the cool blast of the liquid run down her throat on this hot day, Meana lets out a sigh of relief. She lowers the beer down to her side and continues to look about the white sands of the beach. Turning her focus to the ocean itself, she can see the murky waves of Myrtle Beach crashing over the many people swimming around. She watches people getting crushed by the large waves for a while and admires the glisten of the sun off the water in the distance. Feeling completely relaxed and at peace, Meana looks down toward the shoreline and sees Ian standing in the water. Like watching a movie, the water glistens on his olive-colored skin, and even from up on the sandy hill, she can see his radiant-blue eyes stand out among the murky water. He looks back at her and smiles, lifting both arms and flexing as hard as he can. His biceps bulge, and his abs harden while Meana looks upon him and lets out a small laugh. She lifts her beer up in the air and gives him a tip of acknowledgment and approval.

With half of her cigarette gone, Meana lets out a hopeful sigh, thinking about the days she will be able to have fun on the beach again. She takes a few more puffs of her cigarette, and when she feels she has had enough, she throws it out of the small window of the pillbox. Feeling more relaxed than before, she has but to wait a little longer for shift change to occur. Everything has gone smooth as usual, and she has yet to see any reason for her suffering in this small and torturous building to continue. She gives the interior of the compound one last glance then turns around to face the outside world once more. She looks out to the sands and scans the area. To her surprise, she sees a large plume of sand in the air, and as she stares at it, she realizes it is forming a trail.

While she was daydreaming of better times and enjoying her cigarette, she missed the small, tan car coming directly for the forward operating base. With the car only a few hundred yards away, Meana lifts her rifle and looks through the scope to see the driver and vehicle better. Unable to see much through the thick cloud of sand, the only detail she can make out is the car approaching is not a military vehicle. She waits one moment longer, hoping that the vehicle will turn away, but she has no such luck. The car continues to closes in, and has not changed direction. It is still heading for the small lift gate that separates the Marines from the outside world. Deciding she has no other option; she lifts the radio attached to her flak jacket to her face and keys the radio.

"Gate Guard to HQ, over!"

An old and soft voice comes over the other end, "Send it, Gate Guard."

Meana, feeling her nerves on edge, says, "Command, we have a fast-approaching vehicle, located dead ahead of the front gate."

Static fills the air and Meana waits for a response.

"Roger that, Gate Guard. Sending the Quick Response Force to your location. Over."

"Roger that, Command. Gate Guard out," Meana says while trying to keep her cool.

Feeling a small sense of relief that she will have back up at the gate, Meana lowers the radio and lifts her rifle once more to watch the vehicles approach through the scope. Roughly four hundred yards out, Meana can clearly see that the vehicle has not begun to slow.

Still looking through the scope of her rifle, the QRF team leader enters the pill-box and says, "Stay in the pill-box, Corporal. We are going to take the gate. Keep your rifle at the ready incase we need backup."

Meana turns from her rifle scope and looks over to see Ian staring back at her.

With a nervous look washing over her, she replies, "Sounds good, Sergeant. I've got your back," and then gives him a nod of approval.

He turns around and without hesitation, yells a series of commands to his four Marine fire team.

"You two, take position on the right side of the gate," he barks to two young male Marines that Meana has never seen before. "Mendoza and Cortez, I want you both by the pillbox wall at the ready. I'll take point and make contact with the driver."

A uniformed "Aye, aye, Sergeant" comes from the mouth of the other four Marines as they move into position. Ian, being the team lead, stands in the center of the lift gate and raises his left hand to signal a stopping motion. Meana looks away from the team and peers in the direction of the car, less than two hundred yards out. With her rifle at the ready, she dared not look away from the vehicle. The seconds tick by and Meana can feel her heart pounding in her head and sweat pour out of every crack and crevice of her body. Less than one hundred yards, and the vehicle has yet to slow. Meana takes a sequence of deep breaths and she tries to stay her nerves. Less than fifty yards, and still speeding at a high rate, Ian realizes that the vehicle has no intention of stopping.

He looks to his team and Meana as he yells, "Brace yourselves, and ready to fire on my command!"

Just then the male voice on the radio chimes in, "Gate Guard and QRF, we see you. Permission to fire at will has been granted."

Knowing that Ian heard the command over the radio, Meana turns her head and looks at Ian and can see his face is beet red with veins protruding all over his forehead as he yells, "Fire at will!"

She turns back to her rifle scope, aims at the driver side of the windshield, and clicks her rifle from *safe* to *fire*. With the car twenty yards out, the kill shot became nearly impossible to miss. Time slows for Meana as she braces her body for the recoil of her weapon and takes a deep breath just before squeezing the trigger of her rifle. Having fired her weapon many times before, Meana is not surprised with the recoil of weapon fire bombarding her shoulder. A loud and quick series of gun-fire can be heard throughout the forward operating base as Meana and Ian's QRF unleash a volley of lead upon the vehicle. The windshield of the car splinters into pieces and the rounds penetrate and shred through the glass. The vehicle, however, does not slow. Knowing there was no way for the driver to survive, Meana yells, "Move," to Ian as loud as she can. He and his team scramble to move while the car approaches at a high rate of speed through the lift gate and into the camp. With the driver dead, the car just barely makes it into camp before it drifts out of control. It takes a sharp left turn and makes contact with a sand barrier one hundred feet from Meana's pill-box. Meana lowers her rifle, turning from the small slit she was firing from and looks out of the doorway. Seeing Ian lifting himself from the sand and helping his team up, she looks down at her hands and sees they are shaking uncontrollably.

"Wow" she whispers to herself, replaying the incident in her mind.

Still standing in the doorway, Meana looks up and sees Ian looking back at her with a big smile and a thumbs-up toward her. She throws him a weak smile back and places her rifle back into her hands and points it toward the vehicle. Ian turns around and realizes that his job is not yet completed.

He looks over at the two young male Marines and says, "Secure the vehicle."

Wiping the sand from their uniforms, they look up and say, "Aye, aye, Sergeant."

Ian, Victoria Mendoza, and the mousy Elizabeth Cortez stand at a distance as the two Marines make their way to the vehicle. Slowly looking around for movement, they decide that nothing could have survived the gunfire or the crash.

The younger of the two male Marines, walks toward the driver-side door and motions for the second Marine to cover him. He wraps his fingers around the handle of the driver door and lifts his rifle to the ready with his hand. Pulling on the vehicle handle and unable to see through the dark tint of the window, he opens the driver's door with minimal struggle and low visibility. The door swings open, and the Marine takes a swift step back as he places both hands onto his rifle. With the door wide open, they see a young Middle Eastern teenager, with both of his hands taped to the steering wheel and blocks placed upon the accelerator. The younger of the two Marines looks back and mouths, "What the fuck?" to the other Marine. Both Marines shrug in confusion when, all of a sudden, they hear a cell phone go off in the young man's shirt pocket. Meana hears the ringing tone and immediately knows what is happening as she steps from the doorway of the pill-box and screams, "Run," at the top of her lungs. Too late to recognize the threat, the small tan car becomes immersed in flames and explodes in a massive and violent concussion. The two young male Marines standing by the vehicle are quickly engulfed in the explosion as their bodies are shredded into pieces and thrown back like rag dolls. The concussion of the blast sends ripples through the sand while it makes its way outward.

With time slowed once again, Meana manages to see Ian and the remainder of his team thrown by the concussion and into the sand as she, too, is violently knocked backward into the pillbox doorway.

Dazed from the blast, Meana places one hand on her Kevlar helmet and proceeds to sit up. She looks about and sees that she has been blown back into the pillbox, just two feet from the doorway. She stands with aching bones and stumbles her way out of the structure, coughing from all the sand in the air. Desperate to find Ian through the wall of sand, she begins to yell out his name. She hears no response and makes her way forward toward his last location. Swatting the sand away from her eyes and placing a hand over her mouth to block it from getting in, she can see a large mass laying on the ground. She runs toward it with a tear forming in her eyes, and sees Ian lying on top of Mendoza, and Cortez in an attempt to shield them from the violent concussion. Closer, Meana calls out his name once more, and he looks up in confusion.

"Is everyone all right?", he asks the two female Marines he is covering.

Both coughing from the sand and pushing him off of them, they reply, "Yes, Sergeant."

Everyone makes their way to their feet and Meana without thinking, throws herself at Ian and gives him a big hug. He, however, pushes her away and turns toward the car. Not seeing his two young Marines anywhere in sight, Ian falls to his knees and looks to the ground. Meana looks upon the burning remains of the vehicle and the sand retaining wall, and she realizes why Ian is sad. Without saying a single word, she takes a step closer to Ian and places one hand on his shoulder as tears begin to stream down his face.

False Heroism

The sun shines with the ferocity of a thousand blazing fires while Meana sits on her seabag out on a hot tarmac, waiting for her flight home to finish being fueled. Looking around in desperation, she sees not a scrap of shade to save her from the malicious rays of the sun. With it at high noon, she knows the likelihood of finding any shade is slim to none. She abandons the hunt and leans back on her makeshift seat, tilting her military-issued hat a little lower on her face. Looking out at the runway in the distance, she can see the immense heat waves zigging back and forth and distorting the scenery beyond. Through the illusive and waving heat, she sees the sandy and rocky mountainous terrain in the distance. They are peppered with peaks of crumbling rocks that are dark brown in color, and sheer edges with tree clusters growing in random areas. As if the vegetation was clinging to life on top of this decimated wasteland of a peak, the greenery reminded Meana of a random trip that she once took to the mountains of North Carolina. Leaning forward, she places her elbows on top of her knees and begins to reminisce.

It was late January, and Meana was sixteen years of age. Her mother decided to take a spur of the moment trip to the mountains of North Carolina, claiming

she had to drop off a package for her friend Leon, and Meana was forced to tag along. Driving straight from New York to North Carolina, Meana dreaded the thought of only stopping for gas and seldom for restroom breaks. At the time, it was by far one of the worst experiences of her life. Roughly halfway through the trip and freshly entering the state of Virginia, Meana's mother sat silently in the driver seat with both her hands firmly on the wheel. Her mother seemed to be caught up in her own thoughts, and barely acknowledged Meana's presence. Casually stealing glances at her mother, she could see the mixture of nervousness and coarseness that engulfed her facial expressions. Unable to tell what her mother was thinking, she stared at her in wonder, witnessing her biting her bottom lip with ferocity. She looks away and changes her uncomfortable positioning in the passenger seat. Sitting with her feet up on the seat and her body curled into a ball, she couldn't help but wonder why they had embarked on this sudden trip.

For many years, Meana has known about her mother's drug addiction, but even after all the episodes of violence and paranoia her mother had gone through, this, by far, was the strangest of her actions. There was a crazy look to her eye, almost as if she was running for her life. Meana looked out of the windshield in a desperate attempt to gain her bearings but was unable to do so. Having never left the state of New York, the dark scenery before her looked as foreign as it possibly could. She reaches out in front of her and opens the glove box, hoping to find anything to keep her mind busy. As she un-clicks the clasp holding the glove box closed, it's door flops downward, and a revolver falls to the floor. Meana sits in shock, and stares down at this silver-plated, six-shooter of a pistol with pearl grips. Without moving, she keeps her eyes fixed on the pistol and can see that there are rounds loaded into the chambers. She slowly turns to face her mother, and to her surprise, she is still staring out of the windshield.

Meana, knowing that something is up, reaches over with her left hand and places it upon her mother's shoulder and asks, "Mom, is everything all right?"

Without responding, her mother's bottom lip quivers, and tears stream down her face. Her mother leans forward and increases her grip upon the steering wheel in a desperate attempt to keep the car from careening off the road. As the tears continue to stream down her face, the gray clouds holding a grasp on the sky begin to cry in unison. The windshield is filled with the light pitter-pattering of rain, and visibility is drastically altered. Meana, seeing that her mother is not responding, reaches over and turns the wipers, and the low beam lights of the car on. She sits back into her original position and looks upon the revolver once more. Deciding that it would be a bigger issue to leave it on the floor than to pick it up, she reaches down and grabs the pistol with a firm grip. Holding the gun in her hand, she feels a sense of power wash over her and stares at the sheen of the pistol a little longer. Wondering what it would feel like to shoot a pistol, she inches her index finger closer to the trigger. With her finger firmly on the trigger, she fights the urge to pull it. The itch in her finger grows and she continues the fight. "Don't do it," she thinks to herself. Unable to control herself, she fully pulls the trigger of the pistol, and luckily, nothing happens. She lets out a slight sigh of relief as she thinks about the results of a live round going off in the car. Her mother's trance is broken by the load click of the revolver's trigger being pulled, and she is staring at Meana with a deadly glare as she sees her sixteen-year-old daughter brandishing a pistol.

"Are you fucking crazy? What if the hammer had been cocked back?" she says as her right hand leaves the steering wheel and meets Meana's face with a hard and violent smack.

Meana feels a ripple surge through her face and her entire head shifts toward the passenger-side window and makes contact. The sound of splintering glass echoes through her ears, and Meana opens her eyes to see her hair obstructs the majority of her vision. The pistol that she is holding, falls from her hand and lands on the floor of her mother's car with a soft thud. Meana raises both her hands to her head and messages the burning pain that throbs through her face and the side of her head that made contact with the window.

"You broke my damn window, girl!" her mother says, wildly slapping about Meana's head with her free hand.

Taking a couple more blows to the top of her head, Meana says, "Please, Mama. I'm sorry. Keep your eyes on the road."

Her mother, becoming more infuriated with every word out of her daughter's mouth, shouts, "Don't you tell me what to do!"

Meana peeks through the cracks of her fingers at the road and can see their car is swerving between both lanes of the small, two-lane road. Making a split decision, Meana quickly jabs out with her left hand and makes contact with her mother's chin. Her mother, in shock that Meana threw a punch back, sits back in her seat and becomes deathly silent. A wave of fear washes over Meana, and she cries while envisioning the brutal beating that awaits her. However, moments of silence pass as her mother sits in the driver seat, still in shock. Meana, realizing that her mother is motionless, looks up from her hands and can see that her mother is steadily driving the car once more, and her face is pale white. Confused and still scared, Meana looks down at her left hand and lets out a small smile.

Sweat forms on the back of Meana's neck as the sun continues its onslaught of ultraviolet rays. She lifts her right arm from her knee and wipes the sweat away from her neck with a black bandana that she has pulled from her cargo pocket.

"They need to open the damn doors already," she says out loud.

A mousy voice can be heard from a distance and it says, "Hell yeah, they do."

Meana, with a puzzled look upon her face, turns to look for the voice. Directly to her right, Lance Corporal Cortez is seated on her own seabag and has sweat seeping through the armpits of her uniform.

"I didn't even notice you there," Meana says, throwing a smile in Cortez's direction.

"I get that a lot, Corporal," Cortez says, reciprocates the smile.

Meana and Cortez sit in silence as they look about the tarmac, both sweating profusely and cursing the sky in their minds.

Feeling the stagnant hot air between them becoming heavy, Cortez looks over at Meana and says, "So you have anyone waiting at home for you?"

Meana continues to glare at the heat waves in the distance and says, "Nah. We're coming home early, so I doubt anyone will even know I'm on my way."

Clearly lying to Cortez, Meana's body tenses as the words leave her mouth.

"Well, the only good thing that came from that car bomb was us going home early," Cortez says in an effort to lighten the air.

"Yeah, I guess you're right," Meana, glancing over to her left and seeing Ian sitting in a slump on his seabag.

With a pitiful look on his face, he leans against the fence that lines the airport and fiddles with the dog tags of the two Marines he has lost.

Meana continues her soft stare in his direction, and Cortez says, "He seems to be taking their deaths pretty hard."

Meana lets out a small sigh and says, "Yeah, well, they were under his charge, and I guess he somehow feels that he could have stopped their deaths."

Cortez lets out a scuff of disappointment. "We all signed up knowing that this could happen. They died for a worthy cause, and he dishonors their deaths with his self-pity."

Meana, feeling her rage boil over, says, "Why don't you shut your damn mouth and give the man some credit! He blocked you from the blast, didn't he?"

Cortez looks at Meana with a fierce and stern gaze and growls, "What he did was chauvinistic and false heroism! Mendoza and I are Marines just like him, and for your information, Mendoza blocked him from the impact first, and then he climbed on top after the blast had already subsided!"

Not sure whether to believe Cortez or not, Meana sits in silence and ponders the possibility that Ian would really do that.

She shakes her head in an effort to loosen the thought from her mind and snaps, "Whatever, Lance Corporal. Just sit there in silence. That's an order."

Even more frustrated than before, Cortez grits her teeth and grumbles, "Yes, Corporal," and turns her back to Meana.

Fixing her gaze on Ian once again, Meana stands from her seabag and makes her way to his side. Her pace is slow and hesitant as Cortez's words ping around in her head like a bullet ricocheting off a steel plate. She continues to make her way to Ian at a slow and steady pace when, out of nowhere, a headache begins to develop, and she lifts her left hand to her forehead. Rubbing above her eyes profusely, she attempts to alleviate the stress-induced headache. Suddenly a wave of nausea comes over her, and the path before her spins. She stops in her tracks and places both hands on her hips in an attempt to regain her composure. She feels the ham-and-cheese sandwich she ate for lunch creep its way to her esophagus, and the taste of her cigarette lingers in the back of her throat. Unable to hold back any longer, Meana runs to the small patch of grass that buds up against the security fence surrounding the airport. She bends over and grabs her military-issued hat from her head as she begins to vomit the contents of her lunch into the grass. A pain shoots through her back, and the headache that plagued her before intensifies with every heave.

Ian is broken from his trance by the sounds of Meana heaving just a few steps away. He stands from his seated position and makes his way over to her, and his mouth opens in an effort to say something, but the dry, sandy sensation in the back of his throat chokes him. Instead, he stands within an arm's distance of her and watches her unloading the content of her stomach. Having nothing left to throw up, Meana stands in an upright position and spits a stomach-acid-filled loogie onto the asphalt. She turns her head and looks at Ian who stands with a sad and confused look upon his face with mouth still agape. Without saying a word, Meana shifts her body, steps forward, and embraces Ian with a tight and loving hug.

Bundles of Joy

Time seems to bend in the darkest corners of Meana's life, allowing the shadows to loom over her like vultures over a newly found carcass. Yet moments of pure clarity slip through the cracks and shine upon her with absolution. Two months have passed since Meana and Ian have returned from their deployment, and Meana is faced with a new set of challenges. Sitting on the patient table with her legs wide open, Meana looks about the doctor's office with fear in her eyes. She feels the cold sting from the metallic medical stirrups, her legs are propped on and shivers while a blast of the air simultaneously makes its way up her thin white patient gown. *"Hurry up, Doc,"* she thinks to herself, waiting the doctor's return. *"Why would he leave so suddenly like that?"* she thinks while staring at the room door like she has the ability to see right through it. Turning from the door, she looks about the room once more, and not but a few seconds go by when the door opens in a speedy fashion and causes Meana to jump.

"I've got Nurse Jasmin here with me, and she is going to perform an ultrasound on you," the doctor says, walking through the door with a young, Caucasian nurse following right behind.

Seeing Meana nearly jump from the table, the older, tall, lanky, and ghostlike doctor says, "Oh my. I'm sorry to come in like that. I was just so anxious to get Nurse Jasmin over here to you."

Crossing her arms in an effort to fight the cold, Meana says with a shiver to her voice, "That's okay, Doc. You just caught me off guard a bit."

Just then Nurse Jasmin chimes in, "A-all right, sweetheart. I'm going to lower these medical stirrups real quick, then I'm going to run you through the process of the ultrasound."

Not catching the ultrasound until right now, Meana asks, "Wait, hold on a second. Like, I might be pregnant?"

The doctor looks at Meana with a soft, caring face, and he says, "No mights, young lady. You are definitely pregnant." He then pauses to ensure he chooses his words carefully. "We, uh, well, we have to perform the ultrasound because you are still in service, and we would need to report it to your command, and secondly, your records indicate that you were involved in a large concussion not long ago."

Meana turns her head back and forth while she bounces between looking at the doctor's face and the nurse's and places her hands on top of her head in disbelief. "But I didn't have any sex when I was deployed. How can I be pregnant?"

The nurse, noticing Meana beginning to tense up, reaches out and places a hand on her shoulder while saying, "Let's go ahead and get started with the ultrasound, and we will be able to judge the age of the fetus from there. How does that sound?"

Not sure what to say, Meana, in a bit of shock, nods her head in approval, and the nurse prepares the machine nearby.

"So, first things first, I'm going to lift your grown above your stomach, and then I'm going to apply the water-soluble gel just above the uterus. It may feel a little cold, but that's totally normal."

"Okay," Meana says, lifting her gown above her belly and exposing her vagina to the room.

"Oh, I'm sorry, young lady. I forgot to tell you to put your underwear back on," the doctor says, nervously inching closer to the door. "I'm going to step outside while you ladies take care of business in here, and I'll be back when all is said and done." He glides out of the room and back into the main hallway.

Meana's cheeks turn a rosy red, and she grabs her underwear from beside her and slides them back on her body just seconds after the doctor exits the room.

"Doc must have been excited for ultrasound," the nurse jokes, trying to downplay the doctor's clear inability to multitask.

Meana looks at her with a nervous smile as she once again lifts her gown above her stomach. The nurse lifts a large white tub and centers it just above Meana's uterus and gently applies a heavy amount of the gel.

Feeling the cold gel hit her skin, Meana slightly shudders, and the nurse, attempting to make her feel comfortable, says, "Oh, I'm sorry, sweetheart. I know it's cold."

"That's an understatement," Meana replies, turning her attention to the ultrasound monitor while the nurse rubs the transducer back and forth along Meana's lower stomach in an effort to get a clear picture of the baby.

"How much longer?"

"Just a couple more passes, and I should be able to find a nice clear picture of the baby for you," the nurse says while staring at the ultrasound's monitor. "I'm going to push just a little bit harder, and that should do it." A wave of discomfort washes over Meana as the nurse continues to dig the transducer into her lower abdomen. However, only seconds later, the nurse excitedly shouts out, "A-ha, I got you now!" and turns to look at Meana. Staring at the monitor with great intent, Meana can see the clear formation of a baby in her stomach. "Looks to me that you are roughly, five or six months pregnant." The nurse pauses for a second and observes Meana's barren belly with a smile on her face and says, "You aren't even showing yet. That's awesome. I'm sure the baby will start showing any day."

Keeping her eyes on the monitor with a blank stare, Meana slowly turns her head toward the nurse and asks, "Five or six months?"

"Well, yes. You see how the baby is already taking form and how far into the development stage it is? Those are all signs that you're approaching the end of your second trimester."

Meana's face turns a ghostly white, and a mixture of joy and sorrow weigh down on her until she feels her back press against the medical table.

"Are you okay?" the nurse asks, jumping up from her chair and easing Meana's head down to the table. "I'm going to get the doctor in here. I'll be right back."

Watching the nurse run out of the room and frantically search for the doctor, Meana observes the room spinning around in circles, and a cold sweat forms on her forehead as the lights begin to fade. and she blacks out.

A highly stressful hour ticks by, and Meana opens her eyes to see Ian standing above her with a worried look.

"What happened?" She asks in a low, raspy voice.

The nurse, seeing Meana awake, speaks before Ian has a chance, "Young lady, you gave us quite the scare. After I showed you the sonogram of the baby, you blacked out and fell to the table. I just barely had a chase to catch you before I had to run for the doctor. We called your command immediately, and they sent your platoon sergeant to come for you."

While the nurse pauses to catch a breath, Ian takes the opportunity to chime in, "Gunny sent me to get you. We knew you'd be at medical, but not under these circumstances. From what I see on the monitor and from what the nurse has said, you seem to be pregnant. Congrats for you."

Looking at Ian with an extreme level of confusion and trying to shake off the fog from her mind, she says, "U-uhm, yeah, I just found this out myself. Apparently, I was pregnant for those short months of our deployment. She also said that I conceived before the unit even left."

Standing with wide eyes, Ian looks back to the monitor with a hint of fear and asks, "So you were pregnant during the car bombing, the flights, and all of the stress of moving gear and troops around?"

Meana looks at Ian with her penetrating green eyes and nods her head softly to confirm his fears. Without so much as a second thought, he steps closer to Meana and takes her hand. The nurse, who has been standing by and waiting for a moment to speak, looks upon these two Marines holding hands, and a light bulb goes off in her head.

"Oh, I see. I take it that you're not just her platoon sergeant, but you're also the father of this child?"

Turning to look toward the nurse, Ian has a look of panic, and stutters, "I-I-I, um, yes," lowering his head to the floor in shame.

The nurse lets out a large sigh of disapproval because she knows as well as anyone else that two people in the same unit are not supposed to have relations. "Look, because of the circumstances of this child and how it has survived such trauma, I'm going to overlook telling your command…...for now."

Meana stares at the nurse, and as their eyes make contact, the nurse takes a step back and says, "What I mean is, I am obligated to report the pregnancy to your command, but I will say that I found the abnormality in your blood work consistent with pregnancy in about a week. This will allow the both of you the time needed to discuss further actions toward the baby."

Still staring at the nurse with an emotionless gaze, Meana says, "Well, thank you. I guess that's all we can ask for."

Nodding her head while stepping closer to the door, the nurse raises her hand and passes Meana her medical record. Meana reaches out and grabs the records from the nurse, and while the folder slips through the nurse's fingers, she turns from them and exits the room.

"I take it that means you can leave?" Ian asks after turning to look at Meana.

"Yeah, I guess so," she says, having already stood from the table and slid her uniform back onto her body.

Watching her every move and unsure how to address the new situation, Ian places a hand on her shoulder as she bends down to put on her boots, and says with glee in his voice, "I think we should get married!"

All Alone

It's 0720 of the day after her doctor's visit, and the hot and muggy weather saturates Mean's uniform top as she stands outside the regimental building with a singular piece of paper in her hands.

"Thank Odin, it's Friday," she says, glowing with excitement as her time in the Corps is drawing to a close, and she has been instructed to begin the checkout process.

Meana turns her eyes to the paper in her hands, and letting out a defeated sigh, she stares at the multiple line items that require a signature before she can depart. Ten days away from leaving the Marine Corps forever, Meana is determined to get this list knocked out as fast as humanly possible. However, seeing destinations like the dentist, medical, CIF, headquarters, armory, career planner, unit leaders, etc., she allows her shoulders to slump.

She stares at the paper a moment longer, determining which order she must start, and says, "Well, I've already been too medical. I guess I'll hit the career planner next."

She tilts her head back and lets out a small sigh while walking to her vehicle with an excessively dramatic swaying motion. Still driving the same small silver sedan that she began her career with, she approaches it with a smile on her face. Before entering the vehicle, she pauses and places a hand on the roof just above the driver door.

She gives the car a slight tap and says, "We've been through a lot, huh, ole girl?" She relieves her hand from the roof and opens the door of the car. Taking a seat with a soft landing, she places her hands on the steering wheel and says, "Time to start a new adventure."

She turns the key in the ignition and then proceeds to throw the shifter into drive. Placing her foot on the accelerator and giving it a gentle push, she makes her way out of the regimental building parking lot and onto the main road that leads to the career planner. Silence fills the air, and Meana, hearing a ringing in her ears, pushes the radio's power button and gently turns the volume knob in order to drown it out. Kelly Clarkson's *Miss Independent* comes over the radio, and Meana bobs her head back and forth as a spurt of energy washes over her.

Minutes go by while Meana continues to vibe to every song that plays on the radio, and she eventually arrives outside the headquarters building for the entirety of Camp Lejeune and parks her car close to the entrance. The time is 0735, and she exits her car and makes her way to the double doors on the face of the building. Having reached the distant doors in less than sixty seconds, Meana feels winded and places her hands upon her hips in an attempt to catch her breath. Sucking down air like it's going out of style, she feels a sweat form on her brow and thinks, *"No fucking way I'm already getting out of shape this fast."* She reaches for the handle of the doors and gives it a hefty tug. However, they do not budge, and with an angry look upon her face, she tries to yank the doors open. Locked and with no signs that they will budge, Meana decides that she will try the solitary door she saw on the side of the building. Making her way around the building via a thin concrete sidewalk, she looks out into the horizon and can see the sun is almost past the ridge. Stopping to take in the view and admiring the mixture of reds, yellow, and oranges of a new day, she feels the warmth of the sun against her heart. She stands for a few seconds longer, enjoying the view before making her way to the side of the building.

Standing in front of the side door that she hopes will lead into the HQ building, Meana stares at the handle and with, scrunched eyebrows, says, "You better open."

She places her right hand on the knob, and with a small exhale out, she turns it and pulls the door outward. To her surprise, it opens with ease, and she is able to enter the building. Walking through the threshold and into the empty hallway, she stands puzzled, near the main lobby of the building. She, however, is not standing in the lobby, but rather behind the counter where the front desk clerk is supposed to be standing.

She takes a couple steps forward and calls out, "Hello?"

She hears footsteps scurry in the distance and closing in on her position, and as they do, she feels an irrational sense of fear. Standing frozen in the deserted building and wondering what will pop around the corner, she balls her fists and stands ready to fight. The footsteps are louder, and as they reach their peak, an older man, with sunburnt skin, and a small patch of hair on the top of his head, comes around the corner.

"Who the hell are you, Marine?" the older gentleman asks, looking at her like she is an intruder.

"My apologies. I came here looking for a career planner, and this door was the only one open."

Standing stiff and ready to pounce on an intruder, the older man, wearing gym shorts, a scarlet-colored tank top, and tennis shoes, says, "That's because you came before 0800, when we open. You'll have to return then to conduct your business." Meana allows her body to loosen and her fists to unclench and feels her face drop. "Are you trying to check out?" the man asks, glaring at the paper in Meana's hand.

"Yes, sir. I get out in ten days, and my command said I have to get all of these signed by then."

He lifts his hand, reaching out for the paper and says, "I have the authority to sign the paper. Hand it over, and then you can be on your way." Meana hesitates to hand over the paper and contemplates whether to ask a question. Noticing her stalling, the man says, "Give me the damn paper before I kick you out, Marine."

No longer standing idle, Meana quickly hands over the paper and asks, "So I am able to set up an appointment with the career planner since they are not in right now, sir?"

The man looks up from signing the paper and says, "First off, my rank is first sergeant. I am not a sir, and second, I don't set appointments. Call in later, and they'll set one for you over the phone."

Meana stands straighter as she hears the man's rank and replies, "Thank you so much, First Sergeant. I'll do just that. Enjoy the rest of your day," and gently grabs the paper from him as if the slightest incorrect move would set him off.

He gives her a nod of approval just before saying, "Kindly help yourself out the same way you came in," turning away and walking back around the corner.

Without question or hesitation, she does just that. Standing back outside of the building with the sun fully risen, Meana looks down at the paper and says, "Okay, so I got the signature, but no contact with the person that's supposed to help me figure out the rest of my life. Great." Figuring that getting another signature on her massive list is at least a small victory, she gleefully walks back to her car. She starts the car and turns the knob of the air-condition in an effort to drown out the climbing humidity outside.

"Sun's barely up, and it's already humid as shit." She wipes the sweat from her brow. Staring at the list, she contemplates where to go next. Realizing it's still not 0800, and the rest of the required locations will most likely be empty like this one, she pulls her phone from her pocket and clicks on the search engine.

"Might as well go hunt for a job if I'm not going to be able to meet with the career planner."

Typing in, "Jobs near Deerfield, Virginia, that don't require a degree," her screen quickly populates with multiple labor and clerk jobs.

"Ian said we were moving into a rental in Deerfield. Let's see what they have." She taps the first website that pops up, and twenty jobs appear on her screen. She scrolls through each option, and in doing so, she realizes her options are limited to working as a cashier, stocker, etc. Letting out a sigh of frustration, she opens another tab on her search engine and types in, "Population of Deerfield, Virginia." The phone quickly processes her request, and 10,362 shows up on her screen. "Are you fucking kidding me? It's a damn ghost town. No wonder I can't find any real jobs."

Sitting in the driver seat, fuming with anger as the air-conditioning continues to blast her in the face and dry out her eyes, Meana contemplates what to search next. She looks out the windshield of her car and sees the parking lot is still empty. She glances at the clock of her vehicle and can see that the time is 0750. She scrunches her eyebrows and wonders where the Marines that inhabit this building could be. Still brooding, she directs her anger toward her phone and taps a new request into the search engine with loud thumps from her thumbs: "Jobs in the closest town to Deerfield, Virginia." Just like before, the phone populates with many websites, and Meana clicks on the first available. The webpage pops up, and instantly Meana recognizes it to be the same from before.

"Better give me something good," she growls to the inanimate website. This time only seven jobs come across her screen, and she looks upon them with all the rage of a violent hurricane. She can see one titled Luigi's Graphics. "What kind of name is that for a business?" she says as her anger continues to boil. Feeling like she wants to smash her phone, she tosses it into the passenger seat, and it bounces like it had hit a trampoline and smacks the window. The loud bang makes Meana jump, and her temper ebbs while her attention is turned back to the phone. Worried that she may have busted its screen, she scrambles to grab it from the floorboard; and when she finally picks it up, she lets out a small prayer to the All Father, "Please, please, please, don't be broken. I can't afford to buy a new one."

With both eyes squinting as if the phone's about to explode, she slowly turns it so the screen faces her. Fully opening her eyes, she sees the phone has sustained no damage.

"Phew, that could have been bad."

Looking at the screen once more, she scrolls through the options laid out before her and decides that the company she once made fun of, looks like her saving grace. She clicks on Luigi's Graphics, takes a deep breath and braces herself for some ridiculous explanation to a backwater-city-employment option, and begins to read the description:

Luigi's Graphics

Customer Service Associate

Mission Statement:

Looking for customer-service-oriented professionals with the drive to complete their work in a timely manner. No experience needed, but associates must be willing to train and learn all material supplied.

Job Description

Daily work consists of:

- Cleaning work space
- Inventory of floor supplies
- Operating print machines
- Assisting customer in graphic designing
- Helping any and all customer

Requirements:

- High school diploma
- No experience needed

Pay:

- Negotiable

```
Click Here to Apply
```

Staring at the "Click Here to Apply" button intently, she wonders how many people have already applied. *"If I apply, and they call me back, do I really want this job?"* she ponders, looking up from her phone and out the windshield of her car. She sees multiple cars pulling up and parking just a few feet from her own vehicle. Looking at the clock in her car, she sees the time is 0758. *"Must be nice to roll up just before 0800. Gunny would have our asses."*

Meana looks back at her phone and decides she will return to this inquiry later and locks the screen via the small button at the top. She grabs the door handle and pulls it firmly, pushing the door of her vehicle open and stepping outside once again. She makes her way back to the front of the building and looks upon the once locked double doors.

"I swear," she whispers, reaching for the handle and giving it a light tug. The door opens, and Meana lets out a small smile as she walks through the doors and toward the corporal at the front counter. She looks upon the female corporal's face and instantly recognizes that it is Cortez.

"Hey, I knew you switched units, but I didn't know you came here," she says, giving her a friendly smile.

Cortez looks up from her phone and stares at Meana with a blank look. "Oh, hey."

Instantly realizing that there is still tension between them, she says, "Look, I know you and I never reconciled before your leaving, but, well, I'm sorry about how I reacted last time we spoke."

Cortez's face shows a clear sign of surprise, as if she never expected Meana to apologize. "It's fine, Crane. I just wanted to make sure you knew the truth."

Meana, feeling a slight amount of anger rise inside her, says, "Please let's not talk about this again. I just want to move past it. You and I always got along before."

Sensing the genuineness in Meana's voice, Cortez gives her a nod of approval just before asking, "So, anyways, what can I help you with?"

Feeling a little peeved that Cortez has decided to end the conversation early, she says, "The career planner," with some sass behind her voice.

"Just up the stairs, turn right, and it'll be the first door on the left." Cortez points toward the stairs located behind her. Meana looks at the stairs and makes a face of despair, and Cortez says, "I hate stairs too. My knees burn with every step."

Looking back at Cortez, Meana says, "It's not really the stairs themselves. Ever since I found out I was pregnant, my stamina has dropped dramatically"

Cortez looks at Meana with wide eyes and confusion, asking, "Is it his?"

Meana lifts her chin in pride and says, "Yes, it is," and lets a large smile come across her face.

Still staring in awe, Cortez opens her mouth a few times, but nothing comes out. Finally choking some words out, she says, "I didn't realize…," she pauses, choosing her words more carefully. "Congrats to the both of you."

Still wearing the large smile, Meana replies, "Thanks. Anyways, I'll see you later," and she turns from Cortez and heads to the stairs.

Just before taking the first step, she looks back at Cortez and says, "Message me sometime. I'd like to keep in contact after I get out."

Cortez, who is staring at the front door in a trance, snaps back to reality and looks to Meana, saying, "Oh, Sure. I'll send you a message on social media."

Without saying any words, Meana throws a thumbs-up to Cortez and turns to the stairs. Every step feels like her legs are lead, and once reaching the top, she feels winded. She takes a deep breath in and makes her way to the Career Planner office. She reaches the door and sees an overweight staff sergeant sitting at her desk, reading a magazine titled *"How to Lose Thirty Pounds in One Week."*

Meana taps on the door-frame of the office and says, "Good morning, Staff Sergeant. Is now a good time to talk?"

The career planner drops the magazine down in embarrassment and attempts to hide it at her side as she says, "Yes, Marine, come on in. I was just, uh, doing some light reading."

Meana enters into the small twelve-by-twelve room that houses the lone desk and many filing cabinets, and in doing so, the white walls blind her. The sun is entering through a window directly behind the recruiter, and reflects off the white paint.

Meana squints her eyes, and in doing so, the staff sergeant takes notice and says, "It takes some getting used to, but I hear it will increase the temperature in the room and help with weight loss. Command said I could repaint it this color."

Confused at the lengthy explanation from a staff sergeant, Meana says, "It looks good, but I was wondering if you could help me determine a future career path. I'm getting out in ten days, and my command sent me here."

Realizing that she is blabbering away nervously about her weight, the staff sergeant clears her throat and gestures for Meana to sit down in the chair opposite her. "Give me your military ID number, and I'll pull up your certifications and education records."

Meana does as directed, and sits in silence while the career planner pulls her pathetically small record. The career planner clears her throat, except this time it's in embarrassment for Meana.

"Well, I'll be honest with you, not much for us to go off of here." She looks from the computer and at Meana. "According to your admin training and nothing else, you will make a great secretary or admin clerk at an office."

The staff sergeant pauses and gives Meana a nervous smile, hoping to be interrupted. However, Meana stares down at the table, thinking about Luigi's Graphics.

The career planner, getting no response, decides to continue, "If you could enroll in a community college near the area you're moving to, or even an online college, it would greatly expand the options laid out before you."

Meana looks up and says, "I'm not a very strong academic, but I suppose I could give it a try."

The career planner, hearing this, immediately starts to fish through the bottom right drawer of her desk, and after a couple seconds, she emerges with a handful of pamphlets for online colleges that will count Meana's admin training as credits.

"Here you go, Corporal. Each of these will give you a head start. Without college, I can't truthfully tell you that you have much of a future."

Meana looks the staff sergeant deep in her eyes with a fire flickering behind her own, and in meeting her gaze, the staff sergeant stops talking and freezes in place.

Meana outreaches her hand and takes the pamphlets from the career planners sweaty palms and stands and says, "Good day, Staff Sergeant. Thank you for your time."

Silence fills the office as the staff sergeant sits frozen, watching Meana go through her motions and leave the office.

As Meana exits, the staff sergeant lets out a nervous sigh and whispers to herself, "I'd hate to be her spouse."

Meana, back in the second-floor hallway, looks down at the pamphlets she has been given.

"This is bullshit," she says to herself, feeling her heart sink in her chest.

In a depressive haze, she makes her way to her car and sits back down in the driver seat while the air-conditioning hits her in the face. Throwing the pamphlets into the driver seat, she pulls her phone from her pocket and unlocks the screen. Looking upon the application button for Luigi's Graphics once again, she takes a deep breath and presses it.

A Proposal

Having spent the entire day applying for jobs and checking out of the Marine Corps, Meana sits on the lump filled and urine-scented mattress of her barracks room with Ian in silence as they both consider the idea of marrying each other.

"I do love you, Meana. I want you to know that I'm not just doing this for the baby" he says, attempting to look into her eyes while she emptily stares at the ground.

"*Yeah, I'm sure that is exactly what it is, Ian,*" she thinks to herself just before saying, "I know you love me, and I love you too, but I'm not sure if rushing into this is the best idea."

Loudly scoffing, he says, "Look, we already agreed to do a trial run and move in together over in Deerfield, so I don't understand what the issue is. I still have four months left on my contract. You have nine days. This way you can keep the military insurance all the way through delivery. It's a win-win for the both of us."

She lifts her head and looks deep into his eyes and realizes he is right.

"Fuck!" she exclaims.

Ian, leaning away from her, having never heard her actually curse, says, "Hey, that's not very lady-like."

With a dead-serious look, Meana locks eyes with Ian and says, "Lady-like? What am I, some Southern belle?"

Standing from the bed and taking a few steps away from her, Ian reciprocates her angry look just before saying, "I'm not saying you need to be a Southern belle, but I am saying, don't scream 'fuck' in my face!"

"Well, you know what, I don't give a fuck about your ego right now. You're not the one that has to carry around the baby and somehow make a living in Deerfield without the support of the father."

Looking more offended by the second, Ian throws his hands about and shouts, "Don't get an attitude with me! I didn't force you to do anything you didn't already want to do! Don't think I didn't know about Mendoza and Cortez whispering in your ear every single time I turned away from you! I'm not even sure why you talk to them or why we're talking about this!"

Standing from the bed and moving a little closer, Meana's body tenses up, and she balls her fists. "Those women were there for me every time you threw a fit or stomped your feet around like a child and didn't get your way. Mendoza taught me that it is okay to fight for myself, even if it is against the person you love, and Cortez taught me that no matter your size, the sheer will-power inside of me will always overshadow my oppressors." Feeling her emotions bubble over, Meana unloads the rest of her mind with an escalated tone of voice. "I didn't see you standing by my side after the car bombing! I didn't see you holding me at night when I cried! You're not the only one that witnessed those two Marines get blown to shreds, and from what I hear, you faked your so-called heroic act!"

"Shut your fucking mouth, woman!" Ian says, closing the small gap between them and getting right in Meana's face.

Feeling confident in herself for the first time against Ian, she says, "I lost a friend by staying with you, and up until this moment, I never thought twice about it. I ran into Cortez yesterday, and she could barely even look into my eyes. At first, I thought it was about some words we exchanged on the tarmac the day we came home, but now I know. It's because I'm still with you!"

Swiftly and without hesitation, Ian raises his hand, rears it back, and let's loose upon Meana's face. A loud smack can be heard bouncing off the wall of the room, and Meana takes a few steps back and trips on the bed. Landing flat on her back, she grabs the left side of her face where he struck her and cries.

With red swelling across her face, and a mixture of drool and mucus running down her chin, Ian stands with his chest puffed in the air and says with a terrifyingly calm voice, "You will marry me, and we will move to Deerfield where I will raise my child. Do you understand me, woman?" Barely able to keep herself from screaming out in pain, Meana keeps her eyes to the ground out of fear of being struck again and nods her head in approval. "Say the words," he continues.

She sniffles and wipes the mucus from her upper lip and moans, "Yes, I'll marry you."

Dazed and Confused

Employed at Luigi's Graphics and without Ian two months after their expedited courthouse wedding and leaving the service of the Marine Corps, Meana sits in her car and looks about while making her fort-five-minute daily commute to work. It's 0500, and the sun has yet to crest the ridge ahead. She notices there are many street lights burned out on this small back road but doesn't worry because she is driving around with her high beams in full effect. Continuing along her path, she notices the road ahead makes a snake-like pattern, and there is a visible sign that says to slow down to thirty-five mph around the bends. *"That sign can kiss my ass,"* she thinks while maintaining the fifty-mph speed she has the cruise control set too. She rounds through the first turn and blows raspberries at the speed-reduce sign she passes.

She maneuvers through tight turns, and takes them with ease. Feeling confident in her abilities, she maintains her course with her right hand on the wheel, and with her left, she reaches for the warm tea that sits in the center console cup holder. Immediately realizing she can't reach around her protruding baby belly, she decides to switch hands on the wheel and reach for the tea with her right hand, and lets out a slight giggle. *"Can't believe the baby is getting so big,"* she thinks, lifting her tumbler to her lips and taking a sip. Although she doesn't particularly like the bright-pink and flower-patterned tumbler that Ian gifted her, she uses it every morning and thinks of him while doing so. Still sipping her warm tea, she momentarily loses visibility of the road as she lifts the tumbler into her field of view. Turning her head to the right and driving with one eye on the road while still maneuvering through the ever-sharpening turns, she reaches the last bend in the road before hitting the long, straight tunnel, and her rear tires hydroplane. It had rained the night before, and she's paying the price.

The car careens out of control, and Meana grasps the steering wheel until her knuckles are completely white. She screams at the top of her lungs, and tears begin to roll down her face. Time slows, and she looks out the windshield. The world whips by at a rate her eyes can-not perceive. The scenery around her blurs into streaks, and all she can make out are the gray and white colors of the moon in the sky. When all hope seems lost, and the car continues to spin out of control, her military Humvee training kicks in. She rips the wheel to the right as the car spins to the left, and she can feel the tires begin to grip. Just as the tires grip the asphalt once more and the car changes direction, she lets the wheel go, and the car naturally straightens itself out. Going straight, she slams the brakes and comes to a screeching halt, and throws the shifter into park.

With a heavy downpour of tears streaming from her eyes, she gulps for air and her throat feels tight. She pushes the hazard-light button on the car and proceeds to sit motionless, letting time tick by. Gaining her composure, she wipes the tears from her eyes, throws the shifter back into drive, and slowly continues on her route to work. Following the speed limit and no longer laughing about the caution signs telling of sharp turns, she reaches for her tea. The cup holder is empty, and she recalls that as the car lost traction, she was sipping from the tumbler. *"I must have thrown it without noticing,"* she thinks, and starts to look around the car. Realizing that she can't continue to look around the car forever, she takes a break and fixes her gaze upon the road.

In the distance, she can see a dark tunnel quickly approaching. Observing the pitch blackness of the tunnel, she knows that there are no incoming vehicles ahead. She feels this is a good opportunity to turn the interior light of the car on and continue her search for her precious tumbler. The comforting light of the moon is no longer visible and the cold concrete walls of the abyss-like tunnel surround her. Meana turns the car interior light on and quickly looks about for her tumbler. She periodically looks up at the road to ensure she's still on track, but the windshield casts a small glare. With the yellow line of her lane still visible, Meana has no worries about staying in her lane. She decides that a good ten-second look around will do the job, and if she doesn't find it, then it will just have to wait until she hits a stop light. She takes the risk and looks about one last time. Seconds pass, and she still can-not find the tumbler, but just when the last second ticks by and she reaches for the light, the obnoxious pink decor shows its face between the passenger seat and the door.

"I see you," she says in excitement. Looking at the tumbler again, she can see the cap is still on the cup, and it landed right side up. "That's a lucky break. I better grab this before I leave the tunnel."

Meana glances up and can see the end of the tunnel approaching. She hurriedly reaches for the tumbler and soon realizes that her baby belly once again hinders her reach. Deciding that she only needs a couple more inches of reach, she rashly unbuckles her seat belt and forcefully leans herself to the right. Pushing her body with all her might, she accidentally nudges the steering wheel with her large stomach. With this action, the car rips to the left and slams into the opposite wall of the tunnel. The vehicle bounces off the wall, throwing Meana against the driver door and steeply careening toward the right wall. The speed of the car remains relatively unchanged, and as she bounces about the car, she is unable to plant her foot on the brake. Inches from the right wall of the tunnel, Meana desperately grasps at the steering wheel, and luckily, she finds her mark. With the wheel in hand, she rips it to the left, but only manages to reduce the impact of the wall as the car still makes contact. The right half of the car climbs up the tunnel wall, and Meana feels the metallic frame tilting to its side.

She frantically wipes the wheel back and forth, but to no avail. The car flips at a high speed and continues to flip five more times before coming to a grinding and spark filled halt.

Meana, having taken off her seatbelt not seconds before this unfortunate event took place, is thrown about the car like a rag doll. Making contact on multiple points, she lets out a series of grunts of pain and blacks out after her head strikes the top of the car interior with a sickening thud.

Hours pass by, and Meana lies unconscious and helpless in this quiet and lifeless tunnel down a forgotten back road. The sun is in the air, and the heat of a new day begins to climb while she lay in the windshield of the car, facing toward the exit of the tunnel. The sun having crested a large hill, shines on her face, exposing a large gash running along her forehead. With this blinding light in her face, Meana stirs from her involuntary slumber and immediately cries in pain.

"Odin preserve me!" she cries, looking around the wrecked interior of the car through blurred vision.

Her head throbs like never before, and the light of the sun makes the gash on her head, and her eyes burn uncontrollably. She looks around the broken glass and torn fabric for a way out and can see an opening where her driver-side window used to be. Wearing nothing but khaki work trousers and a large maternity-sized shirt, she drags her body through the broken glass and attempts to stay off her belly. Able to keep pressure off her baby by sacrificing the skin upon her forearms, she manages to crawl from the small window of her vehicle and out into the tunnel. Unable to walk, she sits up and leans against the upside-down and badly damaged car. Feeling around the wreckage while looking toward the exit of the tunnel, she manages to locate her phone. She lifts the phone to her face and brings it close, as her vision is still blurred. The screen on the phone is shattered, and there is no hope of using it to make a call. She pushes and holds the *Home* button on the phone in an attempt to use the voice-operated commands, but the phone has no reaction. She throws it across the tunnel and lets out a blood-curdling scream of despair. Just then, a vehicle whizzes around the corner and approaches the scene of carnage. The car comes to a screeching halt, and the driver rips his seat belt off and barrel rolls out of the open car door. Running at full speed, he approaches Meana and stops five feet from her location.

Raising his arms and placing his hands on his head, he says, "What the hell! Ma'am, are you okay?"

The only thing Meana manages to say is, "My baby," before passing out again. Fading into darkness, she hears the faint sounds of the man calling 911 and informing the operator of the situation. In one final attempt to communicate with him, she groans, "My baby," once more.

Flashes of light plague Meana and she struggles to open her eyes. Expecting the blinding sun to still be staring her in the face, she is surprised to see the LED lighting of a hospital room instead.

"Where am I?" she asks out loud, but there is no one present to respond.

She goes to lift her hand to touch her aching face and instead is met with resistance. Struggling to lift her head to look around, she continues to pull against the leather restraints that bind her wrists. Feeling fear rise inside her and helplessness wash over her, she frantically tugs at the restraints. The clanking of the strap's echoes throughout the room, and Meana lets out a small cry for help as she battles with confusion. She manages to fully open her eyes and sees the hospital room she is imprisoned.

Still tugging on her straps, a nearby nurse comes into the room and quickly rushes to her side. "Hush, baby. Everything is going to be all right. There is nothing to panic about. My name is Nurse Angy."

Meana whimpers, "Where am I? How did I get here?"

The nurse looks at Meana sympathetically, placing a calm hand over her wrists and says, "Baby girl, you were in a terrible accident, and you are in the St. Mary's Hospital."

"Why am I strapped down like an animal?" Meana asks with tears rolling down her cheeks.

"Unfortunately, you were in and out of consciousness, and during that time, you were kicking and punching anyone that came near you." She pauses for a second before continuing, "You are fully aware, and as long as the doctor agrees, I can remove your restraints."

Removing her hands from Meana's wrists and quickly rushing the phone on the wall, she punches in some numbers. Within seconds, she is having a conversation with the doctor and explaining the current situation. She hangs up the phone and looks at Meana with a big grin.

"I have approval to remove the restraints. Give me just one second."

Meana lowers her head back to her pillow, whispering, "Okay."

Nurse Angy makes her way back to the bed and begins to undo the leather straps that once held Meana captive. A great weight is lifted from Meana, and she raises her right hand to her face and lightly pushes the spots that hurt the most. Nurse Angy sees this and gently guides Meana's hand back down to her side.

"No, ma'am. You'll tear a stitch if you keep doing that." Nurse Angy makes her way around to the other side of the bed and checks Meana's fluid bag with a few light squeezes and then turns to make her way for the door, "Your husband is here. He said he drove as fast as he could to be by your side. I'll let him know that you're awake."

She turns and exits the door, and Meana painfully says, "Husband? Um, okay, thank you."

Seconds later, Ian bursts through the door and rushes over to Meana's bedside. "Thank Odin. How is the baby?" he asks to her with little concern for her own health.

She hesitates, and just when she goes to open her mouth, the doctor enters the room.

He is looking at a clipboard and says, "Hello, young lady. My name is Doctor Lucian. I'm glad to see you are finally awake."

Meana glances at Ian and sees a look of worry still upon his face and she raises her hand to him. He reaches out and grabs it while they wait for the doctor to continue talking. The doctor approaches and looking up from the clipboard charts, a look of sorrow is cast upon his face.

"I, um, have some bad news for both of you." He pauses and looks away for a moment to adjust his bearing. "There is no easy way to say this, but, due to the extent of your injuries, I am afraid that your baby did not survive the accident." A small glisten appears at the bottom of the doctor's eyes and he continues, "I, um, had to remove your deceased child via C-section while you were still unconscious. I am afraid we had no other choice." Looking gloomy, with a small tear running down his check, the good doctor continues, "I grieve with you, because this has been a very sad past two days."

Meana, in shock from the news that has just been rained down upon her, reaches down and touches her stomach. Realizing that the baby is indeed gone, Ian lets go of Meana's hand and backs away with a cold look upon his face.

"You're absolutely sure you couldn't have saved the child," he questions the doctor.

"No, sir. Unfortunately, the baby's vital signs had already expired before she had even reached my operating table."

Ian looks away from the doctor and from Mean, and lethargically walks to the huge window overlooking the hospital parking lot. Meanwhile, Meana still grasps at the emptiness of her stomach, runs her hands along the laser-seared incision that lay upon her abdomen. The tears from her eyes run dry and she stares at her stomach with a horrified and distant gaze.

"My baby," she faintly says, as her vision darkens, and she blacks out. Her head hits the pillow with a soft thud, and the doctor immediately runs to her side. He takes her pulse and feels her forehead.

Looking to Ian, who is still staring out the window, he says, "She'll be all right. Just give her some time."

Ian continues to stare out the window, ignoring the doctor's every word. Just then, gray clouds begin to roll in on the horizon, and a singular tear sweeps down Ian's cheek.

Dirty Deals

It's been a month since Meana left the uncomfortable room of Saint Mary's Hospital, and she lays in her own bed with overpowering body aches. Staring across the bedroom through pink and puffy eyes, she feels the urge to relieve her bladder and knows she must rise from the bed and make her way to the bathroom. She looks to the ceiling and watches the fan spin in its redundant circular pattern, attempting to summon the will power to move. However, the constant thought of losing her child and never-ending guilt of letting Ian down, pushes her into the mattress like a ten-ton boulder sitting upon her chest. She looks back to the bathroom door which distances itself from her bed, and she blinks profusely in a weak attempt to see. Realizing her vision is blurring from the tears that fill her eyes, she lifts the sheet draped over her torso and wipes the tears away. She looks at the sheet and sees two large wet spots filled with tears, and with raspy breaths, allows the sheet to drop to her chest and lays both of her arms down on the bed. She closes her eyes and pushes the thought of using the bathroom to the back of her mind and fights the urge to fall asleep.

Feeling her body begin to lay limp, she suddenly opens her eyes and shakes her head back and forth to stay awake. Determined that she can no longer wait to use the bathroom, she reaches for the corner of the sheet and blanket that lay upon her and grasps them with an iron grip. With one swift movement, she rips them from their comfortable position and throws them to the side, exposing her half-naked body.

She lies in bed wearing nothing but her black-and-red polka-dot panties and an olive-green tank top that says "Get Some." She places both hands to her side and firmly grips the bed sheets in an attempt to assist herself in sitting. Feeling the pain in her back still very present and the swelling in her legs pulsate, she pulls at the bed and painfully crunches her way up to a seated position. She lets out a low whimper in pain while a singular tear rolls down her face, and her checks feel like fire itself. Having made it to a seated position, she lets her grip on the bed fade and turns her hands to her legs instead. With her right hand, she pushes both her legs to the left and off the bed.

Sitting on the edge, Meana rocks back and forth, preparing to lunge herself to a standing position. She counts in her head, *"One, two, and three,"* throwing her weight forward and thrusting upward on both feet. Feeling a sense of accomplishment as she is standing on her own, Meana lets a smile wash over. The moment, however, is short-lived as she attempts to take a step forward and feels a pain shoot from her left foot, up her leg, and into her lower back. The crippling pain catches her off guard, and she falls to one knee and leans against the night stand next to her bed.

With one arm supporting her against the night-stand and still on her left knee in pain, Meana yells out for help, "Ian, please help!" The clock above her bedroom door cuts through the silent air with its ticking and Meana waits for her husband to respond. Unsure if he heard her, she attempts to yell for help once more, "Baby, please, I need you," with more tears streaming down her face.

Meana places her right hand on her agape mouth and stifles the loud sobs coming from within, and in doing so, she sees the mucus from her nose dribbling across her knuckles. Silencing herself, she hears a distant grunt of irritation and Ian shuffling off the couch. His footsteps slowly make their way to the bedroom, and he enters with a look of annoyance.

He glares down on Meana and sees that she is desperately clinging to the night-stand in an effort to keep herself from falling and says, "What do you need, your highness?"

Meana, with tears still falling from her eyes, says, "Please help me to the bathroom."

Rolling his eyes in a callous manner, he says, "Fine, but stop getting out of bed," and walks over to her. He places each hand under an armpit and yanks her from the floor, and in doing so, she lets out a loud wail. "Ow, it's not that bad. The doctor said you'll recover in no time," Continuing to rudely hold her like a rag doll, Meana struggles to keep pace with his shoving, and her feet drag behind. "Come on now. Pick up your feet."

Feeling worse than when she was lying in bed, she uncontrollably sobs from the humiliation she is enduring and says, "I'm trying, Ian. I swear, I'm trying."

He lets out a scoff while he finishes dragging her into the bathroom and placing her on the toilet without lifting the seat. "All right, you're in the bathroom. Anything else I can do for you?" he rudely asks, performing a curtsey.

Meana wipes the tears and mucus from her face onto the back of her hand and whispers, "No, thank you."

Without any hesitation, Ian turns his back to Meana and storms out of the bathroom and then the bedroom, making his way back to the couch. She sits on the toilet lid and places both hands on her forehead as she painfully leans forward until her elbows rest on her knees.

She takes some steady breaths and reassures herself, "You got this. You're a badass. You're a Marine."

Another month flies by while Meana continues to gain her strength with each passing day. She stands in her bathroom and looks at herself in the mirror with satisfaction, inspects the small scabs that has yet to fall from her face.

Surprising herself with how fast her recovery has gone, she says to the reflection in the mirror, "Looking good. Now what do we do?"

She places both of her hands on the bathroom sink and stares down into the drain, contemplating what to do with the two months of time she has left from her emergency leave. The owner of Luigi's Graphics was kind enough to give her four months of paid vacation so she and her family could properly grieve their loss. The problem was that she had physically recovered faster than the doctors anticipated and was desperate to keep her mind off the crash. She taps her right index finger against the white porcelain sink, and an internal battle of boredom ensues in her mind.

"What to do, what to do?" she asks over and over. Like a light bulb going off in her head, she stands and stares at herself in the mirror and says, "Let's surf the web."

She forces a smile on her face and turns from the mirror to gracefully walk out of her room and into the kitchen. Making her way to the kitchen counter and preparing to pour a nice hot cup of coffee, she glances over to the couch in the living room and sees Ian sitting in his usual spot, eating a bowl of cereal.

"Good morning," she says to him as he brushes her cheeriness off and ignores her.

Meana, hell-bent on having an upbeat attitude, tries not to let Ian's foul mood faze her. Grabbing her favorite unicorn and rainbow coffee cup from the cabinet, she places it down on the counter and lifts the pot of coffee from the burner. Rich black, dark, roasted coffee slips its way into her cup without spilling a single drop of its deliciousness. Meana places the pot back onto the burner and turns the pot of coffee off. She lifts the unicorn cup from the counter and makes her way to the dining-room table where her laptop is located. She sits herself, facing the living room, and places the cup on the table. The laptop is already opened, and she reaches down and clicks on the mouse pad to wake the screen. With a small flash of light, the screen comes to life, and Meana clicks away with her nimble fingers. With her web browser open, she types in, *"Most interesting political stories of the day."* Within seconds, articles fill her screen, and her eyes glisten with excitement.

Scrolling through the headlines, she whispers, "Gun Amendment Bill Hinders Constitutional Rights, Greed on Capitol Hill, Left Versus Right: Who Is Right, Things I Wish I Knew Before Entering Politics."

"Wow, these all suck."

She continues to scroll through poorly titled articles. Just then, she sees one that sparks her interest. *"Senator Burr Implicated in Venezuela Kidnappings."* "Oh shit. That's what I'm talking about," she says with a small but maniacal contortion to her face. She clicks the article and begins to read.

The Daily Confessions
*Senator Burr Implicated in Venezuela
Kidnappings*

A recent political scandal plagues
the United States today as a New York
senator faces allegations of corruption
and ties to the Venezuelan president

who has recently been indicted on multiple charges of kidnapping and drug-trafficking. Members of both the Democratic and Republican parties have refused to comment on the subject, and at this time, few sources are available. However, this past Friday, after a press conference, Senator Burr was not shy as to say, "Any fool that believes I can be tied up in such a scandal, should have their right to vote stripped away." Clearly upset at the allegations laid before him, Senator Burr plans on appearing at multiple press conferences throughout the coming weeks in an attempt to ebb this colossal flame. One thing is for sure, Senator Burr is going to have a very busy couple of months ahead of him, and-

Drooling with excitement, Meana stops reading the article and scoots her chair back, leaping up and running to grab a pen and paper. Moments pass, and she returns with her tools and takes a seat once again. Jotting down the name of the senator, the title of the article, and the country in question, Meana opens a new tab on the laptop and specifically types in, "Senator Burr allegations." Surprised at what she is seeing, the computer screen only populates with two articles, one of which she has just read. Confused as to how such an important subject is not being covered by the major media outlets, Meana sets her pen down on her notebook and sits back in her chair. "

I bet this is going to get covered up like all the rest," she thinks to herself, staring at Ian, still sitting on the couch. *"I wonder what I can dig up on this guy. Not like I have anything else to do."* She twiddles her thumbs and stares at the table with ideas rattling around her head, and she purses her lips at the thought of reaching out to the author of the article. She leans forward and clicks on the original browser page with the first article regarding the senator and scrolls to the very bottom. There she sees the author's name, sitting alone in the left-hand corner, "Archy Brimstone."

"Oh boy, I hope that's a pen name," she whispers, highlighting the name and then proceeding to copy and paste it into a new browser window. Multiple links regarding "Archy Brimstone of New York" pop up on her screen, and the first option is his social-media page. Meana allows her nerves to take hold and taps on the laptop keyboard, considering the consequences of reaching out with so little knowledge on the subject. Allowing her nervousness to run a-muck, she comes to the conclusion that it would be worse not to dig into the dirty dealings of a politician than to dig and potentially come out empty-handed. With her mind set, she clicks on the social-media page and navigates her way to the message center and begins to type:

Dear Mr. Brimstone,

My name is Meana Crane, and I have a few questions that I would like to ask you in regards to Senator Burr and the allegations against him. I noticed that you have taken quite the interest in his recent dealings, and I was wondering if you could use some support, or a partner to help you dig deeper? I don't have much experience, but I am more than willing to learn from a pro. If possible, I would be able to meet if you ever find yourself farther south. Thank you for your time and hope to hear from you soon.

Sincerely,
Meana Crane

She sits back in her chair and reads her message over again, ensuring that she does not come off as distasteful or rude. After multiple readings, she decides that her email is to the point, and she presses *Send*. In doing so, her heart flutters with excitement, and she lets out a sigh of relief.

Making an Unlikely Friend

Days melt by and Meana religiously checks her messenger inbox for a response from Archy Brimstone, and yet the inbox is filled with nothing but random spam. Meanwhile, Ian lives a motionless life, moving from the bed, to the kitchen, and to the couch, without so much as a glance in Meana's direction. She can feel a cold chill in the air as Ian walks by, and knows that he harbors resentment in his heart toward her. Still, she offers to cook him breakfast, and attempts to take him out into town for some one-on-one time. Unfortunately for Meana, he continues to reject her time after time with nothing more than a grunt of disapproval. She is left with a lonely and unhappy feeling deep in her stomach, and every waking moment is spent trying to fill it.

While waiting for Mr. Brimstone to reply, she does research of her own. Within the week of sending the message, she has managed to find numerous articles related to the Venezuelan president and his nefarious acts. She closely follows his trial and even reads about the attempted coup that was staged to relieve him of his power. The amount of information that Meana has ingested in the past week, is enough to make her head spin, and in fact, has done so many times. Although she knows damn well that the doctors still want her to take it easy, she can't help but to rise from her bed in excitement at what she may learn. Having a new purpose, she pursues the truth at all costs. Often spending hours on end staring at the computer screen, Meana's mind continuously races with all the possibilities of the information she hoards. *Tick, tick, tick* goes the watch on Meana's wrist while she spends another day doing research and never allowing her eyes to leave the screen. Scrolling like a madwoman, Meana continues to search for any links that implicate the senator from New York. She rubs her eyes as they feel dry, and scrolls through articles, when a ping echoes throughout the dining room. Meana stops rubbing her eyes, and stares excitedly at their computer. A small message scrolls across the bottom right side of the screen:

New Message from Archy Brimstone.

Anxious to see what is in store for her, she clicks on the notification and begins to read the message from Mr. Brimstone:

Dear Mrs. Crane,

Thank you for taking an interest in the truth. I don't typically receive messages like yours. I usually receive threats or slanderous messages, so I found yours to be quite pleasant. I would be more than willing to share my thoughts on Senator Burr and his affiliation to Venezuela, and at this point, I am willing to take any help I can get. I have taken the liberty of doing a background check on you and have found you to be of exceptional character, and I can always use an extra pair of eyes to keep watch on the senator and the locations in which he travels in the city. I don't know where you are currently living, but if that is not possible, then at least I can task you with specific areas of his life to dig. I should warn you, though, I have caught the senator's eye of late, and he watches all of my activities like a hawk. If you are truly sincere about helping the American people take down this snake, then ever so carefully watch your back.

Sincerely,
Archy Brimstone

With her eyes wide, Meana sits motionless and reads the message a couple more time. *"Do I really want to take this risk?"* she questions herself. Needing to give her eyes a break from the screen, she looks up and around the house. The sun is beginning to fall in the sky, and the house is ill lit. She continues to look about, and per the usual, Ian sits in his favorite spot on the couch. She looks him up and down from her position at the dining-room table and makes a face of disgust, observing his newly found belly protruding from under his white tank top. His face is riddled with stubble, and his hair is equally untamed. Meana leans forward to get a better look at Ian's eyes, and in doing so, she can see the oceanic blue dulled to a bitter gray. She leans back into her chair, and lets out a small sigh of disappointment. Lifting both hands to the laptop, she replies to the message.

Dear Mr. Brimstone,

Although I do not know you, I consider myself to be a patriot at any cost. I have weighed the possibilities of my future actions and have decided that I will aid you on this venture to unveil the truth. Let me know what my first task is to be, and I will get it done. Thank you for your time, and I hope to hear from you soon.

Without hesitation, she hits *Enter*, and the message is sent. Turning her upper body side-to-side in an effort to crack her back, she lets out a soft wince of pain as she turns too fast. Giving up on cracking her back, she sits straight in her chair, and prepares to lean back when, all of a sudden, a reply message comes across the screen.

I am glad to hear you have weighed the risks and come to the determination that we can be partners at any cost. If possible, I would like for you to scope out the senator's home. It lays just outside the major city and deep in a forest of trees, guarded by a massive block wall. I'm not asking you to break an entry. I'm asking that you at least confirm the location of the home and try to get pictures of it. I cannot seem to find pictures, videos, or even any real mentions of it online. The only thing I have manages to scrape together are the building plans. I have attached them to this message, and you

should be able to pull them up and
download them if you'd like too. If this
is not a possibility for you, please let me
know as soon as possible. As I stated
before, the senator knows my face, and
I am unable to get close to his home
without his guards recognizing me. I
foolishly confronted him outside of a
press conference and gave him a piece
of my mind. Needless to say, I need to
lay low for a while. Let me know what
you think, and we'll get the ball rolling

"Fucking spy work," she thinks to herself and she smiles from ear
to ear. *"Oh wait, how am I going to get to New York?"* Realizing that she
has little money for a plane ticket to New York or for a hotel, Meana
clicks reply on the message and begins to type with a frown.

I would absolutely be on board
with a sting type operation. However, I
am unable to pay for the expenses
needed to travel from Virginia to New
York. I apologize if I have wasted your
time, but I am willing to conduct any
home-based research for you if needed.
Thank you again for the willingness to
accept my help.

Clicking *Enter* with a soft and depressed tap, Meana's eyes sink to
the table and she thinks, *"I messed that one up. I guess I'll just keep doing my
own research, and keep an eye on Mr. Brimstone's articles to see if he ever catches
that asshat."* She places both hands under her chin and props her head

up with both elbows on the table, contemplating what she will do with the rest of her time at home, since she is unable to help. A full minute goes by, and the messenger dings once more. Meana, wondering what else he might have to say, maneuvers the mouse and clicks the message.

> Mrs. Crane, I do not think you fully understand how dire of times these are for me. I have no one else to turn to, and without my ability to post articles online, I would have already been shut down. If I don't uncover more details on the senator and reveal his crimes to the public soon, I'm afraid he will be out of reach forever. For that reason alone, I am willing to cover the expenses of a two-way flight, hotel, and rental car for you. Do not misunderstand my intentions. I will seek repayment after we have taken this man down. I am by no means wealthy, but I believe you can-not put a price tag on the truth. Let me know what you want to do from this point on.

Meana's hands shake and the reality of her situation sinks in. This man just offered to fly her to New York in an effort to spy on a United States senator, and all the while, he himself has to hide.

"What the fuck are you doing?" she whispers.

Meana places both of her hands on the top of her head. She contemplates what would be lost from her going down this rabbit hole. She once again glances at Ian, and within seconds, she determines that he may already be lost to her. Turning her gaze to the computer and lowering her hands to the keyboard, she types.

> Mr. Brimstone, you can count on me. If you are truly willing to pay for the trip, I will cover the cost of a hotel for one night and the return ticket home. I am available to leave anytime that you are able to dish out the funding, and please send me an itinerary as soon as you're able. Will I be able to meet you in person? I feel that, given this very odd set of circumstances, I should at least be able to meet you face-to-face. I am taking a huge risk, jumping on board like this, and I want to make sure that I'm not engaging myself in anything illegal. Thanks!

Meana once again hits *Send*, and within just seconds, Brimstone replies.

> I understand how odd this all seems, and I am not without empathy. I will meet you at the airport when you land, and during our meeting, we will discuss further details. It is a nice public place where we can sit, and you can feel safe in my company. I can-not thank you enough for taking this risk. I'll see you soon.

She reads the message, and her heart starts to flutter in her chest. Attached to the message is an itinerary detailing the time of her flight and the hotel she will be staying at. Skimming through the details, she sees that he has paid for three nights instead of the one and that her flight will be leaving the following morning at 0600.

"He paid for the whole damn thing," she says, feeling a little nervous.

Meana pulls out her phone and clicks on the message and downloads the itinerary and the blueprint. She rises from the table, closes the laptop, and makes her way to her bedroom. Closing the door softly as to not alert Ian, she turns toward her dresser and begins to pull out clothes.

Secret Agent Crane

The plane lands with a hard jerking motion on the crowded tarmac of the John F. Kennedy Airport, and Meana feels a knot form in her stomach while the time to disembark is close at hand. She looks out the window nearest her seat, and sees the workers on the ground directing the plane to its docking station and opening the hatch to unload the luggage. With the plane coming to a halt, the "fasten seat belt" light above her head turns off, and she can hear the stewardess say, "Ladies and gentlemen, thank you for flying with Quantum Airlines. You are free to move about the cabin, and we hope you have a blessed day."

Like roaches caught in the light, the passengers on the plane scurry from their seats, grab their luggage, and begin to push each other forward in an effort to get off the plane. Meana sits in her seat and waits for the crowd to dissipate. Once she feels confident that she won't be shoved about, she stands form her seat, grabs her singular bag from under the chair, and walks down the aisle. She makes it through the threshold of the airplane and a mixture of hot air outside and cold air from inside hit her, and a sudden chill runs through her veins. Like a sixth sense sending her a signal, she freezes just inside the passenger-boarding bridge and hesitates to move forward. Forcing herself to push on, she attempts to loosen the feeling of dread by shaking her hands at her side. Feeling better than before, she continues down the bridge and makes her way out into the overly crowded airport. Peeling her eyes from the large crowd, she looks up at the directional signs and quickly locates the exit leading to baggage claim.

Mr. Brimstone said to meet him near baggage claim, and once she felt comfortable, they would part ways, and she would begin her task. While following the signs, Meana makes her way down an escalator and out of the baggage claim section labeled "Terminal C." There she looks for Mr. Brimstone, and within seconds, she can see him standing by the exit doors of the airport. Taking her time to assess the situation, she sees he is wearing black leather boots, lightly faded jeans, a black V-neck T-shirt that poorly hides his small belly, and a pair of black horn-rimmed glasses. He appears to be alone as promised, and he has a nervous look upon his face.

"I guess I'm not the only nervous one," *she thinks to herself, making her way in his direction. Taking only a few steps off the escalator, she can see that Mr. Brimstone has spotted her and is hastily making his way over.*

He closes the gap in a surprisingly quick manner and says, "Mrs. Crane, I apologize, but there is going to be a slight change of plans." *He pauses for a moment and looks about as if being watched. Leaning forward and lowering his voice, he says,* "I think I was followed, and we need to leave immediately. I have a car ready to go if you'll just follow me."

He outstretches a hand in the direction of the exit and gestures for Meana to follow. However, an uneasy feeling shoots throughout her body, and she hesitates to move, skeptically staring him down.

"Please, Mrs. Crane, I insist we move this instant," *he says, raising his voice with a look of great concern.*

Meana, still not feeling that everything is as seems, takes a step back from Mr. Brimstone, and in doing so, the look on his face goes from a soft and concerned look, to a stern and maniacal stare. Fear shoots through her, and she turns to run. She manages to get a couple steps away and she feels a hand graze the back of her head and miss grabbing her by mere luck. Continuing to run away, she glances back and sees that Mr. Brimstone stands in place, brandishing a pistol and aiming it straight at her. Meana lets out an ear-rupturing scream and looks around for help, but to her surprise, the crowd completely ignores her. She reaches out for the closest person and grabs on to his shirt, but the random stranger continues to ignore her presence. Feeling sheer terror and desperation, she looks back at Mr. Brimstone and sees an evil smile form on his face as the loud sound of a gunshot rings in her ears, and she feels the round strike her in the back of her shoulder.

Meana opens her eyes and sees the nearby passengers staring at her while a flight attendant frantically tries to wake her by shaking her shoulder.

"Ma'am, please wake up! Everything is okay!" the attendant desperately exclaims until Meana comes to her senses and stares the stewardess deep in her eyes as if confused at the whole scene. She sits forward in her chair and feels her sweat-drenched shirt sticking to her back. "Ma'am, you were screaming and kicking in your seat. Are you all right?" the flight attendant asks.

"Oh yes, I am all right. I apologize. It was just a bad dream," Meana says, leaning back into her seat to sit in silence.

The flight attendant looks at Meana with a skeptical stare, but with little time on her hands, she walks down the aisle to the front of the plane.

She turns around to face the passengers and says, "Ladies and gentleman, we are about to start our descent. Please fasten your seat belts and turn off all electronic devices."

She turns from the crowd and disappears behind a curtain that separates a small room from the rest of the plane. Meana continues to sit in silence, replaying the contents of her dream in her head. *"I just need to stay calm. I'm sure everything will be okay."*

Minutes pass as the plane hangs over the tarmac of the airport and rumbling sensations rattle throughout its frame as the tires make contact. The shuddering through the plane intensifies, and the pilot chimes in over the intercom, "Ladies and gentlemen, we have arrived at the John F. Kennedy Airport, and it is currently 0830 in the morning, and the weather is just beautiful. We hope you enjoy the rest of your day, and we thank you for flying with Quantum Airlines."

Just then, goosebumps line Meana's arms and neck, and the eerie feeling in her dream returns once more. Taking a series of deep breaths to calm herself, Meana tries to relax in her chair as much as possible while waiting for the plane doors to open. Time ticks by, and the plane comes to a stop. The plane door connects with the passenger cargo bridge, and the door opens, letting in a stream of bright light. Instantly Meana hears seat-belts unfasten and people scamper to their feet as they rush to grab their bags and exit the plane. People begin to push each other forward toward the exit and Meana stares while her dream continues to play through her mind. Almost too afraid to rise from her seat, Meana uses every ounce of will-power to push herself forward and up as she stands in the aisle-way. She reaches down and grabs the singular bag from under the chair and proceeds through the threshold of the plane.

A mixture of hot and cold air hits her as she steps over the threshold, and she whispers to herself, "Just keep going. Just keep going." She makes her way out into the lobby, following the same path in her dream, and to her surprise, the scenery is almost exactly the same. Crowds of people rush about and Meana makes her way to the baggage-claim escalator and steps onto it. She descends into the baggage area and says, "Please, please, please, don't be creepy like my dream."

The ride of the escalator seems to go on forever and the baggage-claim area creeps into view. Just like before, she instantly sees Mr. Brimstone standing near the exit of the airport, only he doesn't look as menacing as she dreamed. He stands there, wearing a pair of brown leather sandals, khaki-colored cargo shorts, and a horribly decorated, tie-dye shirt. He looks older than his pictures online, but Meana isn't about to let her guard down. Stepping off the escalator, she notices Mr. Brimstone glance at her and he starts to approach in a slow and almost painful-looking manner while limps his way to her. Finally standing face-to-face, Meana doesn't have the same sense of fear that she did in her dream, still she casually checks his waist-line with her eyes.

Seeing no weapon or bulge around his shirt, Meana initiates the conversation with, "Nice to meet you, Mr. Brimstone. I recognized you from your pictures online."

He says, "Same here. I made sure to look you up before coming in. Didn't want to wander around the airport looking like a lost tourist," letting out a small chuckle.

Meana reciprocates the laughter and asks, "So, you have some place for us to talk?"

"Oh yes. I thought we could go sit at the coffee shop, here in the airport. It would give us both a little piece of mind," he says, lifting his hands and gesturing at a small coffee shop on the far end of the baggage area.

"Sounds good to me. Lead the way," Meana says, strategically staying behind him.

He turns and slowly leads the way to the coffee shop, and about five minutes go by before they finally arrive.

"Sorry about my speed. Nasty accident has left me a bit useless these days," he says, sitting in a chair at a two-seater table in the far corner of the cafe.

"I know what that feels like. I had a nasty accident myself not too long ago," Meana blurts out without any thought.

He lets out a sigh and looks at her with pity. "Yes, I am aware. I researched you extensively before sending a response to your first email. I'm sorry for your loss." He glances down at the table, avoiding any awkward looks.

"Oh, well, I guess this makes a little more sense. How far into my background did you go?"

Looking deep into her eyes, he says, "All the way." He places both of his hands on the table and interlocks his fingers. "I know about your combat experience, your humble upbringing, and the unfortunate loss you have recently sustained. Overall, you are a solid and worthy person on paper." Feeling flattered, Meana looks down at the table and lets a smile crack her serious façade and she feels her cheeks turn rose red. "A person with your background reaching out to me is like fate telling me now is the time to take the senator down. I couldn't pass this chance up," he says, lifting his hand in the air and gently waving at the waitress walking around.

She glides her way to the table and asks, "What can I get y'all today?"

Meana, having gotten used to hearing a country accent, thinks nothing of the way the waitress speaks, but Mr. Brimstone, on the other hand, says, "What a lovely accent. You must be from the South?"

The waitress blushes and responds with a big smile, "Oh yes, sir, born and raised in North Carolina."

He looks back at her, and with a big smile of his own, says, "I'll just take a coffee, black please. Mrs. Crane, what would you like? It's on me."

Meana, still looking down at the table, looks up at the waitress, and while staring at the red bandana that holds the excessively curly brunette hair out of her face, says, "I'll take the same please."

"Coming right up," the waitress replies with a gleeful sound to her voice.

Mr. Brimstone looks to Meana and continues with what he was saying, "Look, I don't want you to feel pressured into this. I need to know that you have the same desires to bring justice that I do."

Interrupted once again, the waitress brings them two small ceramic cups with black coffee in each. "Y'all enjoy those coffees, and let me know if you need anything else."

Meana looks at her and says with a false smile, "Yes, ma'am, we will."

Waiting for the waitress to walk away, Meana stares into her black coffee and says, "I don't feel pressured. I just want to make sure it doesn't follow me home."

Mr. Brimstone unslings a small bag from around his shoulder, and Meana stares at it, wondering how she didn't notice it before. "I brought you this camera. It's my favorite because you can take an excellent picture from a distance."

Still staring at the small black bag, Meana scoots her coffee a little closer to make more space. He opens the bag and pulls the camera out. Immediately he shows Meana the ins and outs of operating it, and in no time, Meana reciprocates the actions flawlessly.

"You see, you're a natural at this."

She looks him in the eye and sarcastically says, "Oh yeah, I didn't tell you, I'm Secret Agent Crane!"

They both let out a chuckle, and he says, "Well, close enough, I guess," while simultaneously pulling a small room key from his pocket. "I almost forgot. Your hotel room key, as promised, and I also have the key to your rental vehicle here as well." He pats his pockets down as if he has lost the car key, and after a few seconds, he says, "Aha," and pulls the key from a cargo pocket.

Meana reluctantly takes both keys and the camera bag and says, "So, when do I start?"

He looks at her with an inquisitive look. "Well, I assumed you would jump right on it since we only have four days to get as much info as possible."

Meana, a little embarrassed at her question, says, "Yes, that makes sense. My apologies."

She stares at the table once more, and without saying a word, he slides a small blue flip phone across the table and into her view.

"Should you need to contact me, use this. I programmed my number in there as Mr. Contact." Meana, thinking the name to be a little silly, snickers and looks at Mr. Brimstone. He stares back with a smile and then proceeds to take a large gulp of his hot black coffee. "Well then, you have everything you need. I'll be in contact to check in on you," he says, pushing his chair back, standing, pulling a twenty-dollar bill from his pocket, placing it on the table, and walking off without so much as another word.

Meana looks down at the set of items before her and whispers to herself, "No turning back now."

An Unwanted Reality Check

Parked in a run-down alley, littered with trash, Meana constantly checks her mirrors for any suspicious activity. She sits in the seat of the cool-blue Toyota Camry that Mr. Brimstone was kind enough to rent for her, and her nerves are on edge. She feels a knot forming in her stomach as she begins day one of her four-day spy session.

"I can't believe I told Ian I was going to visit my mom. Doesn't he know we aren't in contact? I could really use a cigarette right now," she says, fiddling with the car keys. "Just stay calm, Meana. Just stay calm. Focus on the mission," she whispers, reassuring herself that all will go as planned. After performing her usual routine of breathing in and out to calm her nerves, and shaking her hands violently, and reaches over to the small camera bag sitting on the passenger seat. She lifts it by the small black handle on top and positions it on her lap with the utmost care.

"Don't have the money to replace this guy," she mumbles, looking at the fancy camera after unzipping the bag. She pulls it out and attaches the long lens like Mr. Brimstone showed her, and with the press of one button, the camera makes a light dinging noise and comes to life. The digital display turns on, and Meana sees nothing but black. "Oh boy, did I break it already?"

She fiddles with the camera and flips it over a couple times looking for damage when she finally realizes that she never took the lens cap off the camera, and as she removes it, she lets out a whistle and acts like nobody saw what she did; she, however, is wrong.

While she sits in her cool-blue car located in the alley roughly fifty yards away from the front gate, a man dressed in an all-black satin suit and white-collar shirt with slicked-back, black hair stares her down through a security camera. He pans the camera in her direction and pushes a series of buttons to zoom in on her face. Seeing her clear as day, he pushes the camera button once more and takes an almost-perfect image of her face.

"Have the team run her face through the database and get it to me ASAP," he says to a middle-aged woman sitting nearby.

"Yes, sir. I'll get it out right away," she says to the man.

He continues to gaze through the camera, intent on burning a hole through the screen with its intensity.

"I see you."

He cracks a creepy smile and continues to pick at the details on the monitor. "A camera in your hand, young and pretty, a rental vehicle. I bet you're a reporter of sorts, and not a very good one since you're parked so close."

Using one of the front-gate cameras, he takes a picture of the vehicle's front license plate and sends it to the middle-aged woman, telling her to run it through the database as well. To his surprise, the middle-aged woman already has the results of the first inquiry.

She gives him a rundown on Meana's past, and when she finishes, she says, "She seems pretty clean."

The man looks at her and barks, "Anyone can seem clean! We just need to dig a little deeper," and turns his attention to the screen once more. "Go ahead and dig on her. I want to know everything we can about her and why she is sitting outside."

The woman looks at him and replies, "It'll take me a day or two, but I'll get you what you want, sir, and I assume this is off the books?"

He turns to her once more. "Isn't it always?"

Two days pass and Meana commutes back and forth between the senator's estate and her hotel with as little deviation as possible. With nothing to show for her time, she feels as if she is wasting her energy on this wild goose chase.

"Mr. Brimstone is going to be so pissed that I waste his time and money," she says, tilting her head back and pressing it against the headrest of her seat.

Letting out a sigh of defeat, she stares at the gray interior upholstery of the rental vehicle and starts to count the tiny threads that make its structure. Feeling out of place and bored out of her mind, Meana looks to the gate of the estate once more, and the large iron plate opens. Quickly sitting up in her chair, she scrambles to grab the camera from the passenger seat. Three midnight-black SUV's pull out from inside the property line, and when they do, Meana raises the camera and zooms in on what lies behind. She sees nothing but vast, thick greenery in every direction behind the gate.

"Damn," she exclaims, realizing she will be unable to capture an image on the estate. "Think, think, think," she says, watching the vehicles turn onto the main road leading away. She lifts her hand to her head and grips her hair tightly and gives herself a few tugs. Her eyes light up as an idea runs through her mind, and she returns to the camera. Turning toward the vehicles themselves, she zooms in and captures an image of each one's license plate. "Got you now, fucker," she says with the utmost confidence in her voice.

Excited that she finally has something to report, she reaches into her gray jacket pocket and extracts the small blue telephone from Mr. Brimstone. She pushes a series of buttons and navigates to his number. She pushes the green *call* button, and the phone rings.

Within a split second, he can be heard on the other line, saying, "Hello, Mrs. Crane? Is everything all right? I haven't heard from you in days!"

With an abundance of energy, she yells, "I'm great, and I finally have something to report!"

Hearing the excitement in her voice, he says, "Yes, yes, well, what is it?" She explains how she was becoming frustrated with sitting and how three vehicles finally departed the estate lines, and in a snap decision, she took the photos of their license plates. "That's fantastic news. I've never seen a vehicle leave before. This means we have a way to track him or at least his affiliates." Already briming with excitement, she feels like her heart is going to pop with joy after hearing Mr. Brimstone's praise. "Send me the photos as soon as you get to your hotel room and can access the Wi-Fi. I'll run the plate numbers once I have them."

Still overflowing with excitement, she says, "Yes, sir. I'll get right on that, and I'll head that way right now. Take care," and ends the call abruptly. "Oh shit," she says, realizing that she never gave the man a chance to respond. She shrugs her shoulders and decides it's too late to call back.

She starts the car, and blasts the music while singing along and dancing side-to-side in the driver seat. Finally making her way back to the hotel after about thirty minutes of traffic, she gleefully bebops to the elevator and ascends to her room. Once inside, she walks straight to her laptop, opens it, and clicks on the thread of emails between Mr. Brimstone and herself. She plugs in the camera using the cable that is inside the bag, and with a few clicks, sends the pictures as instructed. She lets out a sigh of relief, and after a stressful day of sitting in the car, Meana takes a long and steamy shower. Having finished her shower, she speedily prepares her clothes for the next day, and then lays in bed. Feeling totally at peace, she closes her eyes, and with a smile on her face, falls fast asleep.

The alarm clock on her phone goes off, and the light of a new day shines through the cracks of the curtain mounted in front of her hotel window. Meana reaches over to her phone, disabling the alarm and crunching up to a seated position. She yawns loud and slinks her way out of bed and over to the armchair where she staged her clothes. Taking the next ten minutes to dress herself, brush her teeth, and tie her shoes, Meana is ready for her last day of sitting around and waiting for action. Following the same routine as the prior days, she sits outside the senator's property line, hoping for a glimpse at what's further behind the gate. Meana rubs her temples in an attempt to alleviate the headache that is forming. Getting no relief, she lifting Mr. Brimstone's camera, and looks at the digital screen displaying the young gate guard sitting carelessly in a stationary chair inside the nice brick and air-conditioned guard-house. She observes the young woman, and in doing so, sees they have many similar features.

Staring at the screen, she says, "Ew. That is creepy. I could be sitting there, and they wouldn't even notice." She shakes her body in an attempt to alleviate herself from the eerie images from the movie, *"Invasion of The Body Snatchers,"* and in doing so, the camera slips from her hands and falls to her lap. She looks down and says, "Oh shit," looking the expensive piece of equipment over for damage. "Mr. Brimstone specifically asked you not to break his favorite camera, Meana," she says, scolding herself.

Upon picking up the camera and gazing through the windshield once more, she sees a shadow looming next to the driver-side window. She glances left and nearly jumps out of her seat and she sees a man in a suit and tie staring her down. He gestures for her to roll down the window, and she looks at his face, but is unable to steal a glance at his eyes. The sunglasses upon his face are so darkly tinted she is uncertain if this generic robot of a man even has any. Still looking him over, she sees the all-black satin suit, black tie, and the classic white under-shirt. Instinctively, she knows that he works for the senator.

"Ma'am, this is the fourth day in a row that you have been watching this property. Is there something I can help you with?"

Meana, feeling a sense of spite rise up, says, "Yeah, actually. You can tell me why the senator hides behind these gates, and what a puppet like you is doing at my car door."

The man says with little emotion, "Ma'am, I have to inform you that if you continue to sit and stalk this property, I will be forced to call the police."

Without hesitation, Meana loudly says, "Freedom of the press, my man. I'm here working on a story that links the senator to the president of Venezuela, and if you have a problem with that, call the police, and they'll explain to you how you're oppressing my constitutional rights!"

He stands silent, pondering what to say with the utmost precision. "Venezuela, huh. I'll make sure to let the senator know that you're interested, Mrs. Crane. And as for the police, I bet they'd be more willing to side with me."

Glancing down at the badge upon his black, leather belt, and hearing her name, she sits traumatized, knowing that all of Mr. Brimstone's warnings went to waste, because they know her identity. Her breaths become shallow, and she gasps for air, and places one hand above her right lung. The man, satisfied with his warning, turns from her car and proceeds to a black SUV that is parked in the distance. Meana sits in the driver seat, still gasping for air like someone is squeezing her lungs.

Moments pass by, and just before the man is able to enter the driver seat of his vehicle, Meana sticks her head out of window and yells, "I don't care how long it takes! I'll take you and that piece-of-shit, kidnapping, raping, drug-dealing senator down!"

The man pauses, with his fingers touching the handle of his vehicle. He turns his body and head midway to look back toward Meana, who sits laboring for breath in her car. Lifting one hand to his face, he removes his glasses to reveal his dark and cold-looking eyes. Meana leans back in her seat, and a shot of terror runs down her spine while the man stares deeply at her with a maniacal smile contorting his face. Frozen in her seat, she watches the man enter his vehicle, turn it on, and slowly pull away as he continues to look at Meana.

Pulling out of Meana's sight, he looks to the gentleman sitting in the passenger seat and asks, "Is it done?"

A man with midnight skin and eyes to match looks at the man in the satin black suit and says, "Just as you instructed, Agent Cavanaugh."

With that said, the two turn to the windshield and sit in silence while driving down the road.

Meana frantically scrambles for her phone, and managing to grab it, she dials for Mr. Brimstone. The phone continues to ring on and on without answer, and Meana continues to dial away. Deciding that it's useless, she pulls out a small piece of paper from her pocket and stares down at the address written upon it. Mr. Brimstone supplied Meana with his physical address in the event she could not reach him. Pulling her personal phone from her other back pocket, Meana pulls up the GPS app and punches in the address. It populates, and she can see that he lives not but fifteen minutes from the senator's estate. Dramatically slamming the shifter into drive, she peels out of her hide-away spot and beelines toward his home. Her legs shake, and tears are forming at the corners of her eyes, and she panics.

"Please be home," she says to herself, envisioning the FBI agent chasing her down and kidnapping her.

Faster than anticipated, she arrives to see a two-story home, with a minty-blue color engulfing the exterior. She whips the car into the driveway, and the tires make a loud screeching sound as she does. Throwing the car into park and jumping out of the driver seat, she moves faster than she has in a long time. Allowing herself to trot to the door, a sharp pain shoots through her left rib, and she halts.

She grabs her rib and lets out a painful grunt and bends over to says, "Fuck me. Not now."

With sweat beading above her brow, she pushes through the pain and lifts herself from her slumped position. She reaches for the doorbell and gives it a firm push. She can hear the ringing bounce off what sounds like empty walls inside the house. She presses the button a couple more times, but no one comes to the door.

"Fuck, fuck, fuck," she exclaims, fighting back the urge to panic further.

Looking around the porch, she sees a side entrance that leads to the backyard. Without hesitation, and still grabbing her rib, she makes her way to the side of the house and pushes the gate open. To her surprise, the gate is slightly cracked upon arrival, and she walks into the backyard. Rounding the corner of the rear side of the home, she can see the grass is a dark brown with a mixture of yellow.

In all her panic, she says, "Damn, that shit's dead," and turns to look for a back door.

Seeing the rear, glass-French-doors that lead into the home, she approaches them with swiftness and begins to knock. Yet again, there is no answer, and in desperation she decides to peer through the glass of the door. Barely able to see through the partially opened blinds, she tilts her head until the room becomes visible. Upon the visibility clearing, she sees there is no furniture on the first floor of the home.

"This guy gave me a false address," she blurts out in frustration.

Reaching down into her jacket pocket to retrieve the phone he supplied her, she pulls it out and flips the lid open. Right as she starts to scroll for his contact, a singular drop of blood descends upon her hand. She stops and stares at the droplet.

"Oh, no," she says, hesitating to look up, and imagining what lies in wait.

Another droplet falls from the sky and lands on her hand, and Meana, having had enough of it, looks up and sees exactly what she

155

was dreading. Taking a step back and letting out a terrified gasp, she looks upon the lifeless body of Mr. Brimstone. With a black cord tied around his feet, he hangs from the second-story window of his home, upside down. All color is drained from his face, and his eyes stare down at her with a cloudy-gray tinge, and Meana stands frozen, staring back. She continues to look upon his corpse, and sees a piece of paper pinned to his chest by a small dagger, and upon it, reads: *How fast can a Crane fly?*

Adrenaline pushes its way through her veins and she reads the message over and over. Her hands begin to shake violently, and the pain in her side disappears as she runs back to her car. Absolutely void of any proper decision making, she rushes to her hotel room and packs up all her belongings, including Mr. Brimstone's camera. She rushes down from the hotel room and makes her way to the car once more. Ripping her way out of the hotel drive, she makes her way to the airport in the quickest manner she can. Everything's a blur for her and she pictures the hanging body of Mr. Brimstone. The blood still on her hand, she frantically wipes it on her jacket pocket. She arrives at the airport after driving on autopilot with tears in her eyes. Not bothering to take the car to the rental place, she hops out of the vehicle and makes her way to the airline front desk. With nothing but her lone duffle bag and the camera, she approaches the man at the counter.

Wiping the tears from her eyes in an attempt to seem as normal as possible, she says, "Excuse me, sir, do you have any flights to Deerfield, Virginia, so I can purchase a ticket? I'm looking to leave as soon as possible." He looks her over and makes a face of concern, seeing her puffy eyes and the blood upon her jacket. Meana notices him looking at the blood and says, "Look, I'm trying to escape my abusive boyfriend, and I think he's right on my tail."

The man, looking even more concerned than before, says, "Say no more. I have one that is going to be leaving within the next hour. Will that work for you?"

She nods her head and pulls out a small wad of cash from her pocket. They exchange the currency for the ticket, and the man guides her to security. With no one currently in line, she passes through security with ease, getting strange looks from TSA along the way. She looks down at her ticket and sees that she must make her way to terminal C, gate 42. Looking up from the ticket, she sees the female restroom ahead and decides it best to make a pit stop first. She enters the restroom, looks about suspiciously, and then proceeds to lock the door. Turning from the door, she stares at herself in the mirror and sees the puffiness of her eyes and smear of blood on her jacket. She rips the jacket off and immediately throws in the trash receptacle nearby. Leaning against the counter, she turns the faucet of the sink on and washes cold water over her face. Looking up from the bowl of the sink, she stares into her eyes and lets out a steady breath of relief.

Working in the Shadows

Agent Cavanaugh enters the overly tight and pretentious area of a U.S. senator. The office space is lined in white marble, and the white tile floors shine with the intensity of the sun.

"Like the floors?" Senator Burr says, noticing Agent Cavanaugh staring at them.

"Not particularly, sir," the agent says. "That repulsive white is giving me a headache."

"Good for you," the senator smugly remarks just before he changes the subject.

"Give me a status report."

"We have a nobody sniffing around your estate, sir. She's poked in and out and made mention of her findings on the Venezuela incidents," says the agent with a stern look on his face.

The senator shifts in his vintage black leather chair that looks like it costs more than the agent's entire wardrobe.

"I'm sorry. Say that once more," the senator says sarcastically. The agent opens his mouth to repeat his report, when the senator cuts him off and says, "Are you serious right now? That was rhetorical. I don't actually want you to repeat it."

He reaches down to his left-hand drawer of his black and polished desk and pulls out two crystalline glasses and a bottle of aged scotch. He pauses for a moment and stares at the agent. Letting out a snicker to himself, he grabs one glass and places it back into the drawer and then proceeds to put ice cubes from the mini fridge behind himself into the glass. He pours the scotch gently over the ice cubes and watches Agent Cavanaugh's face with a facetious grin on his own. Forcing the agent to stand and wait on him, he lifts the glass to his mustache-riddled face and takes a neat sip. He smacks his lips in approval and lets out a loud and obnoxious sigh of pleasure, looking the agent in his eyes.

Placing the glass on to a coaster nearby so as to not damage his desk, he opens his mouth and asks, "How much does she know?"

The agent, still staring the senator down, says with disdain in his voice, "More than you'll appreciate, sir. In our brief moment together, she stated that she had evidence to link you to multiple crimes."

Squinting his eyes and pursing his lips, the senator sits and thinks for a moment. He takes a deep breath and exhales to ask, "Can you take care of this problem?"

"Yes, sir, if that's what you want," the agent says, puffing his chest.

"No, I asked because that's not what I want," the senator says with high amounts of sarcasm to his voice.

The agent grits his teeth and he fights back the urge to let a barrage of words leave his mouth and instead gives the senator a maniacal smile as he pictures wrapping his hands around the man's throat and strangling him.

"I'll get it done," says the agent, attempting to turn around and leave.

He makes it to the door of the office and manages to get one hand on the knob, just as the senator loudly says, "Oh, and do it quietly."

The agent turns around and shoots the Senator a death glare accompanied by a sarcastic salute. He turns toward the door once more and smoothly transitions to the other side. He looks back at the senator as he cracks the door and grins because he knows the senator hates when the door is left open. He bobs and weaves through the hallways of this oversized mouse trap of a building that houses a plethora of politicians, and in doing so, he thinks, *"I wish I could burn this mother-fucker down."* Having navigated his way completely through the building and out to his large, midnight-black SUV, he firmly sits in the driver seat and pulls out his phone.

Pushing a series of digits and dialing an unknown number, he lifts the phone to his face and says, "I have a name and phone number. I need the location of this target ASAP."

The voice on the other line reassures him that he'll get the information in no time, and Agent Cavanaugh abruptly ends the call. He looks out of the window and smiles, thinking about all the things, he has planned for Meana.

Nights pass by, and Cavanaugh sits down a dark and gravel-filled road. He has committed an excessive number of hours on this sting, and as he lies in wait, he takes a sip of black coffee from his Styrofoam cup. Setting the coffee down in the cup holder, he looks out the windshield of his SUV and gazes upon Meana's property. It's an average-sized house, a three-bedroom, two-bath home with a small basement fit for a small family. Luckily for him, the blinds are wide open, and he can see Meana and Ian sitting at the dinner table. Looking through his binoculars, he sees they haven't made eye contact all night, and neither has spoken a word since they sat down.

He sets his binoculars down and says, "Awkward," in a high-pitched and joking manner to himself.

Lifting the binoculars back to his face, he continues to observe this depressing couple. Time passes on and they finish dinner, pick up the house, and prepare themselves for bed. He sits up in his seat, excitedly watches the couple make their way to bed, with blinds still open and the moon light illuminating their room.

Licking his lips, he says, "Time for a show." Wearing a sad expression as the young couple lays in bed and instead, rolls to opposite sides with as little as a good-night kiss. "Fucking lame," he says, dropping the binoculars in disappointment.

The night presses on, and he waits until he is sure that they are asleep before exiting his vehicle. Standing outside his SUV, he pops the trunk and grabs the lone black fabric bag from inside. The bag holds the surveillance equipment he needs to keep an eye on the couple from a distance. Cavanaugh throws the bag over his shoulder and jogs his way to the edge of the wood fifteen feet from the house. He double checks the perimeter, and when he is sure that it is clear, he progresses forward. An hour or so goes by with Cavanaugh masterfully setting up surveillance cameras and microphones around the front porch, back porch, and wood line surrounding the home. Satisfied that his work is complete with no flaws, he jogs his way back to his vehicle, throws the bag in the trunk, and speedily leaves the scene. The back roads of this small Virginia town are barren, and Cavanaugh repeatedly slaps himself in the face and pinches his thigh in an effort to stay awake long enough to make it to his run-down hotel room. After an untold amount of time, he arrives at the hotel and whips the SUV into a parking spot, hops out of his seat, and makes his way into his room. Before laying in bed, he plugs in the power cord to his government-issued laptop and logs into the surveillance feed. With the cameras panning over the screen, he turns the volume up as high as it will go and then proceeds to flop back on the single twin-sized bed. Still wearing his shoes, black jeans, and black zip-up hoodie, he falls asleep, and all that can be heard is the light snoring of a sociopath.

The night passes by, and dawn arrives and Cavanaugh is startled awake by the sound of movement over the cameras. He leaps up from his sleeping position and groggily observes the laptop screen. It's the young female leaving for work, dressed in a green-collared shirt with the logo of Luigi's Graphics upon the chest, khaki-colored slacks, and a basic pair of black tennis shoes. He clicks away on the laptop and pans to another camera to get a better angle of her face. The new angle clearly shows a sad and depressed look as she gets into her vehicle and starts it. With her hands and forehead resetting on the wheel, she sits in the driver seat of the running vehicle for ten minutes before driving off.

He looks at her car driving away in the distance through the camera and says, "I'll see you later, Meana. Let's look at this waste of flesh over here." Clicking on the laptop once more, he has an angle overlooking the open-blinded bedroom that houses the young man. He is still lying in bed, and Cavanaugh looks at his watch to check the time. "Get up, bum," he says, seeing it is seven-fifteen in the morning.

Cavanaugh continues to watch the young man as hours melt by, and he has yet to roll out of bed. The clock strikes eleven, and the young man lethargically rolls out from under the covers. Cavanaugh, originally sitting slumped on the bed, perks up and zooms the camera screen in. The young man makes a bathroom pit stop with the door wide open and then casually makes his way to the kitchen. Looking at the young man in disgust, he watches him leave the bathroom without washing his hands, and he says, "Nasty little shit." The young man sloppily pours himself a bowl of cereal and creates a mess on the counter. Watching the young man make his way to the living room, Cavanaugh wonders why all the blinds are left wide open.

The young man sets his bowl of cereal down on the living-room table and plops down on the couch while still wearing nothing but his salmon-colored boxer briefs. Grabbing the remote, the young man flips the television on and grabs his bowl of cereal. After eating with his mouth open, the young man sits and watches the television for hours without moving. Cavanaugh, having decided that the young man is of little interest, takes a shower, combs his jet-black hair back, and shines his black leather boots. When he returns to the laptop screen, the young man is still sitting in front of the television.

Cavanaugh, smelling better, dressed in some casual clothing and black combat boots, smiles at the monitor and says, "You'll do just fine."

He closes the laptop and proceeds to pick it up and pack it into a nice tan one-strap leather pack. He picks the pack up by the handle and rips his car keys from the night-stand. Strolling out of the room and locking the door behind himself, he makes his way to his vehicle and sits in the seat as he turns the key in the ignition. The vehicle roars to life, and Cavanaugh places his bag into the passenger seat.

"Holy shit, this leather's burning," he exclaims, feeling the fire being emitted by the black, leather interior, of his government-issued SUV.

He turns the knob of the air-conditioning system to full blast and ensures the temperature knob is set to ice cold. Feeling the sweat slide down his back, he throws the shifter in reverse, pulls out of his parking spot, and makes his way out of the motel parking lot. Driving down the road, he grips the steering wheel with intensity, thinking about his next plan of action. Allowing the curvature of the road to guide the vehicle, Cavanaugh lets a small grin slip and he continues to think about all the horrid things he has waiting for this unsuspecting, young man. Pulling off of the main road and onto a thin gravel road with rocks shooting out from under his tires, Cavanaugh makes his way to Meana's home. Glancing left and right to ensure there are no random cars sitting in the small clearings on either side of the road, he continues his course with little concern, and sees the coast is clear. No longer worrying that anyone else is present to help the young man, he pulls his vehicle right up to the front door and positions it with the trunk facing the house. As Cavanaugh throws the shifter into park, he glances into the rearview mirror and sees Ian still staring at the television.

He opens his door, and just before stepping out, grabs his leather bag from the passenger seat. Standing in the gravel driveway, he slams his driver side door in an effort to get Ian to look out the window. Unfortunately, Ian is locked into a trance, and Cavanaugh stares grumpily at the front door. He places his bag down onto the floor, unzips the front pocket, and pulls out two black leather gloves. Zipping the bag closed, he stands straight and slides a glove over each of his hand. Pulling the edge of the gloves to ensure they are snug; Cavanaugh reaches for the doorbell with his left hand and pushes the button. He hears the doorbell ring, and after seconds, the televisions loud sound-effects cease. Watching through the open shades of the huge window to his right, Cavanaugh sees the young man peering outside at the large black SUV just before he sluggishly makes his way to the front door.

Hearing a series of clicks and snaps from the door unlocking and the chain being undone, Cavanaugh tenses his body and prepares to pounce. The door swings open, and the young man stands before him. Before pouncing, Cavanaugh takes a second to look upon his prey. The young man has a thick stubble upon his chin, and his black hair is in desperate need of maintenance. His white tank top has what looks to be a mustard stain, and a small belly pushes its way forward from beneath the soiled tank top. Cavanaugh looks at Ian in disgust and allows his face to reciprocate. Ian, without saying a word to the man, looks at him with extreme confusion, and with his dull blue eyes, stares at the man's face. Cavanaugh determines that he can no longer look upon this out-of-shape slob and, swiftly lifts his right hand and thrusts the section between his thumb and index finger into the young man's throat. Ian instantly gasps for air in a loud fashion and falls to his knees. Grabbing his throat with both hands, he manages to lift his head to look at the stranger before him.

Just as Ian fully erected his head, Cavanaugh scoffs and says, "You're weak," and proceeds to punch Ian square in the nose, rendering him unconscious.

A Serpent's Bite

There is a silent stiffness in the air, and Meana sits at the front desk of the photocopy company known as Luigi's Graphics. Although she once hated sitting at this very desk, she is grateful to return four months after the accident. Upon the day of her return, the small team of five employees had a box of chocolate and a bouquet waiting in the break room. They welcomed her back with open arms, and even the owner was present to welcome her back. Until that day, she had believed that she was another unnoticed face among the crowd. Grateful to have the small team of employees that care for her well-being, she lets out a smile and reminisces on the unit cohesion that she used to have in the Marine Corps.

Sticky sweat rolls down Meana's back while she stands in the light of this hot and humid day. She lets out a loud and expressive grunt, lifting her right hand to face level and thrusting it forward as hard as she can. Making contact on the face of Lance Corporal Mendoza, her face smooshes to the side, and her head follows suit. Mendoza loses her footing as Meana moves in for the kill. Caulking her right foot back behind her body, she thrusts her hips forward, and her leg cuts through the air at Mach speed. Her leg makes contact with Mendoza's left ribs, and Mendoza lets out a painful grunt, attempting to lower her left arm to catch Meana's

leg. Successfully capturing Meana's leg just above the knee, Mendoza, with a small trickle of blood running down her face, propels her right hand forward and pushes Meana to the ground as she simultaneously kicks her left leg out from under her. Meana lands in the fighting pit made from a mixture of sand and shredded tires with a loud thud and a small bounce. Feeling the air rapidly exit her lungs, Meana clutches at her chest and tries to regain her breath before Mendoza has the chance to finish the fight. With Meana still unable to catch her breath, Mendoza straddles her legs and lets out a volley of punches to Meana's stomach. Meana lets out a series of painful grunts as spits flies from her mouth. Satisfied that Meana can no longer fight back, Mendoza reaches forward and places her forearm on Meana's jugular and presses with all her might. Feeling the blood pound through her neck as her face turns a deep purple, Meana desperately thinks of a way out. Knowing she has seconds before she will lose consciousness, Meana propels her feet as high as she can and manages to straddle Mendoza's face with her heels. Pulling with all her might, Mendoza's head is lifted backward, and her forearm soon follows.

Feeling the air return to her lungs and the blood leave her face, Meana knows that she has an opening. Seeing Mendoza's stomach wide open, Meana unleashes hell and can hear Mendoza cry out in pain. Still pulling Mendoza's face with her heels, Mendoza begins to weaken. Holding onto Meana's shirt with her left hand, Mendoza reaches out with her right and attempts to place Meana in a front choke. To no avail, Mendoza cannot reach and eventually loses her placement on top of Meana as she is sent flying backward into the shredded tires. Meana wastes no time as she leaps off of her back and races toward Mendoza who is lying face-first in the pit. She jumps on Mendoza's back and immediately places her in a rear blood choke. With little energy left, Mendoza weakly tries to pry Meana's arm away, but eventually gives in. Feeling Mendoza's body begin to go limp, Meana lets out a loud battle cry of victory. Knowing she has been defeated, Mendoza reaches up to Meana's arm one last time and taps it three times. Meana instantly let's go, and both women lay side by side as they both attempt to suck in as much air as possible.

Minutes of silence pass, and feeling herself stabilizing, Meana says, "Holy shit, Victoria. You are one tough chick."

Wiping away the small amount of drool from her chin, Victoria looks back at Meana and asks, "How the hell did you get your heels to reach my face? My back hurts just thinking about it."

Meana looks at Victoria and shrugs, and both women begin to laugh.

Still sitting with a smile on her face, Meana wonders if anyone in the office has ever even been in a fight before. The thought of watching anyone in the bleak office fight wipes the smile from Meana's face, and she sits with a blank look. Moments pass with her sitting in silence. The rhythmic ticking of the small clock on the wall echoes throughout Meana's head, and feeling herself go stir-crazy, she pulls her phone from her back pocket. Unlocking it with the push of a button, she maneuvers to her social-media app and stalks the senator's page. Looking at his social-media page with a disgusted look upon her face, Meana can't help but wonder how it is that a man like him stays in power. *"Must be a lot of corrupt politicians saving his skin,"* she thinks to herself. Using her thumb, she motions it upward, and the cell-phone screen transitions and reveals new posts from the senator.

Just as Meana is about to click on an article about fighting child kidnapping that the senator has posted, the small jingle of the business doorbell reverberates around the office. Surprised and shocked to see a customer, Meana looks from her phone and to the man standing in front of her without saying a word. Moments pass and the man stands a few feet from the door and stares back at Meana. She takes a deep breath, setting her phone down, she remembers to say, "Good morning, sir. Welcome to Luigi's Graphics. How may I help you?"

Silence fills the air and the man continues to stare at Meana. Feeling a knot form in her throat, she opens her mouth once more to recite her scripted welcome and the man finally speaks up, "Are you Meana Crane?"

Looking at the man suspiciously, Meana says, "Yes, sir. How may I help you?"

"Some gentleman outside gave me twenty bucks to hand this envelope to you," says the man, approaching the desk with a manila envelope under his left arm.

"Okay. Who was the man?" asks Meana, standing from her seat.

"Not a clue, ma'am. Just figured it was an easy twenty bucks."

Meana, getting irritated with the vague answers, asks, "Well, what did he look like?"

The man lets out an annoyed sigh as he reaches the counter and says, "I don't know. White guy, with black, slicked-back hair."

He places the envelope on the counter, and without waiting for Meana to speak, he turns around and leaves the shop. Meana, staring at the envelope, attempts to say thank you but is too late as the man is already out the door. She stares down at the envelope in confusion and decides she might as well see what's inside. Lifting the envelope from the counter, she undoes the small clip that holds it closed and flips the small flap back. She turns the envelope over and pours the contents onto the counter. Just as she does so, her manager, Mark, walks out from his small back-room office and approaches the counter while holding a small Styrofoam coffee cup in his left hand.

Before Meana has a chance to look down at the contents, Mark asks, "So how are you feeling today? Body aches finally gone?"

Meana, looking at Mark and shooting him a false smile, says, "Not completely, but the doctors said I'll probably have some for close to six months."

"Yikes," he exclaims, lifting the cup to his face and taking a sip. "So, what are you looking at?" He points a finger at the envelope.

Meana, realizing that she is holding the Manila folder in her hand, says, "I don't know. Some weird guy asked for me by name and then gave it to me."

Mark lifts his eyebrows in surprise and lets out a sigh while saying, "That's what happened to me when I got the divorce papers from my wife. I'll give you a minute by yourself," and he turns to make his way back to his office.

"Thanks," Meana says with confusion to her voice.

She watches Mark walk to his office and close the door before glancing down at the contents of the envelope. Satisfied that he is no longer going to be a nuisance, Meana looks down and sees that the contents are photos, but she dumped them out blank side up. She places the envelope down on the counter and scoops the photos up. As she flips them around, her facial expression goes from a blank stare to that of sheer horror. The color drains from her face, and she feels dizzy. No longer able to stand, she allows herself to fall backward into her chair. Still clutching the pictures in her hands, she feels her stomach begin to ache. Just before projectile vomit makes its way up her throat, she reaches out for the small trash can located under the counter and unloads the contents of her stomach inside its dull and silver structure. Vomiting up the oatmeal and peanut-butter toast she had for breakfast, Meana continues to clutch the picture.

Minutes pass, and Meana is able to regain her composure. Lifting her face from the trash can and setting it down, she gazes upon the photos once again. With tears streaming down her face, she sees a tortured and gagged Ian. His face is swollen and bloodied, and his mouth looks to be taped shut with duct tape. He's laid in the back of a large, black SUV with his hands and feet hogtied together. Meana looks at the picture in disbelief and turns her attention to the other ones. In one photo, Ian is strapped to a chair, and his head hangs as he sits unconscious in the chair. Around his neck is a small cardboard sign that says, "I'll pay for your sins." Meana drops the photos to the ground and places her hand over her mouth to muffle her sobs. Struggling to keep quiet, she stands from her chair and grabs her belongings. She beelines for the front door, and in doing so, Mark comes out of his office.

Seeing Meana up from the counter and heading for the door, he shouts, "It's not quitting time yet!" Meana turns to face Mark, and he notices the tears streaming down her face and looks at her with great concern. With shakiness in his voice, he asks, "Meana, what's wrong?" Without saying a single word, Meana points to the photos she left behind the desk and storms out of the building.

Outside in the parking lot, she rummages through her purse for her keys while running toward her car. Nearly dropping her bag, she locates her keys and unlocks the vehicle. She rips the driver door open, leaps into the seat, and shoves the key into the ignition. The car roars to life, and Meana hastily makes her way out of the parking lot and on the main road home. The tires let out a loud screech as she slides the car onto the road, knocking over a couple construction cones in the process. Meana, driving as fast and as furious as she possibly can, and shakes her left leg back and forth in anticipation. All her nerves are firing, and her mind is running wild with the thought of Ian being tortured as she makes her way home. She presses on the accelerator even hard and whips the car around slower vehicles and around multiple tight bends. Looking ahead, she can see the same tunnel that she once crashed, and without hesitation she continues to keep her current pace. The light disappears as she enters the tunnel, and sweat forms on her upper lip, she grips the steering wheel until her knuckles whiten.

Muttering to herself, "Just breath. Get through to the end. It's the fastest way home," she fights the urge to close her eyes. Still gazing out of the windshield, Meana can see the end of the tunnel and the sunshine coming through. With the accelerator already maxed out and Meana going just under one hundred miles an hour, she breaks free of the oppressive tunnel and is approaching the last of the curves before reaching her road.

Minutes fly by with Meana keeping her focus and sliding the car down the gravel road leading to the house. Sending dust and rocks in every direction behind her, Meana sees the house ahead. Quickly approaching the house, she slams the brakes, and the car slides, desperately attempting to grip the gravel. Timing the brake just right, the car comes to a halt with a wave of dust behind it. Throwing the car in park, Meana leaps from her seat and runs to the front door. Standing in the open doorway, she puts her hands on her head and frantically looks around. Stepping into the living room, the only thing she can see is a bowl of cereal sitting on the table and the television paused on Ian's favorite show. Running from room to room with tears in her eyes, Meana sees no trace of Ian and scrambles for her phone. She calls Ian and lift the phone to her ear as the ringing tone continues to drone on. Seconds pass when, all of a sudden, Meana hears a ringing noise nearby. Looking around the house, she realizes that it's coming from the couch. Walking over to the couch with the phone still ringing, she reaches down and pulls Ian's cell phone from between the cushions. She immediately drops Ian's phone on the couch and proceeds to end the call on her own. Feeling an extreme amount of depression wash over her, she softly sits down on the couch and stares at the floor in defeat. Lifting her phone one last time, she dials 911 and waits for the operator to answer.

Still staring at the floor, she can hear the operator answer the phone, "Nine-one-one. What's your emergency?"

Meana hesitates, and after taking a few shaky breaths, she says, "I need to report a kidnapping."

It's All My Fault

Flashing red and blue lights illuminate the entirety of Meana's house while she sits on the couch with her phone in her hands. She stares off into the distance as a police investigator rambles on about the proper procedures for a kidnapping and then proceeds to ask her questions. Meana, still in a trance, hears nothing but muffled noises around her, pictures her husband bleeding somewhere dark and crying out in pain. Tears stream down her face and the horrid images of Ian being tortured run through her mind as if she is watching an old horror film. There is a ringing sound in the air, and Meana's body feels cold. She shivers, sitting on the couch, and even though she knows the police-man is talking to her, she is unable to respond. Minutes go by, and the police-man finally reaches down and touches Meana on the shoulder. Like breaking a spell, Meana snaps back to reality, and all at once the noises around her begin to clear. She can see and hear the multitude of investigators walking around her home, poking through drawers, opening closets, and taking pictures of every small detail. She looks up from the spot on the wall she was staring at and sees a gentle-faced policeman staring her back. He looks young, maybe twenty-four in age, not a wrinkle in sight. His fair-colored skin has a youthful shine to it, and his smooth-looking, shaved face smells of aftershave.

She looks deep into his dark-brown eyes, and he says, "Do you want to step outside, ma'am? Maybe some fresh air will help some."

173

Meana, without saying a word, nods to the policeman, and he helps her stand from the couch and hands her a blanket. With one hand under her right arm, he helps to support her as she weakly makes her way through the front door and out onto the porch. Guiding her to a set of outdoor chairs that sit on the porch, he gestures for her to take a seat. Doing so, Meana can see out in the distance that the sun is beginning to go down.

She stares off, and in doing so, the policeman asks her, "Ma'am, did you have any contact with your husband before learning of his disappearance?" Still sitting silent, Meana looks him in the face and shakes her head no. The detective pulls out a small pad of paper and a nice silver pen. He jots down a couple notes and then turns his gaze to her once more. "Is there anything you know or can do to help us figure out what happened here?"

Forcing the words to form, Meana says, "Pictures, I have pictures."

The cop stands a straighter, and with a worried look, asks, "What pictures, ma'am? Are they your husband?"

Meana nods her head yes and lets out a small whimper, trying to hold back more tears. Wiping her face on her sleeve, she turns and looks out to the sun.

"I left the pictures at work. I didn't think. I just ran home," Meana says with guilt lining her face.

"Ma'am, it's understandable. I can't imagine what was running through your mind." The policeman stops and seems to think about what to say next. "I'll give you a minute to collect your thoughts. I'm going to go call your employer." And with that said, he shoots Meana a small smile and walks into the home.

Time seems to fast forward and Meana sits motionless on the porch, and the detectives go in and out of her house, looking for clues. Still in shock and clenching the blanket upon her back, she allows the darkness of the kidnapping sink in. *"Was this me? Did I do this?"* She thinks to herself over and over again, replaying her past actions. A specific memory comes across her mind, and her eyes widen in horror as she figures out what she thinks is the cause of the kidnapping.

Sitting outside the senator's property line, hoping for a glimpse at what's behind the gate for the fourth day in a row, Meana rubs her temples in an attempt to alleviate the headache that is forming. Lifting the camera that was lent to her from Mr. Brimstone, she looks at the digital screen displaying the young gate guard that sits carelessly in a chair inside the nice brick and air-conditioned guard-house. She observes the young woman, and in doing so, she sees that they have many similar features. Still looking at the screen, she says, "Ew. That is creepy. I could be sitting there, and they wouldn't even notice." She shakes her body in an attempt to alleviate herself from the eerie images from the movie "Invasion of The Body Snatchers" and in doing so, the camera slips from her hands and falls to her lap. She looks down and says," oh shit", looking this expensive piece of equipment over for any damage. "Mr. Brimstone specifically asked you not to break his favorite camera Meana," she says, scolding herself profusely. Upon picking up the camera and gazing through the windshield once more, she sees a shadow looming next to the driver-side window. She glances left and nearly jumps out of her seat as she sees a man in a suit and tie staring her down. He gestures for her to roll down her window and as she looks toward his face, she is unable to steal a glance at his eyes. The sunglasses upon his face are so darkly tinted that she is uncertain if this generic looking robot of a man even has any. Still looking him over, she sees the all-black satin suit, black tie, and the classic white under shirt. Before he even has a chance to speak, she knows that he works or the Senator. "Ma'am this is the fourth day in a row that you have been watching this property, is there something I can help you with?" Meana feeling a sense of spite rises up, says, "Yeah actually, you can tell me why the Senator hides behind these gates, and what a puppet like you is doing at my car door." The man still emotionless says, "Ma'am I have to inform you that if you continue to sit and

stalk this property, I will be forced to call the police." Without hesitation, Meana says, "Freedom of the Press my man, I'm here working on a story that links the Senator to the President of Venezuela and if you have a problem with that, call the police and they'll explain to you how you're oppressing my constitutional rights." The man stands silent as if pondering what to say with the utmost precision, "Venezuela huh, I'll make sure to let the Senator know that you're interested Mrs. Crane." As if hearing her name was a dagger to her heart, she sits traumatized, knowing that all of Mr. Brimstone's warnings went to waste as they now know her identity. Her breaths become shallow and she gasps for more air as she places one hand above her right lung. The man satisfied with his warning, turns from her car and proceeds to a black SUV that is parked in the distance. Meana still sits in the driver seat, gasping for air as if someone is squeezing her lungs. Moments pass by and just before the man is able to enter the driver seat of his vehicle, Meana sticks her head out fo window and says, "I don't care how long it takes, I'll take you and that piece of shit kidnapping, raping, drug dealing Senator down!" The man pauses for a second as his hand touches the handle of his vehicle, he slightly turns his body and heads back toward Meana. Lifting one hand to his face, he removes his glasses to reveal his dark and cold looking eyes. Meana sits back in her chair and a shot of terror shoots down her spine as the man stares deeply at her with a maniacal smile upon his face. Frozen in her chair, she watches as the man enters his vehicle, turns it on, and slowly pulls away as he continues to look at Meana dead in her face.

Tears stream down her face and she realizes that her fears are most likely true. She rises from her seat on the porch, just as the young detective walks out of her front door, and she looks him deep in the eyes and says, "I did it. This is all my fault."

The man stops dead in his tracks and looks her in the face with a serious look, and says, "Explain please."

Meana, realizing that she should have worded that phrase better, replies, "Not like I kidnapped him, but I think I'm the reason he was kidnapped."

The detective's body loosens, and he no longer looks ready to fight. A soft look comes across his face, and he asks, "May I sit next to you?" Meana nods, and they both take a seat on the small bench. Both looking outward toward the gravel driveway of her home, he says, "Take your time, and explain your side of the story. I'm here to listen."

An Unexpected Visitor

Meana stares at the ceiling of her room, lying in bed at ten o'clock in the morning. She contemplates getting up and cleaning the house but decides that she's probably just going to stay where she is. She reaches over to her night-stand and grabs her cellphone off the top. She unlocks the phone with the tap of her finger and makes her way to her social-media page. She scrolls through her feed for hours on end. Giggling to herself occasionally at a funny post, she continues to scroll on. Feeling a headache from over her right eye, she puts the phone down on her chest and rubs her temples. She closes her eyes and winces a little as she digs the tip of her fingers deeper and deeper into her temple. Feeling a little relief, she opens her eyes and once again looks up at the ceiling. She averts her eyes and looks at the small, black, square-shaped alarm clock that rests on her night-stand. The clock strikes one o'clock, and Meana realizes her stomach is aching from hunger and decides to get out of bed. She rips the covers off of her body in a smooth, effortless movement and wiggles her body to the edge of the bed. Tossing her legs over the side, she sits up and leans forward with both hands on her knees. She stands with a crack and a pop from her back and knees to accompany her as she prepares herself to make her way to the restroom. Wearing nothing but a black tank top and some skin-colored panties, she limps her way to the restroom. Her knees and ankles feel swollen, and arthritic aches wash over her.

"Getting old," she says while letting out a small chuckle.

She uses the restroom and proceeds to the kitchen for her lunch. Opening the refrigerator in a lethargic manner, Meana sees only food that she would have to cook. Not in the mood to cook, she opens the freezer and looks for the easiest item to warm up. She rummages through the freezer and eventually comes out with a boxed lasagna.

Reading the label, she says out loud, "Set the oven to 350 degrees, place the tray in the oven for forty minutes, and blah, blah, blah."

Not bothering to read the entirety of the instructions, she takes the lasagna out of the box and places it on the stove top. She turns the oven on and sets it to four hundred degrees as she picks up the lasagna and tosses it into the oven. She closes the oven door and starts setting up the coffee machine. Moments slip by, and Meana is holding a fresh mug of coffee and eating an un-toasted piece of white bread that's three weeks past it's due date. Not giving a damn at the moment, she stuffs the piece of bread into her mouth and sits in a chair located at the dining-room table, not but ten feet from the kitchen. Her laptop sits upon the dining-room table, and she flips the monitor up and powers on the screen. She types in her password and immediately makes her way to a fresh Internet page. Typing with nimble fingers on the keyboard and maneuvers her way to a federal police site. She scrolls around the FBI website and clicks on the missing-persons tab. With little hope flickering behind her eyes, she continues her daily search and keeps her expectations low. The webpage finally loads, and Meana scrolls through the long list of missing persons. Curiosity gets the best of her, and she clicks on the missing person's profile of each individual as she searches for Ian.

Many missing children haunt the webpage, and Meana, feeling a knot in her stomach, decides that she is going to move on without clicking on the kids' profiles. She scrolls on through and sees a plethora of missing women. The list of the lost seemed to be riddled with women, and here Meana sat, looking for what seemed to be the only man at the time. An hour slides by and Meana jumps from the FBI website, the local police website, surrounding-area websites, and so on and so forth. She finally decides that she's going to try one last search, and she types in the closest police station to her location that is across state lines. The page load time seems to drag on, and Meana finally makes it to the home screen. She navigates to the missing-persons section, and within seconds, she stops and sits in shock. Looking upon her computer while wearing a face of disbelief, she sees Ian's profile and the word *Found* next to his name. She abruptly erupts from her chair, causing it to slide back and eventually landing with a loud bang on the floor. Not noticing she knocked over the chair, she leans in toward the screen and looks for the phone number to that station. She reaches for her pocket in search of her phone and quickly realizes that she is still in her underwear and never brought her phone from the room. She quickly runs to the room, leaps from the door on to the bed, and wrestles with the covers until she finds her phone. Making a mad dash for the computer, she unlocks her phone and dials the number. With the speaker on, her phone rings, and she paces back and forth in the kitchen and the ringing seems to drone on. Biting her nails in anticipation, she lets out a frustrated sigh as the phone continues to ring.

"Pick up the phone," she yells.

Just then, a feminine voice comes over the phones and says, "Sergeant Anderson. How may I help you today?"

Meana, at the top of her lungs, explains how she scrolled through their site and saw her husband and how she wanted to verify his finding.

The officer on the line says, "Well, yes, ma'am. Patrol found him last night, wandering outside a bar."

Meana sets the phone on the table and takes a series of deep breaths, attempting to calm herself.

Lifting her head up and fighting back the tears that threaten to fall from her eyes, she says, "When can I come get him?"

"Ma'am, you need to bring proof of marriage and proof of his and your identification, but you should be able to come get him by the end of today."

"The end of the day," Meana screams, unsatisfied with the timeline.

The officer calmly replies with, "Yes, ma'am, the end of the day. We need to finish processing and questioning him before he can be released." She pauses for a second before saying, "He is currently being held at the Mercy emergency center. I'm sure they'd allow his wife to enter."

An over-excited and energetic Meana gasps out loud and says, "The hospital," with extreme confusion in her voice.

The officer hesitates and replies with, "Ma'am, I apologize, but I can't explain the situation over the phone, but we can brief you once you get to the hospital."

"Sounds good. I'm on my way. Thank you, ma'am," Meana says, already walking to her bedroom and thrusting her legs through some jeans. She ends the phone call with a tap of the red button and tosses it on the bed.

She runs to the bathroom and opens the drawer as she pulls out a deodorant stick and heavily applies it to her pits in an effort to mask her two-day old musk. She puts her messy, brunette-shaded hair into a ponytail, throws some socks on, and makes her way for the door. She slips on some lace-less shoes and grabs her keys from the pink, butterfly-patterned key holder mounted to the wall. Just as she is about to open the door, she remembers her phone. Running back to her room once again, she scrambles around, looking for her phone. Nowhere to be seen, she panics.

She puts her hands on her head in frustration and exclaims to herself, "Think, Meana, think!"

Just then she remembers throwing the phone on the bed. She skydives for the bed, and with a violent landing, sees the phone bounce up and into the air. She quickly grabs it mid-air and proceeds to hop off of the bed. Feeling like she has lost precise time, Meana makes a mad dash for the door. Having reached the door, she smells smoke coming from the kitchen. Realizing that she has forgotten the lasagna in the oven for hours, she quickly turns from the door and makes her way back to the kitchen. She throws the oven door open, and in a desperate attempt to be speedy, she grabs the lasagna from the oven bare-handed. She winces in pain but manages to lift the lasagna container to chest level and throw it on to the stove top. She looks down at her hand and sees that the skin has instantly turned a deep red, and her hand burns like never before. She turns to the sink and places her hand under the cold-water faucet. Once satisfied that she'll survive, she grabs the kitchen hand towel hanging nearby and wraps it around her hand. Not worrying about anything else, she launches herself through the front door and doesn't dare to look back.

In the vehicle and turning the key in the ignition, she simultaneously clicks her seat belt into place. She throws the car into drive and peels out of her driveway like a drag car racer, and onto the main interstate. She punches the coordinates into her phone and sees that it is a four-hour trip to Ian's location in Tennessee. Not giving a single care, she happily places the phone on her lap and makes a beeline for the hospital. Without stopping for as much a bathroom break, Meana drives straight through to Mercy Hospital and runs her gas down to the red line. She whips her car into the hospital parking lot and just barely misses hitting a few pedestrians as she makes her way for an open parking spot. Seeing one toward the back of this busy hospital, she sharply turns into the spot and the car halts in a crooked position. Throwing her door open and allowing it to slam into the car next to her, Meana lets out a wince and proceeds to close her door. Feeling like she can't control her emotions any longer, she starts to run for the main door with tears in her eyes. Bawling her eyes out, Meana steps through the main threshold consisting of automatic sliding doors.

She sees a nice-looking nurse sitting in her chair with a smile on her face. Meana dashes to her, and the nurse's smile fades as she sees this young woman approach with tears streaming down her face.

"Honey, are you all right?" the nurse asks, standing from her chair.

"Meana, struggling to control herself, manages to blubber out, "I'm here for my husband."

"I just need his name and to see your ID, honey," the nurse says in a caring tone.

Meana frantically scrambles through her purse and pulls out her whole wallet and hands it to the nurse. The nurse gives her a smile and proceeds to take the entire wallet and opens it to locate the ID.

She looks up at Meana and says, "What's his name, baby girl?"

Meana, still crying, lets out a weak "Ian Pierce."

With a couple clicks of her mouse and a few taps on her keyboard, the nurse is able to direct Meana to Ian's room. She hands Meana her wallet back accompanied by a tissue and gently touches her shoulder as she says, "Stay strong, baby."

Meana, holding the tissue to her nose, gives the nurses a thankful smile of affection. She turns from the desk and proceeds toward the elevator doors. She presses the button on the elevator controls and stashes her wallet back into her purse. Waiting for the elevator to reach the lobby level, she stares up at the floor indicator and taps her foot anxiously. At last, the elevator reaches the ground level, and the door opens wide as a rush of people make their way off. Meana doesn't hesitate to push forward, and forces her way on the elevator, pushing people out of her way. Getting nasty looks cast her direction, Meana pushes the number *four* on the elevator and begins to smash the *close-door* button as well. The doors closes as the last person jumps through and nearly gets a leg caught. Meana leans in the far corner of the elevator and blows her nose once more with the tissue before balling it up and stuffing it into her purse. She pulls a small mirror from a side pocket of her purse and opens it, inspecting her face to ensure she doesn't have any random buggers laying about and to ensure her eyes aren't swollen from crying. Satisfied that she is going to look as good as she can, she closes the mirror and places it back in its original location.

The elevator chimes, and the door slides open to the fourth floor of Mercy Hospital. She steps from the elevator and makes a right turn. Walking briskly down the hallway, she makes her way to room 402. Looking upon the doors and reading the numbers, she realizes that she turned the wrong direction off the elevators and is on the odds side of the hallway. Quickly turning about, she increases her speed and zooms past the elevator she had just gotten off. Just as she passes the elevator, she can see that room 402 is the first room on the left. She approaches the door, reaches for the handle, and as she places her handle upon the cold metal, she pauses. Suddenly a different set of emotions wave over her and she starts to think of Ian.

One and a half years prior, Meana lays in a hospital bed. Bruises riddle her body, and cuts can be seen along the entirety of her forearms. She was the survivor of a horrific car cash that sadly ended in the termination of her soon-to-be child. Ian sits in an armchair a few feet from her hospital bed, and, with tears in his eyes, stares down at his young wife with pity and anger brooding in his heart. Meana, hearing the soft sobbing of her husband, lifts her head and opens her eyes.

Seeing Ian looking down on her, and she says, "Don't cry, babe. We'll be just fine."

She reaches for his hand, and Ian, who is irrationally upset with Meana, snaps back with a, "Will we?" as he rips his hand away from her. Confused and aching all over, Meana attempts to sit up and speak with her husband. He, however, wants nothing to do with her at the moment and walks over to the window located on the other side of the small all white hospital room. Meana winces in pain, realizing that she is unable to lift herself without help. She calls out to Ian to return to her side. He ignores her furthermore and continues to gaze out of the window. Meana, still woozy and sleepy from the drugs she has been given, lays her head back onto the pillow and softly calls out Ian's name.

Meana takes a deep breath and she looks upon the burnt hand wrapped in a kitchen towel that lays upon the hospital-room handle. *"I've always sacrificed my well-being for you comfort, haven't I?"* she thinks to herself. Looking up from the handle and through the small window on the door, Meana pushes the handle forward, and the door follows suit. The wooden structure glides open, and Meana sees a middle-aged man wearing an all-black satin suit with hands in his pockets, standing by Ian's bedside. He has fair skin, black, pit-like eyes, and jet black, slicked-back hair. Looking upon this man, Meana's body shudders and she feels goosebumps riddle her arms and neck. The man stares at Ian intently and doesn't lift his gaze until Meana steps form the shadowy doorway. Looking upon her with his lifeless eyes, the man steps forward and takes his hands from his pockets.

"Nice to see you," he says to Meana with a cold smile upon his face. Not knowing what to say to this stranger, Meana stands motionless. The man takes long and drawn-out steps as he approaches Meana. She feels herself wanting to step backward but instead pushes herself further into the room. Standing toe-to-toe, the man caulks his head at an angle and inspects Meana. "You're much prettier in person," the man creepily says.

Meana takes a loud gulp and asks, "Who are you, and what do you want?"

The man, still checking Meana out, walks a small circle around her and brushes their shoulders together.

Standing face-to-face once more, he says, "You pushed your luck one to many times, and my employer didn't appreciate it. He wanted you dead, but I decided to make an example out of you instead."

Feeling her sense of fear spike, Meana whispers, "Who is your employer?"

Once again smiling at her with a devilish grin, he says, "That's not of your concern. The only thing that matters is that you learn to keep your nose out of others' affairs."

Without letting Meana reply, the man makes his way to the exit.

As he approaches the threshold, Meana exclaims in rage, "You son of a bitch! You did this to him!"

The man stops in the doorway and contemplates whether to humor her any further. Deciding that his time is up, he proceeds onward. Meana, feeling brash, turns and runs out into the hallway.

She sees the man standing at the elevator, and as the doors open, she screams for all to hear, "I'll find you, and I'll kill you and your employer, you son of a bitch!"

The man places one hand on the closing elevator doors to prevent them from doing so and takes a small and arrogant bow toward Meana. Lifting himself upright, he turns and enters the elevator that is bound for the lobby. She stands motionless in the hallway with bystanders look at her in terror. With the elevator doors closed and the man gone, Meana replays the scenes of this meeting in her head as she slowly makes her way back to the room. Standing just inside the room, Meana stares at the floor, went all the puzzle pieces fall into place, and she knows exactly who the man works for.

"The fucking senator," she whimpers to herself, walking to Ian's bedside.

She shakes her head vigorously from side to side in an attempt to shake the thoughts away and turns her gaze upon her husband. He lays

186

in his bed with breathing tubes shoved down his throat. A needle and tube hang from his arm and leads to a clear bag of hydration fluid that was placed next to him. Meana, with tears well in her eyes, starts to inspect the damage inflicted upon her husband. His thick, black hair is butchered and cut to ribbons. He has large gashes cut along his arms and face from being tortured. Meana takes a large gasp as she places her hands upon her mouth and continues to look him over. A small piece of his right ear is missing, and stitches are lining the wound. He has rope burn around his neck and around his wrists. Both of his legs are in casts from the knee down, and when Meana removes her hands from her mouth and is about to grab his hand, she sees that some of his fingernails are missing, and those that aren't, are overgrown and chipped. The horror on her face continues to rise with every glance she takes of him, and her legs beginning to fail her. Unable to look upon him anymore, she takes a few steps back and throws herself into an armchair nearby. Lifting her legs up to her chest and burying her face between her knees, she no longer holds back and cries hysterically.

Valkyrie Rising

Two months have passed since Ian was released from the hospital, and Meana has come to hate every day that followed. Having gone back to his old routine of sitting on the couch and bathing in his own self-pity, Ian's health has barely improved. He still looks sickly and frail, and although his hair has grown back, he refuses to leave the house to get it cut. His once-oceanic-blue eyes are emptier than before and have permanently turned to a cold gray as he stares at the television in a zombie-like trance. *"Well, some things haven't changed,"* Meana thinks to herself, looking at her pitiful excuse of a partner. Deciding that she has had enough of his self-loathing, she walks over to him, bending over the back of the coach.

She places a hand upon his shoulder and says, "How about we go for a drive? We can whip around some of these back roads and get some fresh air?"

Ian, however, complacent with lying where he is, shrugs her hand from his shoulder and lets out a disapproving grunt. Feeling her heart sink, Meana leans back to an upright position and places her hand at her side. She hangs her head low, turning away from Ian and sitting at the dining-room table with her head buried in her hands. *"What am I going to do with him?"* she thinks to herself, staring at the floor below her feet. Still staring down, she sees a teardrop make impact and disperse in a wide pattern. Lifting her head from her palms, and her body from the table, she walks to her bedroom and shuts the door. Turning her back to the door and leaning upon it for support, Meana lets her body slide down until she is seated with her legs outstretched before her. With tears still in her eyes, she lifts her phone to her face and unlocks the screen. Scrolling through the plethora of photos she has taken; she marks her way back to when they were still in the Marine Corps. There upon her screen, sat two young Marines, happy as can be, holding each other at Myrtle Beach.

"How did we get here?" she questions herself, staring at the picture.

Scrolling through the photos with her thumb, she lets out a small smile and she comes across a picture of them playing mini golf on an Emerald Isle putt-putt course. Ian stands tall with a short club in his hand and raised to the sky as Meana hangs from him on his other side. Both of them wore a large and genuine smile, and as she continues to look at the picture, memories come crashing back.

Humidity lingers in the air while Meana attempts to concentrate. She peers down the worn and banged-up eleventh hole of the small mini golf course they have visited. Taking in a small breath and holding it as the club smoothly swings back and forth, she makes contact with the ball, and it glides down the small fairway.

"Go, baby, go!" she screams out in excitement as Mendoza simultaneously yells out, "Turn, bitch, turn!"

The ball keeps pace as it approaches the small hill on the far end of the fairway. It goes over the edge and picks up immense speed, but just as it approaches the hole, it hits a small clump of mini-golf carpet that has bunched up from age. Both Mendoza and Meana raise their hands to their heads as they watch the ball fly into the air. Watching it in slow motion, Meana turns to Mendoza and sees the large smile on her face, as she knows Meana's ball isn't going to make it to the hole. Turning back to her ball, she watches it reach its peak and begin the descent.

Coming down faster than it went up, the ball careens toward the dark-blue creek of water that cuts through the course. With a big splash, Meana's ball lands in the center of the creek.

Mendoza looks to Meana and says, "Booyah, baby. Looks like I'll be the winner since you don't have a ball anymore!"

Ian, watching these two-bantering back-and-forth about the fairness of mini golf, speaks up and says, "Here, babe, you can have mine. It's too hot for me anyways."

Meana turns from yelling back and forth with Mendoza and says, "No, wait, you can't just leave. We are supposed to be having fun together."

Rolling his eyes, and giving Mendoza a cold look, he says, "You guys play. I'll just watch," and throws the ball at Meana.

Looking up from her phone, her eyes are tearless.

"You've always been an asshole. I just never saw it before," she says, standing form behind the door. "I know exactly what I have to do."

Meana faces toward the door, places a hand on the doorknob and turns it as a new fire is lit in her heart. She makes her way over to Ian and stands in front of him, blocking his view of the television.

"Get out of the way," he growls with a grainy-sounding voice.

Meana leans forward and relieves him of the remote and turns to the television with her hand held high. She clicks the red *power* button on the remote and watches the television switches off. Turning back to Ian, she sees him looking at her with his pale-gray eyes, and for a second, a surge of fear hits her and goosebumps riddle her arms.

"You and I have a lot of stuff to fix, and I know what you went through was in no way acceptable, but I still love you. Even with all of our flaws, I think we can fix our issues."

Ian, still lying motionless, opens his mouth and says, "How can I ever love you again? They told me why I was kidnapped. They told me what you did."

More confused than ever, she asks, "What are you talking about, Ian?"

Struggling to sit up, he looks Meana dead in the eyes and says, "You killed an FBI agent and strung him from a window, and I paid the price for it. They tortured me to get information on you, and in the end, they offered me a way out, and guess what, Meana? I fucking took it. After hearing about what you did, I willingly shot up heroin!"

"You have to be fucking kidding me! Why would you do that?" she asks, backing from Ian and nearly tripping on the coffee table behind her. Struggling and grunting, Ian stands to look at Meana. She looks upon him with disgust and says, "Here I was, about to give you another chance at redeeming our relationship, and you fucking drop this on me! You are a coward and have always been a coward! I stood up for you at the hospital when they showed me the toxicology reports!"

Showing a flash of anger, Ian raises his hand and attempts to slap Meana in the face. Seeing his movement, she raises her hand and catches his arm mid-air. Looking him in his eyes, she squeezes with all her might and twists his arm behind his back. Standing behind Ian and wrenching his arm toward his upper back, Meana pushes him forward until his face is on the couch. He flails about as it becomes increasingly harder for him to breathe. She stares at him thrashing about, and with a wild look in her eye, smiles. Thirty more seconds of commotion happen before Meana realizes what she is doing. With Ian barely able to fight back and moving slower by the second, she lets her grip on his arm go and allows his face to lift from the couch. Taking a desperate gasp for air, he rears his head back and lands on the floor between the coffee table and the couch.

"I knew what they said was true. You are a killer," he barely gets out, still gasps for air.

"No, you're wrong. That man they said I killed; he was a reporter. The men that took you were corrupted federal agents looking to frame me for his murder and silence my efforts against them." Turning from Ian and walking over to the dining room, she pulls out two chairs and then proceeds to sit in one. "Come sit with me," she says, looking at Ian.

Looking up from the floor with a pale face and look of fear in his eye, he struggles to stand and makes his way over to the table as requested.

Taking a seat with a light thumb, he allows himself to fall into the chair, and Meana says, "You getting kidnapped was my fault, but you taking drugs to forget your past, that's all you. You need to understand that I'm done being a victim. I've had a lot of time to reflect over the past few months, and I see a lot of my memories much differently now. You have always been my oppressor, and I always gave you the benefit of the doubt, but I'm done." Pausing and straightening in her seat, she continues, "We are done. I'm not sure where you plan on going, or what you plan on doing, but I want you out tonight. Oh, and I'd watch your back if I were you. I plan on pushing these guys harder than before."

Too scared to look Meana in the eye, Ian rises from the table and makes his way to their room. Meana can see he is grabbing a duffle bag from under the bed and pulling clothes from inside the dresser. She turns her eyes from him and looks toward the front door. Minutes pass and he gathers his belongings and finally emerges from the room. Still staring at the ground, he lethargically walks past the dining room and toward the door. Pausing as he reaches the door, he lifts his hand and reaches for the car keys.

"No, that car is mine. I will drive you where you want to go if you'd like," she says with as much kindness as she can muster in the moment.

He allows his hand to drop to the door-knob of the front door, and without saying a word, he turns the handle and opens the door.

Passing through the threshold of their home, he quietly says, "Goodbye, Meana," and closes the door behind himself.

She sits in the quit home all alone once more. An hour of silence passes with sitting motionless, replaying the events of that night in her mind. Feeling her stomach tense, and a wave of emotion rise to her throat, Meana scrunches her face as hard as she can, but to no avail.

She bursts out in tears and lets out a loud cry, "Goodbye, Ian!"

Friendship Anew

Cement formed block and cracking mortar joints sit in view of Meana. Upon the crumbling wall of her basement, there lay a detailed map of a grand estate surrounded by many acres of wooded land. On the map it seems as if the land is in its own separate world. Looking like a mini–Central Park, Meana knows that she must be able to trek across the dense wood in a timely manner. Everything will hinge upon her ability to move without hindrance. She turns her gaze from the map and looks down at her desk. Her desk is made of cheap particle board and is macaroni yellow in color. It may be an eye-sore to anyone else, but to her, it is her battle station, where everything she is trying to obtain will come to fruition. Every detail of her plan begins here on this small five-by-two-foot desk.

"*I never thought I'd use this desk,*" she thinks to herself. "*I let it sit here for so long in the dark.*" Sitting there, wondering why a desk she once found useless now has so much sentimental value for her, she lifts her right hand and reaches for the glass of bourbon on the rocks that has been sitting nearby. Lifting it with care, she presses the glass to her lips and takes a well-placed sip. The only noise to be heard in the basement is the clinking of the ice in the glass. Finishing her sip, she tilts the glass away from her face, and the ice once again clinks about. She places it on the table with a soft thud, and uses a microfiber towel laying nearby to wipe the excess condensation off the glass before it has a chance to roll down the exterior and onto the table. She tosses the small hand towel off to the side and then sits straight in her chair. Placing both hands on the back of her head just under her high ponytail, she tilts her head up to the ceiling and takes a few relaxing breaths.

The stress of the mission has been weighing down on her since the very beginning, and the planning and late-night hours are starting to come together. Now that she has the groundwork laid out, all that's left to do is gather a team whose loyalty has no bounds. She ponders the candidates in her head and wonders if they're even still alive. Deciding that she has to at least reach out, she leans forwards in the chair and pulls her phone from her back left pocket. She unlocks the screen of the phone and scrolls to her social-media app and gives it a hefty push. Tapping away on the screen, she searches for her candidates and comes across a familiar face. A beautiful Latina woman with a serious and intense look engulfs the screen of her phone.

Meana looks down at the profile picture she has clicked on and says, "Hello, Mendoza." She navigates over the message section of the app and types, "Long time no see, Vic. I have an emergency situation and was wondering if you'd be able to help me?"

Satisfied with how she worded the message, Meana hits *Send*. Not but a couple of seconds goes by, and she hears the chime of a sent message. Without the opportunity to remove her eyes from the cell phone, she sees that Victoria is already replying. She waits patiently for the message to be completed, and as she does, she takes another sip of her drink. Placing the glass down and wiping it again, the message from Victoria finally populates, and it says, "Anything for a sister. Send me your number."

Meana looks at her phone with wide eyes and is extremely surprised at the response she has received. She taps away on the phone and sends her personal number to Victoria, and within seconds, the phone begins to ring. Meana pauses, looking at the phone, and knowing that if she answers it, she will have to divulge all her private information. Deciding that the risk is worth the reward, she hits the green *Accept Call* button and lifts the phone to her ear.

"Hello," she says.

Victoria wastes no time in saying, "You said you have an emergency. Did he hurt you?"

"Oh no, no, I'm physically fine," Meana says, starting to formulate the delivery of the information she is preparing to tell.

A second goes by before Victoria responds, "Physically?"

Meana, knowing that Victoria would catch that, lets out a heavy sigh as to inflame the dramatics of her situation.

"Well, yes," she says before pausing for dramatic effect. "I'm in a bit of a peculiar situation."

"Uh-huh" Victoria says, trying to egg Meana on.

Feeling her nerves beginning to hit their boiling point, Meana blurts out the information she wants to convey, "Ian was kidnapped by an evil senator after I confronted him about his drug-dealing and child-kidnapping scheme in Venezuela, and they returned him addicted to heroin and ruined, and I want to get revenge on him and his lackeys."

Having blurted all the information out at a high speed, Meana takes in a large gasp of air in an attempt to calm herself. The phone goes silent, and Meana looks down at the screen, thinking that maybe she hung up, but to her surprise, Victoria is just silent.

A full minute goes by before Victoria replies, "So where do we start?"

A week goes by, and Meana sits in a small dinner a couple miles from her home. She looks around while sipping on her coffee, and sees the red and glitter-filled booths that line the window-filled wall on the front side of the older-styled restaurant. *"Looks like it's straight from the 1950's,"* she thinks to herself as she watches the waitress move around the restaurant in skates.

The waitress approaches, and with a smile, asks, "More coffee?"

Meana smiles back and replies, "Yes, ma'am, and also I'm ready to order."

"Go ahead, sweetheart," the waitress says.

Meana decides that she is not going to hold back and orders the champions breakfast which consists of five pancakes, hash brown, sausage, bacon, Canadian bacon, and three scrambled eggs.

The waitress looks at Meana with concern on her face and asks, "Are you expecting company?"

"Actually, I am. She'll be here any minute," she replies, looking the waitress in the eye with a seriousness.

Allowing herself to slide back from the table, the waitress says, "Ok, well, I'll be back to take her order. Enjoy your coffee," and she skates away.

Meana sits in silence once more as she stirs her newly poured coffee and stares at the door of the diner. Minutes pass, and she sees a silver sedan pull up with Victoria in the driver seat. Meana perks up in her seat and watches Victoria park and step from her car. She walks to the front door of the diner and swings it open hard. The door hits the wall behind it and makes a loud clanking noise. Victoria, not caring at all, walks right into the diner and toward the back corner where Meana is seated. Surprised that Victoria knew right where to go, Meana slides her coffee to the side and clasps her hand together on the table-top. Victoria approaches with a stern look and throws a small wave toward Meana. Meana responds with a smirk while Victoria slides her way into the opposite side of the booth.

"Been a long time," Victoria says, inspecting Meana's face.

Feeling Victoria's stare reach her soul, Meana breaks contact and glances away. "Yes, it has. Thank you for flying all the way to Virginia for me." Meana lets out an awkward cough and says, "So, about what I said on the phone, it's uh." She pauses and engages in eye contact once more before continuing, "Well, it's true. I want to take the senator down."

Victoria, hearing the confirmation of Meana's plan, lets out a smile as her dark-brown eyes stare Meana down. "Okay, how big of a team do you need?" Victoria says, whipping her phone out of her purse.

"Wait what?" Meana says in confusion. "I thought you'd try to talk me out of it."

Shaking her head, no, Victoria says, "Why would I try to stop you from doing what I have been wanting to do for a while?" Meana, confused, glances down at the table and collects her thoughts. Seeing Meana thinking to herself, Victoria explains her side, "Look, Meana, you and I go way back, and we've seen some shit together." Victoria takes a steady breath and prepares herself for what she's about to say. "I live in New York, and this same senator pushed a bill forward that will literally rip the Hispanics in my area from their homes. Hundreds of people will essentially be homeless." Victoria sits up straight in her chair, feeling her emotions getting the best of her. Continuing with a shaky breath, she says, "This asshat owns a large portion of the poor-income areas, and I have seen the aftermath of his extortion." Tensing her jaw and increasing the intensity of her gaze, she says, "If I help you, I will be able to help the impoverished people of my area in New York City. It's a win-win."

Meana having heard every word of what Victoria said, sits in shock and awe. "Holy shit, Vic. Why hasn't anyone done anything?"

Shaking her head from side-to-side, she says, "My uncle Benny tried, and he, uh," she pauses and Meana can see her eyes start to swell with tears, "Was found dead in his apartment, and the investigation ruled that he hung himself, but I know it's a fucking lie"

"Meana, feeling the pain Victoria is going through, immediately reaches out with her right hand and places it over both of Victoria's. Letting a small tear leave her eye, Victoria looks at Meana and sees a friend looking back. For the first time since they've known each other, Meana is seeing a side of Victoria that she didn't know existed.

Moments pass as they sit in silence, and Meana allows Victoria to regain her composure before saying, "Thank you for your story. I have no doubt in my mind, he needs to die." A maniacal smile comes over her face.

Victoria looks up from the table and looks Meana in the eyes, "So how big of a team did you need?"

Meana leans back and retracts her hand from Victoria's, placing it to her chin, and assuming the thinking-man pose. "You, me, and I'd say three more will be fine."

"Actually, if you can, make one of them an electrician. I have something in mind."

Victoria, without saying a word, nods her head and picks her phone up from the table. With a couple quick taps on her phone, message after message is sent in an effort to rally the troops.

Completed with her task, she looks up from her phone and looks upon Meana once more. "Let's go hunt a bad guy."

Coming Together

A month has passed since Meana and Victoria were once again reunited in that throwback of a diner, and every day since then has been about assembling and training their team. Meana knows she made the right choice by reaching out to Victoria, and Victoria delivered everything she had promised. Standing in an open field of tall green grass with nothing but tree lines surrounding them in the lost woods of New York, Meana looks upon her team. All though only two of the four have any military tactics training, or are in any way related to the military, Meana knows that if Victoria vouches for them, then they are good to go. Before her stand four strong and proud-looking women of Hispanic descent, Victoria Mendoza, Elizabeth Cortez, Joanny Nicholson, and Victoria's cousin, Jennifer Mendoza.

She walks back and forth, looking at the women who stand shoulder to shoulder, facing their new commander. "Well, ladies, I'd say you're all perfect for the job, but I'm sure you already know that." Seeing smiles on their faces, she continues, "There is a dark and rooted corruption in this world that seems impossible to beat, but we have been given a chance to strike back." Meana swallows the excess spit forming in her mouth and continues, "The people of your neighborhoods have been dealing with a tyrant, a tyrant that has been plundering their way of life and their bank accounts for too long."

"This same tyrant took something from me as well, and for that reason, he has united all of us in these desperate times."

Victoria raises a fist in the air, as if to strongly agree with what Meana has said. "She's right. This bastard has trampled on the Latinx community for too long, and she is proof that his reach has no bounds." Looking Meana in the face, she says, "Tell them about Venezuela."

Looking at Victoria, Meana nods her head in approval and says, "This parasite of a man has kidnapped, enslaved, and raped women and children alike in Venezuela, and his ties to the president there are direct. The president of Venezuela has been working with this traitorous piece of shit, and they two have collaborated on many kidnappings here in the United States." Feeling herself getting worked up, she pauses and takes a deep breath. "I did extensive research and interviewed many people on the matter, and I made the grave mistake of confronting one of his men in a rash manner." Tears start to well in her eyes, and she fights them back. "They kidnapped my ex, tortured him, and then released him to me a broke man, all to prove a point that I could not fight back."

Jennifer steps forward from the row they have formed and says, "He is wrong, though. You can fight back. We can all fight back, and we will!" She walks forward and hugs Meana, and as she does, Meana sees Victoria standing behind her cousin with one hand on her shoulder.

Elizabeth, who has been silent up until now, says, "Meana, a cause like this is worth dying for. Putting our past aside, I'm all in."

The other woman, having heard what Elizabeth said, all nod and agree in unison.

Joanny chimes in, "So where do we begin?"

Meana, feeling stronger than she has in a long time, says, "First things first, I need to test your resolve." She lets out a small, maniacal smile.

Joanny has a worried look on her face and says, "Oh brother."

Two days have passed since their meeting in the woods, and Meana stands outside the front door of a tactical training facility for veterans and civilians to learn basic combat skills and to sharpen pre-existing. Looking at her watch, she counts the minutes that melt by and waits for her counterparts to arrive. Five minutes tick by, and the time is 0800 in the morning. Not seeing her team yet, Meana gets anxious. She pulls out a pack of cigarettes from her pocket and lights one of her mentholated kill sticks to calm her nerves.

"I fucking hate that I love you," she says to the cigarette, looking at it with caring eyes and blowing it a kiss.

She takes a few steady puffs, and as she reaches the midway of the cigarette, her team arrives.

The watch on Meana's wrist reads 0804, and she gives her team a look of disappointment while saying, "Promptness ensures effective readiness."

Victoria, having driven the team, looks at Meana and shrugs her shoulders. "Jennifer thought we were going to a beauty pageant and decided to put on her makeup."

Meana, looks at Jennifer with her full attention, and realizes that she is no older than twenty-one years of age. Her look goes from a stern one to an empathetic one as she ponders the heart-break that this child must have endured and what the exact moment that drove her to join this team was.

"Meana," Victoria says, noticing her staring at Jennifer, "You ready to get started?"

Snapping out of trance, Meana looks at her team and says, "Yeah, let's do this shit."

The five members of this all-female team make their way through the front doors of the facility, and they see a young man sitting at the front counter. He is looking down at his phone and is smiling at the video that is loudly playing.

"Excuse me, sir," Meana says to the young man, but he doesn't seem to hear her.

Victoria steps up and says, "I got this," and she slams her hand down on the counter hard and exclaims, "Hey, buddy!"

The young man nearly jumps from his seat as he launches his phone, and it lands on the counter with a loud bang.

Looking at Victoria with a scowl on his face, he asks, "Yeah, can I help you?"

Elizabeth, seeing Victoria's face turn a deep red, steps up and says in her mousy voice, "Yes, sir. We are the Crane party."

The young man, still staring at Victoria with a foul look, reaches over to the tablet on the counter and brings it up to his face. He turns his gaze to the tablet screen and says, "I see your reservation here. Looks like it's already paid in full, and the only thing left is for every member to sign the waiver forms." He sets the tablet down and reaches under the counter for the appropriate paperwork. Having found what he was reaching for, the young man brings out a small stack of papers and distributes them to each team member. "Please fill these out and hand them back to me. I will send you a copy via email after I have had a chance to upload them."

Each of the team members looks at their paperwork in length and then proceeds to fill them out accordingly. Having finished their paperwork, they all hand the sheets back to the young man, and he makes an annoyed face as he collects them and throws them under the counter.

"All right. Now that I've gotten those, you ladies can proceed down the hallway to your right and into the women's locker room, and you can put your personal belongings in the lockers provided if you should choose to," he says, pointing to the small all white hallway located just to the right of the front counter. "Azul's Combat

203

Simulations is not responsible for any theft should you choose to use the lockers." He pauses to ensure they are listening and then proceeds, "Once you have dropped off your personal belongings, come out and head through the red double doors at the end of the hall. Your instructor will be waiting for you there."

The young man, having finished his long-winded intro, swings his arm about and toward the door as if shooing the team away like flies. The women proceed down the hall, drop off their belongings in the ill-lit and musty-smelling locker room, and then proceed to the red double doors.

Approaching the doors, Meana pauses and turns to her team. "All right, ladies, remember, everyone needs to approach this training like it's the first time you have handled a weapon. There is no room for arguing with the instructor."

With the words leaving Meana's mouth, Victoria lets out an annoyed sigh and knows that particular message was for her. Meana gives her a playful wink and turns around to open the doors.

"Let's go, ladies," she says, turning the handle and pushing the right-side door open.

The door opens with ease, and the team is back outside in the heat of the morning. Just to the left of the doors stands a tough-looking woman, standing roughly five feet six inches tall, with jet-black hair and skin to match. She wears black fabric boots that say Danner on the side, olive-green-colored spandex pants, and a black, form-fitted collared shirt with the name Azul above the left chest pocket. The black hat upon her head says, "Play stupid games, win stupid prizes."

As she sees Meana's team walk through the doors, she turns and addresses them in a professional manner, "Good morning, ladies, my name is Rebecca Azul, and I will be your combat instructor for the duration of your course."

"Go ahead and stand side by side for me and face my direction." She makes her way in front of Meana and places her hands firmly behind her back. The team does just as asked, and Rebecca, noticing how fast and well they listened, says, "I take it that at least some of you are prior military or law enforcement. You move with precision and have a certain air about you." She navigates her way to Meana's right and stands toe-to-toe with Victoria. "I can tell you have an attitude on you. I like that."

Victoria lets out a small smile of approval and looks Rebecca up and down. "Looks like I'm not the only one."

Rebecca takes a few steps back to observe the women that stand before her and yells, "You ladies have all enrolled in my basic combat arms course! That includes the basic firearm movement and firing as well as basic self-defense. This course will last for a duration of one week unless you need further training, and in that time, you ladies will be able to successfully protect yourself and your team should the need arise!" She stops for a moment and adjusts the cap upon her head and then continues with her speech. "Should you all pass my class, you will be eligible to move forward with my intermediate course then eventually the advanced tactics class! Mind you, it is very expensive but very worth it!"

With her hands still firmly clasped behind her back, Rebecca walks over to a small wooden table approximately ten feet away. Meana, looking upon the table, can see five safety glasses, five earplugs, four pistols, five rifles, six flak jackets, and an arsenal of ammo. Rebecca reaches the table with some well-placed and effortless steps, picks up the olive-green-colored flak jacket, and places it upon her body.

"This is a standard flak jacket with a reinforced Kevlar weave that will stop up to a 9-mm round. It can be made more effective by adding a ceramic plate into the front and back pouches." She then taps the front and back of her flak jacket so that the team can hear the thud of the ceramic plates. "These plates will increase the impact absorbance to approximately a 7.62 mm round, depending on the distances of the shot." She simulates a rifle round striking her in the center of the plate. "These flak jackets, however, do not protect your arms, legs, neck, or face from taking damage. They are only designed to protect your vital organs."

A cold sweat pours down Meana's back and suddenly she sees blood and limbs flying before her as the images of her own traumatic combat experience flashes before her eyes. She breaks eye contact with Rebecca and looks toward the floor, and she can feel a small amount of guilt rise inside her.

Rebecca, taking notice, says, "Moving on from the flak jacket, let's talk about weapon safety. There are a some basic but very important rules when handling a weapon."

She turns from the group and picks up a matte black AR-15 rifle from the table and cautiously points it to the floor as she turns back to the team. Victoria, noticing Meana still staring at the floor, reaches out with her elbow and nudges her a few times until she finally looks up and comes back to the present.

Rebecca continues with her lesson in the background as Meana and Victoria look at each other, and as if reading her mind, Victoria says, "Brought back some memories, huh. We can talk about it later. Let's get our money's worth from this first." She throws Meana a small playful smile.

Meana and Victoria bring their sidebar conversation to an end, and Jennifer raises her hand like she's in a classroom.

"You don't have to raise your hand, young lady. Just ask your question," Rebecca says, looking at Jennifer like she would a child.

Jennifer, with a clueless look on her face, says, "Oh, sorry. So, are we going to shoot today, or are we going to be getting lessons all morning?"

Just then, Victoria cocks her hand back and sends it flying toward Jennifer's head. She makes contact with the back of Jennifer's head, and her loose ponytail is sent flying about as her head whips forward from the force.

"Don't be so damn rude, Jenny."

Victoria then looks at Rebecca and says, "Sorry, just ignore her. Please continue," letting out an embarrassed sigh. Jennifer stands with her hands crossed over her chest and wears pouty lips while glaring at Victoria from the side.

Rebecca stands in awe, and says "Okay, anyways, the most important rule is to treat every weapon as if it is loaded." With the rifle still pointing toward the floor, Rebecca pulls the charging handle of the rifle back and peers down into the chamber to ensure no road is loaded. Letting the charging handle go, the bolt is sent forward, and the rifle makes a loud metallic, clanging noise.

Joanny jumps from the loud sound of the bolt being sent forward, and Rebecca looks at her with a smile and asks, "First time next to a rifle?" Joanny nods toward Rebecca with a nervous look and watches as she sets it down on the table. "I will be giving you all a copy of the weapon safety rules at the end of our class today, so don't worry if you can't remember everything I say." She turns and looks at Jennifer who stands in silence. "To answer your question, no, you will not be shooting today. You ladies will be suited up in your gear and will conduct dry runs around the obstacle courses and range." She looks the five women over and says, "Let's get you fitted."

Meana looks at her team and gestures with a nod to walk over to the table where the gear is located. They follow Meana's subtle command and begin to pick up the gear as Rebecca instructed. Meana, Victoria, and Elizabeth, quickly equip the flak jacket and begin to adjust the sling on the rifle within seconds.

Rebecca, watching the team intently says, "I guess I know which of you are prior military," with a smile on her face.

The three look to their two civilian counterparts with empathy and watch them struggle to put the flak jackets on.

Meana steps forward, and as she does Victoria places a hand on her shoulder, and says, "We got them, boss lady."

Victoria and Elizabeth smoothly throw the flak jacket over Jennifer's and Joanny's shoulders and show them how to fasten the Velcro straps to make the fit comfortable. They then hand them their rifles and teach the two rookies how to properly wear the sling and hold the weapon. Not but a couple minutes goes by, and the team is geared up and ready to train.

Rebecca looks at Meana's team and sarcastically and jokingly exclaims, "If I wasn't such a badass, I might actually be intimidated by you ladies! Now that you're ready to kick ass, let's walk over to the obstacle course, where I will show you basic moves for handling a weapon in a team environment and how to take cover!"

Meana nods at her team and then gives Rebecca a thumbs-up as they prepare to descend down the small cement staircase that leads to a football-field sized obstacle course with small buildings and rubble scattered about. Rebecca leads the team down the stairs and to the starting line of her obstacle course. She gives the team a breakdown of movements and shows the civilians in the group how to successfully follow behind a team-mate without pointing their weapons at each other.

"The most important thing when following a team-mate is to watch their back and never ever point your weapon at them!" Rebecca says as she has them line up one at a time by the starting line. She looks at Meana and gestures for her weapon.

Meana clears the chamber and hands it over to Rebecca and says, "She's all yours."

"Watch me closely. I will perform and move my rifle about carefully as I scan the horizon for enemy contact while simultaneously taking cover." She walks up to the starting line, readies herself to run, and shouts, "Go," and as she does, she bolts from the starting line like a flash of lightning and performs a series of moves that are flawless.

Having completed her movement, she makes her way back to the line, performs the task once more, and then hands the rifle back to Meana after finishing. She looks at the team with a stern look and says, "I want you to perform the moves I just showed you, one at a time. If you can get these down by lunch, I'll teach those of you that don't know how, to break your rifles down and clean them."

She moves to the side of Victoria who is first in line and pulls a whistle from between her breasts, located just behind her flak jacket. As she lifts it to her lips and pursues them against the whistle, Victoria can feel her heart begin to race as she is first to conduct the set of moves. Rebecca places one hand in the air and then drops it to her side in a speedy manner, while she blows the whistle.

Victoria shoots past the starting line and quickly runs to the first piece of cover she can see. She then waves the rifle around the corner of rubble and screams, "Bang, bang!" simulating sending rounds down range. She fires a few more imaginary rounds and then quickly scrambles to her feet and sprints to her next area of cover beside one of the small buildings while yelling, "Moving!"

Reaching the building, she stacks up against the wall, and Rebecca blows her whistle and yells, "Clear the course! Great job, Victoria! Love the communication!"

Feeling proud of herself, she lifts her rifle into the air and yells, "Oorah!"

Rebecca smiles and yells, "A jarhead, that explains a lot. All right, get back into line!" She then turns back to the team and points to Joanny next. "Come on, little goose. Let's see what you remember."

Joanny creeps to the starting line and fumbles with her rifle.

Rebecca watches her approach the line, and once she has, Rebecca adjusts Joanny's grip on the rifle and says, "Don't be nervous. You're here to learn. No one's perfect on their first attempt."

She lifts the whistle to her lips and gives Joanny a nod of approval. Joanny looks forward at the course, and a bead of sweat rolls down her face as the high-pitch tone of the whistle goes off. Joanny, having run very little in her life, slowly takes off, and just a few feet into the course, trips and falls straight into the ground. Knocking her eye protection clear off her face, she lays on the ground for a moment before pushing herself up to her knees and staring down at the ground in embarrassment.

Meana and Elizabeth look at each other, and Meana says, "Oh shit. We have a lot more work to do than I thought."

Climbing the Hill

It has been six months since Meana and the team have started training with Rebecca at Azul's Combat Simulations, and with earth passing day, their skills continue to sharpen. Glaring out the window of her upstate New York hotel room, Mean lifts a glass of scotch to her lips and takes a hefty sip. One day left until her plan comes to fruition. One more day until she can cleanse the world of one more parasite. As she continues to gaze outward into the world, she is amazed at the numerous amounts of light that still live throughout the night. It's eleven o'clock, and still the streets are buzzing with activity. *"Why don't I remember this as a kid?"* she thinks to herself, sitting in silence *"The small town of Deerfield, Virginia would be dead right about now."*

Just then a knock on the door interrupts her train of thought, and she stands from the arm-chair in which she was sitting. Still holding the glass of scotch in her hand, she reaches for the knob of the hotel room door with the other and swiftly opens it. Looking directly at her is Jennifer, and behind her is the crew.

"Getting the party started without us, I see," Jennifer jokingly says, staring at the glass of scotch that Meana is brandishing.

She nods at Jennifer and peers around her as she smells the fresh scent of pizza in the distance.

"Did you get the goods?" she says, staring past Victoria and Joanny and directly at Elizabeth, who is standing dead last in the line of eager women before her.

While smiling back, Elizabeth raises the two large boxes of New York-style pizza toward Meana and sniffs the boxes in a teasing manner. "Hell yeah, we did!"

Victoria scoffs, pushing her way past Jennifer and Meana. "I'm starving! Let's eat before I die!"

Meana rolls her eyes and gestures for the rest of the team to enter her room and Victoria plumps herself down on the hotel-room bed. They all lazily lay about the room, one in the arm-chair, one on the small sofa by the far end of the room, and two on the bed.

Sloppily eating pizza by the handfuls, Victoria stares out the window of the room with a serious look upon her face. "So, tomorrow night it all begins?"

Meana, sensing a slight bit of worry in the women that usually acts as the rock for the team, says, "We've been practicing for months and have perfected our plan of action. As long as we follow the details, everything will fall into place."

Victoria looks over at Meana with fear clouding her eyes and nods while she says, "You're right. I trust you to lead us."

"Hell yeah," Jennifer says in the background as Elizabeth and Joanny, both with pizza in their mouths, raise a fist in approval.

Looking at her team and feeling pride well up in her heart, Meana starts to remember a time when she had no one by her side.

An eleven-year-old Meana sits on a rusty and cold metal bench just outside of the public school she has been attending. In the background, the sun starts its inevitable descent, and police sirens can be heard all around in the distance. Her

neighborhood is no place for a young girl to be sitting outside alone. However, there was no other place for her to go as she was forced to sit in silence and await her mother. As she raises her legs up to her chest and wraps her arms around her knees, a group of young girls burst from the front door of the school, erupting in laughter as they joke about. Not noticing her presence yet, the girls continue along their path, snickering and poking each other in amusement. Recognizing the voices of the girls that bully her, Meana buries her head behind her knees in a hopeless attempt to hide from them. Her efforts, however, are in vain as the leader of the group, Denease, stops her laughter and points in Meana's direction. In unison, the mean girls turn to look and change from their original path and head straight for Meana.

Closing the gap with speed, Denease immediately pokes Meana in the back and she says, "Hey, ugly. Your mommy forget you again?" The group of five girls laugh obnoxiously as their leader continues to berate Meana with petty insults. "Oh look, Meana, I see your dad waving over there." She points across the street. "Oh, wait… He left you and your mother!"

With the girls laughing even louder than before, Meana tries to dig her head further into her knees.

"Are you going to cry? Are you getting upset?" Denease continues to taunt.

She looks at her group of bullies and gives them a nod. They all begin to poke Meana with a single finger, and as they continue, each one pushes harder and harder. Feeling the pain increase as the girl's poke, tears start to roll down Meana's face and down her leg, and she keeps her face against her knees. Denease hears Meana sniffling and continues to poke her while saying, "Wah, wah, wah. The baby cries again!"

Meana feels a fire begin to burn in the depth of her stomach. Listening for Denease's voice more intensely than before, Meana is able to locate her exact position just before launching a pinpoint-accurate elbow behind herself. She makes contact with Denease's nose, and Denease instantly cries out in pain as the impact violently causes her head to whip backward. Blood spurts from her nose and lands on the girl beside her, and Meana can hear, "Ew, gross, Denease!" as the girls all stop poking and stare in disbelief. Denease grabs her face and cries out in pain, stumbling away from Meana. Burying her head back into her knees, Meana continues to cry. The

213

group of girls all scurry away as the pained moans of Denease can be heard for blocks and she recedes from the school. Just then, Meana's mother approaches, and seeing her daughter crying, assumes she is being dramatic.

"Stand up, you crybaby. You're weak, and that's why your daddy left us in the first place!" She smacks Meana on the top of her head and then wraps one hand around Meana's left arm as she yanks her to her feet. "Get moving. I don't have all day to wait on you."

Struggling, Meana slinks her way to a standing position as her mother continues to pull her away from the school.

"Boom!" Joanny mimics, describing a war movie she had been watching the day before. Her dramatic reenactment of the movie snaps Meana back to the present, and she turns to look at the strong faces of her team.

Letting a smile slip through the cracks of her stern facade, Victoria says, "Ladies, I have to say, we have all come a long way, and even though we are a bunch of amateurs, I can say that I honestly trust each of you with my life."

The team all look at her with a glisten in their eyes, and Jennifer says, "Ah, Vicky, I didn't know you could be so sweet."

Victoria's face instantly changes as she grabs a pillow from the bed and launches it into Jennifer's face. "Shut up, Jenny!"

After recovering from the high-speed projectile to the face, Jennifer picks up a cushion from the coach and launches it back with a vengeful force aiding her.

It makes contact with Victoria's face, and as it does, she exclaims, "Oh, it is on, girlfriend!"

Suddenly the women erupt into a full-blown pillow fight, and faces are being bashed in by the rough exterior of the cheap hotel pillows. Taking multiple strikes to the face, Elizabeth shouts, "Parley," at the top of her lungs in an effort to alleviate the beating. She, however, is unsuccessful, and Joanny ceases the opportunity to strike her from the side. Elizabeth flies off of the arm chair and lands on the floor with a thud.

"Oh shit," Joanny says, looking upon the petite and motionless body of her friend.

Feeling her heart fill with panic, Joanny drops her pillow and lifts her hands to her head. At that moment, Meana launches her own surprise attack and slams Joanny in the face at full force. Following Elizabeth's lead, Joanny, too, lays on the floor and dramatically acts like she is dying. The remainder of the women look each other seriously in the face and then instantly begin to uncontrollably laugh as they turn to their overly dramatic peers.

"I hope you leave all that melodrama in the hotel. We don't need that for tomorrow!" Jennifer jokes continuing to laugh.

Joanny and Elizabeth raise themselves from the floor, both with a red mark upon their faces, and Elizabeth, acting as a child, sticks her tongue out at Jennifer and crosses her arms.

Meana rolls her eyes and says, "Okay, ladies, let's settle down and get to work."

Instantly the team wears stern-looks and cleans up the room. Meana, originally sitting on the bed, slides herself to the side and opens the top drawer of her hotel nightstand. She pulls out a large and detailed blueprint of the estate and lays in on top of the bed.

"Let's review the estates property lines and our plan of action at the gate one more time." The team nods toward Meana, and she says, "Joanny and Jennifer, you two are still taking care of the gate and the guard buildings' power. Victoria and Elizabeth, you two are my insertion team." Stopping to point to a black duffle bag in the corner, Meana says, "Do not forget the bags I gave each of you. Your equipment and weapons are inside, and without them, the mission cannot succeed."

Jennifer looks Meana in the eyes and asks, "Where did you get the equipment?"

But before Meana can answer the question, Victoria pounds her first into her palm and says, "I can't wait to take this scumbag down. This is for all the lives he has destroyed."

Meana looks to Victoria and gives a nod of approval before returning to the blueprint. "My job is simple. I'll take care of the lone guard at the gate and plant myself as a double. This will help us gain entry behind the wall." Looking up at each of her teammates with seriousness to her face, she says, "We each have a part to play, and if even one of us fails, we all go down in flames."

A large gulp can be heard from Jennifer just before she places her hand in the center of the blueprint and says, "Until Valhalla!"

Each member places their hands on top of the other and repeats the phrase, "Until Valhalla!"

An hour or so goes by and the team continues to fine-tune their plan of action, and once satisfied, Meana folds up the blueprint and places it in her black duffle bag located in the corner of the room.

"I'll be taking this with me in the event we need it at the last minute," she says, waving the blueprint just before placing it in the bag.

Joanny gives her a thumbs-up and head toward the door. Victoria and Jennifer do the same, and as each one reaches the door, they first bump with Meana.

"Remember, no contact until it's time to take action, and most importantly," she pauses and looks to Joanny and Jennifer. "Don't talk over the radios. Use the clicking signal I taught you."

Jennifer rolls her eyes and says, "We got it, boss. Get some sleep. We'll see you tomorrow."

Meana takes one last look at her team as they walk down the hotel hallway and out of sight. She closes the door softly and walks over to the night-stand. Carefully refilling her scotch glass, Meana picks it up and heads back to the armchair by the window.

She takes a seat, and raises the glass to her lips while whispering, "I won't be getting any sleep tonight."

Cataclysm

Meana is broken from a transient hold by the beeping of her G-SHOCK watch and snaps back to the present. Still sitting in the small chair located in the lonely brick guard-house, she lifts her left arm and checks the time. Pushing a button on the watch to disarm the alarm, she sees that it is thirty minutes past midnight, and she knows that the Bravo Team is in place to initiate phase three. Slowly pulling the small black radio from her pocket and keeping it hidden behind her back, she hits the key three times, and after a few seconds, two clicks of acknowledgement are sent in return.

"If all goes to plan, Bravo Team will be arriving on sight in less than five minutes," she thinks to herself. Just then, a Chevy Tahoe, very similar to her own, pulls up to the guard-house and stops perfectly in line with the guardhouse window.

"Hmm, they're early," Meana whispers with a small smirk.

She stands from her chair, keeping her head tilted downward in an effort to keep her identity concealed. Before she even takes her first step, the gate guard's radio goes off, "Command, to Gate Guard, over." Meana lets out an irritated sigh but is not surprised at the call.

"Gate Guard to Command, I hear you," she replies.

The gruff voice demands, "There is no one scheduled for a visit at this hour. Approach the car and check the driver's identification."

"Will do," she says with a sarcastic tone, tossing the radio onto the table nearby.

She looks through the guard-house window at the dark and mysterious silhouette in the driver-seat and casually winks. Walking over to the edge of the building with extreme confidence, Meana slides a small window open and gestures for the driver to roll the driver's window down. The Bravo Team leader cracks the window in an effort to conceal her masked face from the cameras. The team leader slides a piece of paper through the crack of the window, and Meana reaches out to grab it. Just then she can hear the radio in the background going off, and the gruff man is yelling for her to get the vehicle's driver to roll the window down. She purposely acts like she cannot hear the radio and opens the folded piece of paper. Reading the message her team leader has handed her, she smiles and lets out a small giggle. The paper reads as so, "You're a bad bitch. Let's do this shit." Meana looks up from the paper, lifts her right hand to eye level as she mimics a pistol and imitates shooting, saying, "Pew, pew," out loud just before proceeding to push the gate entry button.

A voice can be heard over the radio once again, and this time Meana can here it clear as day, "What the fuck are you doing, Jasmine? Stop that vehicle!"

This time, Meana turns around and walks to the table, while also keeping an eye on the black SUV. Without letting the vehicle leave her sight, she reaches down and grabs the radio from the table-top. Standing like a statue, she watches gate creak and groan its way open, and the vehicle makes its way past the steel mammoth that once stood between her and the mission. With the vehicle clearly through the gate, Meana reaches for her back pocket and pulls her personal radio out.

Keying the radio, she says with conviction in her voice, "Alpha Team, kill the lights in fifteen seconds."

Two clicks of acknowledgement can be heard as usual, and Meana clips her radio to her flak jacket.

The gruff voice frantically shouts, "Jasmine, come in! What's going on? Report!"

Staring at the radio with contempt, Meana takes a deep breath, holds it for a count of three seconds, and then lets it out at a slow and steady pace. She lifts the radio, and with all the arrogance in the world, calmly says, "Sorry, Jasmine can't come to the radio at the moment."

Seconds pass, and the man on the radio unassumingly questions, "What the fuck?" just as the lights and cameras around the gate and guard-house go dark.

With the gate wide open, Meana lowers the volume on the guard's radio and stashes it in a side cargo pocket of her black tactical pants. She picks up the gate guard's old and unmaintained rifle and tosses it around her shoulder. She takes a few seconds to adjust the sling before deciding it's time to head through the gate. Walking with a brisk pace, she reaches the door of the guard-house but stops at the threshold and hesitates to step out. Turning from the door, she heads for the utility closet, unlocks its door, and opens it. Looking inside the utility closet, she can see the female gate guard awake with tears running down her face and a puddle of piss beneath her.

Meana, with a blank look on her face, tilts her head and says, "Wouldn't want you to be forgotten, Jasmine," before throwing a devilishly playful smile in the guard's direction.

Satisfied with herself, she turns away from the utility closet and proceeds to exit the guardhouse exterior door. She trots past the huge steel gate and is within the estate grounds. Just past the gate, lays a long, thin gravel driveway, and the night sky conceals the end of the drive from Meana's sight. She, however, knows the exact pace count she must run in order to be in position for the next phase of the mission. She makes her way over to the right-hand side of the driveway and maneuvers her way into the thick, wooded area surrounding the estate. Tracking of every step she takes, she occasionally stopping to takes a knee, and check her watch. She uses the compass feature of her digital watch and her pace count to navigate these dark and endless woods. Perfectly following her azimuth, she approaches the midway point of her journey to the estate. Having stayed no more than fifty feet from the gravel driveway at all times, Meana sees the black SUV her team was piloting. Knowing that her team has already dismounted the vehicle and made their way to the rally point, she sits and watches the vehicle with little worry. She pulls the guard's radio from her cargo pocket and brings it to her ear. Listening for any intel on the other guard's location, she steadies her breath and keeps her eyes fixed on the SUV. She hears the gruff voice barking commands back and forth to his other guards, and after a couple minutes of listening, she finally hears what she's been waiting for.

The gruff voice says, "The cameras are still down at the front gate, and where the hell is that vehicle? It should have already made its way to the main drive."

A much-younger-sounding male voice responds on the radio and says, "We are not sure, sir, but I have deployed the quick response task force to search for it."

Keeping the radio to her ear, Meana smiles. Voices continue to argue back and forth over the radio and time continues to tick by. Meana, still in a kneeling position, starts to get irritated while waiting for this quick response task force to appear. She allows the arm holding the radio to drop down to her side, and she shakes it about in an effort to get the blood running again. She closes her eyes and rotates her neck in a clockwise direction and multiple cracks can be heard. She lets out a sigh of relief, opens her eyes, and her face returns to being stern and focused. Staring at the SUV, she lifts her head in curiosity and thinks she sees motion around the rear end. It only takes her a split second to realize that the quick response task force is smarter than she had anticipated. They had approached in the dark of night in all-black uniforms and black ski masks, concealing themselves in the shadows just as she had, and they had come on foot without the use of flashlights.

"Sneaky bastards," Meana whispers, pulling a cell phone from her front right pocket.

She watches the enemy combatants close in on the vehicle, and soon realizes that there are eight in total. She sees one member motioning for the others to move in, and two of the combatants stealthily push closer to the driver side. Meana leans forward in excitement.

"Just a few more feet," she says as she tries to keep her excitement in check.

Time seems to freeze for Meana while she smiles so hard her face hurts. Without saying a word, she pushes the green *Call* button on the cellular device. A second passes by, and as the enemy team takes one last step toward the SUV, it ignites in flames, and before any of them can turn to run, it explodes with a brutal and bloody concussion that engulfs the entirety of the quick response task force. Meana looks upon the carnage, and even in the darkness of the night sky, she can see their limbs separating and flying about the gravel path and even farther out into the woods.

Satisfied, she takes one proud look at the ruin she has caused and turns toward the woods. No longer worried about the first wave of guards or noise, she starts running at a rapid pace. She has to put distance between herself and the vehicle, as she knows it will draw more guards in. She sprints through the woods while keeping the trail in sight. She can see light breaking through the tree line in the distance and knows that she has finally reached the main estate. Sweating profusely and little winded, she decides to kneel at the edge of the wood just out of sight. Down on one knee, she puts her hands on both hips, erects her back as straight as possible, and takes a series of steady breaths. Regulating her breath, she feels herself regaining her composure. She reaches into her cargo pocket for her bandana in order to wipe her sweat away when she remembers that she used it to gag the gate guard.

Having nothing else to use, she rubs her coarse uniform sleeve across her forehead and says, "Damn, that fabric's hard."

Having cooled down from her midnight stroll through the woods, she turns her attention to the estate. There is a large gravel parking area out front, and the estate seems to be made of pure stone. Gray cobblestone makes up the entirety of the structure, and Meana sees a plethora of large, stained-glass windows lining the front. Dead center of the estate is a massive stained window depicting a curiously demonic-looking knight in armor. The background of the window is fiery red and has flames sprouting over the knight's shoulders. The armor is pitch black and has numerous shades of gray intertwined to depict slashes and dents from battle. It has long black horns, red glowing eyes, and both hands are resting on the hilt of a large claymore, its tip plunged into the ground. It stands on a dark, rocky ledge with its head tilted down, looking as if it was gazing upon the entrance. Underneath this massive piece of artistry is a large cedar double door with black metallic handles and two large lion-head door knockers. Meana kneels with her mouth hanging open at the ridiculous quality of the stained window and overall detail of the estate.

"Going to be a damn shame when I burn it down," she says maniacally to herself.

Refocusing, she turns her attention to the guards patrolling the perimeter. She counts five guards standing stationary near the entrance and at each edge of the structure. She also sees an additional four running around like chickens with their heads cut off. Her assumption is that they are freaking out about the explosion nearby. Her assumptions are solidified when she sees the additional four guards jump into a golf cart and speed down the gravel path. Smirking while they blaze past her, she reaches for her radio.

With the radio in hand, she keys it. "Bravo Team, additional reinforcements are on the way. There are four in total."

A double click acknowledgement over the radio lets Meana know that her team heard her loud and clear. She sits in position and continues to survey the guards around the property, hoping to find an opening to make a run for a shadowy spot by the edge of this mammoth-sized building. Just as she is certain that the guards are living statues, the one on the far-right corner of the building reaches down and pulls a cigarette packet from his jacket pocket.

"Aha," she lowly exclaims, readying herself to pounce on her prey.

The guard looks at his fellow guards in suspicion and rounds the corner, turns his back to the front of the building, and lights the cigarette. Meana, seeing her opening, makes a mad dash for the guard, and within seconds, closes the gap. A few feet from the guard, and without hesitation, she attacks. Reaching for the long Ka-bar she has tucked into her right boot; she swiftly pulls it out and thrust it as hard as she can toward the guard's neck. With perfect precision, she makes contact, and her knife sinks into the guard's throat. His body immediately goes limp, and blood decorates the cobblestone wall close by. Minimizing the noise of her kill, she catches his lifeless body before he can hit the ground. With the guard firmly in her grip, she quietly pulls him away from the corner of the building and stashes his body in a bush nearby. With him concealed, she steps away and flattens herself against the cobblestone wall. She steadies her breathing and looks about for any other guards. Looking around, she notices the smoke of the cigarette wafting in the air. She bends down, picks it up, and proceeds to take a long and steady drag. She lets out a satisfied sigh as she exhales and flicks the cigarette into the grass.

Knowing that there is only one route to go, Meana makes her way down the cobblestone side wall of the estate and maneuvers her way up a balcony nearby and through a plain cedar double door leading to a large vacant room. As she slides her way in through the open door, she thinks, *"Fucking rookies don't even lock doors."* Looking around the room to ensure that it is indeed empty, she sees a snobbishly decorated room with expensive white furniture and a large, deep-red, Victorian-style rug in the center. Meana stares at the rug and shudders as it reminds her of a drab, run-down hotel she once stayed in. She catwalks her way to the door leading to the main hallway of the second floor, and gently turns the handle and slides the door open just enough to squeak through. Closing the door behind her, she works her way down the dark and ominous hallway and keeps her eyes peeled for signs of movement. Surprised that the guards are nowhere to be found, she pushes forward and thinks, *"The diversion outside must have worked better than we thought."*

Duck-walking through the hallway and checking each room as she goes, she makes her way to the large room located in the back of the estate. Crossing her fingers for good luck, she presses on, just inches from the large oak double doors that separate her from her prey. Pausing at the doors and pushing her back against the wall, she checks the magazine of the rifle to ensure all is operational and inserts it back into the magazine well. She slightly pulls the slide of the rifle back and confirms there is a round chambered. Having completed her weapons check, she closes her eyes and takes a series of deep breaths. Allowing the emotions of fear, anger, grief, and embarrassment to wash over her, she opens her eyes, and a wildfire spark throughout them. Exhaling with intensity, she turns toward the door, and bursts her way through with her rifle pointed forward. She steps into a dark and mystical room of colorful books and shelves as high as the three-story open ceiling. Not allowing any of it to distract her, she turns her attention to the figure sitting in the antique-style brown-and-red leather chair, facing the fire on the other side of the room.

Still staring at what she knows to be the senator, she hears a deep and gruff voice say, "So you came to kill me?"

Without hesitation, she cockily says, "You're fucking right, I did. I'm here to get mine."

"It's a fool's errand. You'll die here" the voice says.

Meana, boiling with anger, steps forward and makes her way around the senator's chair and proceeds to push the barrel of her rifle close to his face. Feeling the blood drain from her body, she looks upon the senator's corpse sitting in his chair, clutching a glass of alcohol with half melted cubes of ice. His throat lays open with his tongue pulled through the large gash. Wearing an expression of agony and terror, his pale skin and gray eyes look Meana in the face, and she glances upon the wet blood soaked into his silken robe. Not allowing his death to bother her any further, she rashly starts waving the rifle around in an attempt to locate the gruff voice. Maniacal laughter echoes around the ill-lit room, making it difficult for Meana to pinpoint its location. The corners of the room are pitch black, and the darkness is impossible to see through. The only light in the room is from the crackling and quickly diminishing fireplace.

"Marco," the voice says with malice in its tone.

Meana, knowing that she has walked into a trap, does the only thing she can think of.

"Polo," she nervously says in reply.

"At-a-girl. Why don't we play a game?" the hellish voice says. "I've watched you for so long."

With her heart pounding uncontrollably, the blood in her neck bulges and forcefully pumps its way to her brain. The adrenaline in her body is red-lining, and she finds it difficult to concentrate on any one area of the room.

"Fine, I'll give you a hint," the voice says in a playful manner. "In Odin's name we fight and die. On Valkyrie's wings we glide, in hopes of reaching Valhalla in the sky."

Still swinging her rifle frantically around the room while listening to this mad voice spew nonsense, Meana thinks about it and attempts to control her blinding frustration. Wiping the sweat from her eyes and whispering to herself, "What do I do? I have no clue what he's talking about." the answer suddenly pops into her head, and she glances up. With her rifle still at the ready, she gazes up toward the high ceiling and sees a man in an all-black satin suit standing on a circular balcony that wraps its way around the ceiling's curvature.

Clapping his hands, the man says, "This room always did have great acoustics. My voice can project in every corner from up here. I'm so glad you decided to join us. I'm sorry the senator couldn't make it." He gestures to the stiffening body in the chair by the fire. "He's not feeling well. I think he said his throat was hurting."

Squinting her eyes, Meana still can't make out the man's face in the tall and dark room, but his maniacal laughter can be heard loud and clear.

"Who are you?" She screams out in an effort to get her voice to reach the top.

"We've spoken before, Meana. You don't remember threatening me?" As the voice explains their connection, Meana glances at the floor and runs through the memories in her head, and only seconds later, the familiarity of the voice washes over her. She looks up in awe and shouts with fury in her voice, "You son of a bitch. This is all your fault!"

Once again clapping, Agent Cavanaugh leans forward over the high balcony and into the dying light of the fire, and his designer black satin suit with his slicked-back, black hair becomes clear to Meana.

"Now that you know who I am, let's get started." He snaps his fingers, and the main door to the large room swings open, and armed guards' storm in with automatic rifles raised at the ready. Having previously known that she has walked into a trap, Meana lowers her rifle to the ground and then proceeds to erect her body perfectly straight, and she raises her hands. "Smart move, my girl" Cavanaugh smugly says, gesturing for the guards to remove her. "Take her to the basement and prepare her for information extraction. I'll be down in a bit," he says to a singular guard standing outside of the formation.

Glancing to his fellow guards and nodding his head, two other guards lower their rifles and proceed to advance to Meana. One guard stands in front of Meana while the other grabs her wrists and begins to cuff them with a pair of zip-tie-style cuffs. Waiting until the rear guard slips the cuff on Meana's right wrist, she quickly jumps into the air and kicks the front-facing guard square in the chest. She and the guard are sent flying in opposite directions, and she collides with the rear guard, sending them both to the floor with a loud thump. Wasting no time, she instantly wraps herself behind the rear guard, grabs his pistol from his holster, and lets out a barrage of bullets while making her way to her feet. With bullets flying in every direction, the remainder of guards in the room instinctively lower their heads and run for cover. Knowing this is her only chance, Meana runs full force toward a large window facing the outside world. Jumping with every ounce of energy she can muster, her body shatters the stained window, and just before she clears the frame, she takes a round clean through her right shoulder. Time slows, and Meana sees the blood from her shoulder fly in front of her as her limbs flail about. Without an opportunity to observe the scenery, she swan-dives toward a large holly-berry bush. She lands directly into the center of the bush, and its sharp leaves cut through her skin like a hot knife in butter. Ignoring the pain, she immediately removes herself from the bush and sprints full force into the wood line nearby. Bullets make contact with the ground near her feet, and clumps of dirt go flying in every direction from the lone guard hanging out the shattered window with his finger firm on the trigger of his weapon. Not daring to look back, she runs deeper and deeper into the night and presses forward through the thicket. She has no clue how long she has been running, but she knows she can-not stop. Feeling extreme exhaustion setting in and feeling the increasing pain of her gunshot wound, Meana can no longer sprint at full force.

Her footing becomes sloppy, and the night seems a little darker as she fights to keep her head up. Still pushing onward, Meana reaches for the radio, and just as it clears her pocket, her uncooperative and uncoordinated hands drop it into the darkness. With vision blurring steadily, Meana stops in her tracks and falls to her knees. She frantically lets her hands scrape at the vegetation of the wood and attempts to find the small black radio while the pounding in her head grows louder and louder. To no avail, she can no longer hold her body up, and finally, she collapses to the ground. Laying in the dark wood, scared and alone, the cold of the night sets in, and the leaves on the ground poke and irritate her skin. A sharp pain continues to grow in the small of her back, and she lethargically tries to adjust her position. Attempting to alleviate the pain, she reaches back and removes the item trying to pierce through her. In her hand, she holds the small black radio. Letting out a pain-filled chuckle, she keys the radio and says, "All teams, Valkyrie down. I say again, Valkyrie-" Before Meana can relay her message once more, her eyesight fades, and she collapses into a death-like stillness. The silence of the dark wood fills her ears, and while struggling to take slow and labored breaths, a double-clicking tone of acknowledgment comes over her radio.

Coming Soon:

Odin's Bane

By
C. M. Schrecengost

About the Author

C. M. Schrecengost is an aspiring author living near the salty seas of North Carolina with his wife and daughters. When he's not hanging out with his wife and children, playing video games, running his business, or enjoying a good book, he often stares at a computer screen, letting his hands paint an emotionally thrilling story. Drawing his stories straight from his dreams and slapping them onto paper, he devotes numerous nocturnal hours pushing his mind to the limit for his readers.

www.ingramcontent.com/pod-product-compliance
Lightning Source LLC
Chambersburg PA
CBHW060426180626

46817CB00007B/2682